THE
ESCAPE
ROOM

THE
ESCAPE
ROOM

L. D. SMITHSON

bantam

TRANSWORLD PUBLISHERS
Penguin Random House, One Embassy Gardens,
8 Viaduct Gardens, London SW11 7BW
www.penguin.co.uk

Transworld is part of the Penguin Random House group of companies
whose addresses can be found at global.penguinrandomhouse.com

First published in Great Britain in 2024 by Bantam
an imprint of Transworld Publishers

A CIP catalogue record for this book is available from the British Library.

ISBN 9780857504807

Typeset in 12/16pt Minion Pro by Jouve (UK), Milton Keynes
Printed and bound in Great Britain by Clays Ltd, Elcograf S.p.A.

The authorized representative in the EEA is Penguin Random House
Ireland, Morrison Chambers, 32 Nassau Street, Dublin D02 YH68.

Penguin Random House is committed to a sustainable future
for our business, our readers and our planet. This book is made
from Forest Stewardship Council® certified paper.

For Joanne and Tom.
You are an inspiration.

1

Bright, white snow blanketed the streets in every direction as Kevin Yates turned left into New Lane. The sun was only just up, it was early in his shift and his bag was heavy, but he marvelled at how something as simple as snow could make even the most ordinary places look beautiful. Not that he would ever think of this road as ordinary or beautiful after today.

His boots crunched against the snow as he delivered mail to the first few houses.

In his twenty-two years as a postman, he thought he'd seen everything. Working in one of the few professions licensed to trespass on other people's property, he had witnessed lovers climbing out of windows, naked people making their morning coffee, family fights, fleeing burglars and more people passed out on their lawns than he could count. 'We glimpse the grim reality behind the façade,' his first boss had told him all those years ago, 'and it is our duty to look away and forget what we've seen.' Kevin had always taken pride in living up to this standard, but that was about to change.

Number fifteen was halfway down. He knew someone famous lived there. Well, when you say famous it wasn't anyone who'd ever achieved anything as far as he could tell. In Kevin's mind to be famous you needed to be a skilful sportsperson like Gary Lineker or a talented musician like the Gallagher brothers. The woman at number fifteen was just one of those famous-for-being-famous types. As far as he could tell she had a pretty face and a good body and at some point had dated a film star Kevin had never heard of.

The first time he'd seen her in person was when he had knocked with a parcel. She'd answered the door cradling a baby, which had surprised him because the fact she had a kid had never been mentioned in the papers. After that, she would wave when she saw him and call out a cheery hello – he had to admit he'd bragged about that in the pub.

As Kevin approached the house, the child was waddling down the path with both podgy arms held out for balance. The smile that touched his lips left pretty swiftly when he clocked that the kid was wearing only a nappy. As a father of four, Kevin felt a wave of disgust and increased his pace. It was minus degrees out here. What was the woman thinking?

The curtains of number thirteen twitched as he passed.

At the gate Kevin's cold breath caught in his throat as he stopped to take in the scene. He would wonder later how long it might have taken him to spot the truth of things without the snow. It created the perfect canvas: a bright white backdrop for those little red footprints. Footprints that tracked back to the half-open front door.

Kevin's eyes followed the route the child had taken with growing horror; the footprints became darker and redder as they neared the front door. He couldn't see inside from where he stood, the interior was too dark. He focused again on the child, who had begun waddling in his direction.

Placing his post bag on the ground, Kevin removed his coat.

'Now then, little one,' he said, scooping up the child and wrapping it tightly inside his coat, 'let's get you nice and warm.'

'Mummy sleeping,' the child said as it nuzzled into Kevin's chest.

'OK, sweetheart. OK.' He rubbed the toddler's back as he walked towards the half-open door, treading on fresh snow to avoid the gruesome footprints. Once there, he placed a protective hand on the back of the little one's head to ensure the child didn't see inside, then he pushed the door wide with the toe of his boot.

Everything Was a Clue

2

Expect the Unexpected Podcast
Season 2, Episode 1: 'The Fortress'

'*Welcome to the show. I'm Shane Fletcher, ex-police detective and mystery fanatic and this is* Expect the Unexpected, *the podcast that blows your mind with crimes that beggar belief.*

'*Today we have an exclusive. For those of you who haven't heard of* The Fortress, *seriously, where have you been, people? It's the news story of the year. And despite all the press inches and speculation on social media, the police still have no clue why this thing happened or who was responsible. I'm hoping my guest today can help change all of that because she was there.*

'*She is a twenty-four-year-old woman who was studying at Leeds University for her PhD when she chose to take part in what was pitched to be the next big thing in reality TV. What happened next is the stuff of nightmares.*

'*It is a story of puzzles within a puzzle, one I'm sure you will find fascinating. But we also need your help because, like we always say on* Expect the Unexpected, *someone, somewhere must know something.*

'*Please bear in mind that this is all incredibly fresh and sharing her story may at times be tough for her. So, without further ado, here we go. Bonnie Drake, welcome to the show.'*

'Thank you. I'd like to say it's great to be here but . . .'

'Who wants to be a guest on a podcast called Expect the Unexpected? *Not one for the life goals, hey? But here you are, and I for one am delighted about it. To date you have refused to speak to anyone so perhaps we could start with why you chose to share your story with me today.'*

'To be honest I agonized over it for a long time. I don't want to . . . glamorize any of it. I've not really spoken to anybody about the details, well, other than the police. But progress is really slow. There don't seem to be any answers coming and I need them. So when you contacted me, and I read about how your podcast had helped to solve all those other cases, I saw an opportunity to do something productive.'

'Well, all of us here at Expect the Unexpected *want to help you find answers and hopefully some closure. I'm confident we can shed some light on this with your help. The world deserves to know the truth. We've done some research that I'd like to get your take on, but first can I ask you what I ask all my guests: how did this start for you? When did you first hear of* The Fortress?'

'Right, OK. I don't think I was aware of it at all until my sister mentioned it. There was a lot going on at the start of the year – we'd just lost our mum – and I wasn't using social media so I missed all the hype. It wasn't until she started talking about this new show they were recruiting for on Channel Five that I knew anything about it.'

'Are you and your sister fans of reality TV?'

'Clara is but I'm not really. I don't mind watching the odd one but I'm more of a documentaries and drama person.'

'So how on earth did you end up on the show?'

'That was down to Clara. Her heart was in the right place, but there's no way I'd have gone anywhere near reality TV without her.'

'She must feel awful.'

'She had no way of knowing what would happen.'

'For anyone listening who doesn't know what happened, we will be going into all the details in the next hour. And if what Bonnie is telling us is true, it's an unbelievably elaborate set-up.'

'It is true. Everything I've said is true.'

'I didn't mean to suggest—'

'Look, the whole thing was awful, horrifying. No one would have believed what happened to us was possible. But it did happen to us. *To me.* I wasn't even supposed to be there and now I'll never escape that place.'

3

Three Months Earlier

Clara Drake tried to check out her competition without lifting her head from her phone too much. She moved her eyes to the limits of their sockets to take in the anorak-wearing middle-aged man who had a dirty canvas bag leaning against his leg from which he had taken a crumpled magazine. A few seats along from him was a suited man, probably in his early twenties like her, who stared directly ahead as he silently moved his lips as if reciting some secret tactics. Then there was the only other woman she could see, a Chinese girl who looked young enough to be a teenager but whom Clara expected was probably older from her neat, knee-length skirt and polished flats. Clara glanced at her own battered Converse trainers. Maybe she should have worn something smarter – this was an interview of sorts. Would it matter? Would they be looking at things like that?

The TV on the wall opposite displayed the logo of the brand new reality TV show that had been all over social media for months.

THE FORTRESS

Are you smart enough to unlock its secrets?

CAN *YOU* GET OUT

Clara had completed a few escape rooms over the years and loved them. She wasn't as good at the puzzles as her sister Bonnie, but then she had never been as good at anything as Bonnie, apparently. Her nickname growing up had been Scatty-cat and she had been proud of it; it had sounded so affectionate when her mum and grandpa used it. That was until Bonnie pointed out it was because they all thought she was scatterbrained. After which it had become less of a term of affection and more of an irritation.

'Goodly morning, folks!' The man with the clipboard appeared from behind Clara and took his place under the TV screen. 'Eyes up, look in. That's better. How are you all today? Ready to solve some puzzles?' Before any of the people sitting before him had a chance to speak, he started reading from his paperwork. 'You will each enter your own room along this corridor at the same time. Each door will lock behind you and can only be re-opened with a four-digit key code. The first person to unlock their door and exit will join us on *The Fortress*.' He paused and looked at the group as if expecting a gasp or wow. 'Please hand in your signed forms to me before selecting a door to stand in front of. They're all the same inside, folks, so no need to fight.'

There had been a good few hurdles to cross before this one. First she'd had to complete an application form that asked her to list five talents and five flaws, and then solve a puzzle about how she would escape a cellar with a locked door and only one window that was out of reach. She'd thought her answer about using the sink and washing machine to flood the room so she could swim up to the window was a little ridiculous, especially as she couldn't swim, but somehow her crazy solution took her through to the next round. That was the moment she realized she might really be able to do this. Perhaps she wasn't the stupid, useless sister after all. Maybe she could be the one to save them.

Clara unconsciously played with her mum's ring on her third finger.

After that she'd had to send in a two-minute video on *Why I think I'm smart enough to unlock the fortress*. Then she'd finally been invited here, presumably to prove it.

Clara handed her signed disclaimer form to the cheesy TV guy. Somewhere in her gut she felt a tingle of excitement – or was it fear? She *had* to be the first one out. She needed to focus and think fast. She saw the applicant in the suit yawn and felt a little more confident.

It was not a plush hotel. The carpet beneath her feet was a strange orangey brown and the door handles were square and old-fashioned. It was a new production company and this show for Channel 5 was their first commission. It was pretty low budget she sensed but the £100k prize money was healthy enough.

'Ladies and gents, are you ready?' Mr Cheesy held his iPhone in front of him, his thumb hovering over the screen. Between Clara and him were the other contestants, all looking as tense as she felt. 'Three, two, one . . . ENTER!'

Clara opened her door and stepped inside. The room was completely empty. There were no tables or chairs, no curtains or blinds, no pictures with naff motivational phrases on the walls, no water glasses or water, no pens or paper. Nothing. Clara half turned to check if this was right as her door clicked closed behind her. There was no handle on this side, only a punch code lock with the numbers zero to nine.

Think fast and find the clues, she thought to herself as she took a short walk around the small space. The carpet in here was mottled grey and she could see a few bits of old Blu Tack on the walls but that was it. She walked to the window and breathed heavily over its surface a few times in the hope it might reveal the numbers, but it didn't. She ran her hands across each wall then stood in each corner to look closely along their surfaces before getting down on her knees and checking the carpet. She felt the panic rising. She needed four numbers. Quick. But there was nothing here. No clues, no instructions and nothing to count.

She paused and took a moment. Or maybe there was. There were four walls, one window, one ceiling, one floor. She tried 4-1-1-1, then 1-4-1-1, 1-1-4-1 and finally 1-1-1-4 but the door stayed locked.

Can you *get out*, she heard in her head. It was the slogan used over and over for *The Fortress*. 'Clearly not,' she said to the empty room as she spun on the spot and willed her brain to see.

She tried to count the remnants of Blu Tack that were randomly scattered over two of the walls, but they presented no pattern or code that she could see. They looked like they had genuinely been left behind by previous occupants. There were four panes of glass in the window, six spotlights above her. How the hell was she supposed to work this out? She was going to fail. Someone else might already be out. Then what would they do? The bank would take the house and she and Bonnie would be homeless.

Don't panic, think!

She expected Bonnie would have worked it out by now. If she was here she'd be explaining it to Clara as if it was the most obvious thing in the world. Bonnie didn't mean to sound patronizing, she wasn't mean that way, but she couldn't always hide her frustration when her little sister wasn't keeping up.

Why did I come here? Why am I trying to do something Bonnie should be doing? It was foolish. I'm foolish. Scatty, Scatty-cat.

Clara stopped moving, closed her eyes and took a few deep breaths. What would Mum say?

You're just as smart as her. Take your time. Think it through. You can do this.

When she opened her eyes she felt calmer. She was being too literal, she felt sure. The secret to getting out of here was not about this room, it was about the show. This was the final selection event. If you cracked this, you were in. She thought of all the Instagram posts she had studied as she obsessed about winning a slot. They showed puzzles, ciphers and codes. So perhaps the answer was a code or a cipher.

She thought about the show's pitch. *The Fortress: are you smart enough to unlock its secrets? Can you get out.* It had always struck her as odd that this final phrase had no question mark. It was either a sign that the show was unprofessional and sloppy, or that the people designing it were a bit slow. But what if there was no question mark on purpose, because it was a clue?

Four words, all with three letters. It was worth a shot.

Clara took two steps to the door and typed in four digits. 3-3-3-3.

4

Bonnie walked into the kitchen to find Clara already up and sitting at the table. Her sister was a big one for lie-ins on a weekend, so this was out of character.

'Morning, Scatty-catty.'

'Don't call me that.'

Bonnie switched on the kettle and reached for two mugs. Why had she said that? It was Mum's pet name for Clara, not hers. She might have known it would upset her sister. Bonnie yawned and put it down to tiredness. If she was honest it was tricky knowing what to say for the best these days. In the months since they'd lost Mum she felt they had also lost the ability to communicate with each other without causing offence.

As Bonnie passed Clara one of the mugs of tea she noted the envelope on the table with its bold, red letters instructing them, DO NOT IGNORE.

'Another one?' she said. When Clara didn't answer, Bonnie sat and cradled her mug in her hands. 'How's your leg today?'

'Still in plaster.'

Clara had come off her bike on her way to work the day before and broken her tibia in two places.

'Did you manage to sleep?'

'A bit.'

'Any pain?'

Clara pulled a face which told Bonnie, yes of course.

'Are you going to call the production company this morning?'

Clara was staring at the envelope.

'You can't do it now. They won't let you.'

'I worked so hard to win that place.'

'I know, but you probably wouldn't have won anyway.'

'Why? Because I'm not clever enough?'

'It'll be about who's most popular or who makes the best TV.'

'And you don't think that could be me.'

Bonnie knew this version of Clara well. If things didn't go to plan, she'd get a downer on herself and assume the world was against her. Mum was always good at pulling her back to reality, but Bonnie had no clue how she used to do it. She should have paid more attention.

Sipping her tea, she tried not to look at all the reminders around them: Mum's favourite mug still hanging on the mug tree, her apron on the back of the door, a note pinned to the fridge saying she loved them both to the moon and back. Everything was duller and less important now, as if the volume had been turned down on life. She ate and drank simply to stay alive. She interacted with others only to be polite. But she didn't want any of this. It was too hard.

Bonnie turned over the envelope so she could no longer see the screaming red typeface.

'You could go in my place.'

Bonnie blinked at Clara a couple of times, her mind still dreaming of flying away to some simpler, happier version of life.

'I've been thinking about it all night and I think you could pull it off.'

'Good God, no.'

'Come on, Bonnie. This could be our way out. And you'll be brilliant at it, you know you will. You were always better at puzzles and stuff. You solved the last two escape rooms we did pretty much by yourself.'

This wasn't strictly true, but still Bonnie couldn't help the pride she always felt when her baby sister admitted to admiring her.

Clara picked up the envelope. 'What if we lose the house? Where will we live? That's not what Mum would have wanted. She'd have wanted us to fight.'

Bonnie felt anger bubble inside her. Clara couldn't speak for Mum. If anything, Bonnie was the one closest to her. As the eldest she'd always had a special relationship with her. They could communicate with one glance, especially when Clara was being dramatic, which was often.

'Bonnie, pleeeease?' Clara let the last word drag out long and whispered.

See?

'No. It would be awful.' What she really meant was, *I'd be awful. People would hate me and I'd either make an idiot of myself or be voted off in the first week.*

'So what if it is. If you win £100k, all our problems are over.'

'They'll know it isn't you. They've met you and have those interview videos you made.' They'd obviously liked her, which was no surprise. Clara came over as incredibly bubbly and fun when she put her mind to it.

'People are always mistaking us. It happened last week. Terry in the newsagents asked me if I could read his mind yet.'

'That's different. Terry's old and his eyes are bad. These people specialize in images. They'd spot a fraud a mile off.'

'So they spot it and throw you off. Nothing lost. At least we tried.'

'I'm not doing it.'

'Why? Because you're scared or because you don't care what happens to us?'

The bitterness in Clara's tone stunned Bonnie for a second. She might be a drama queen, but this was new.

'Clara, of course I—'

'Prove it, then! Prove it.' Clara tried to stand but stumbled. When Bonnie moved to help her Clara waved her away. 'If you're not going to help, leave me alone.'

Bonnie clenched her jaw. 'Don't be stupid.'

'It's just a TV show.'

'It's not. It's my reputation. I want to have a serious career—'

'You'd be going as me. *As me!* It would be my reputation, you jumped-up, precious cowbag. Forget it, OK, just forget it. It's not like I've been working on it for the last two months. It's not like I was doing all that for us or anything. I was just doing it because . . .' Clara threw her arms in the air. 'Oh, I don't know, because I'm a fame-hungry, vacuous something or other. I'm sure you'll fill in the blanks.'

'Calm down.' Bonnie knew the rage inside Clara was nothing to do with her, or even this conversation, but still she could feel her face beginning to flush.

'You're always so selfish. Why am I surprised? When I need you the most, you are never, *ever* there.'

'Why bother asking me, then?' Bonnie knew she shouldn't bite but it was too late. The anger now burned hot on her neck.

'Because I'm desperate, OK? Because no one else looks like me, so no one else can take my place and because I was doing the whole bloody thing for us, for you!'

'Don't make me laugh. You just wanted to be on the telly.'

'Oh, you are such a bitch!'

'*I'm* a bitch? Have you heard yourself? And for that matter

I'm not selfish, I live in the real world and have more important things to do.'

'Oh, please, don't give me the "my PhD is so important"
crap again. I'm sick of you lording that over me. It never
impressed Mum, anyway.'

Bonnie opened her mouth to answer but knew she would
cry if she did, so she left the room, slamming the door behind
her as best she could, considering it had expanded so much
that it didn't fit in the door frame any more. Mum had said
year after year she'd get it fixed, and now she never would.

The arguments were wearing Bonnie out. Despite their
mum's best efforts, she and Clara had bickered ever since they
were little. 'You'll be each other's best friend one day,' Mum
would say, but Bonnie was never sure if this was what she
really believed or simply wishful thinking. Lately it seemed
like they couldn't even talk without it descending into a row.

Bonnie stood looking out to the street from her bedroom
window as she tried to calm down. She wanted to get away
from Clara, the atmosphere, the house. Mum would hate to
see this, especially as the source of all their worries was the
fact she had not taken out enough life insurance and spent all
her savings on the many and varied alternative cancer treatments she could get her hands on. For months they had all
eaten their body weight in organic kale and beetroot and
every dish was smothered in turmeric. Mum ate so much of
the stuff it stained her fingertips a deep golden colour. Now,
with her gone, the two of them were alone and unable to keep
up the mortgage payments. The bank had given them three
months to pay up or sell. Bonnie had been angry at first about
the life insurance, but her mum was not a detail person and
had simply not thought to check. And who could blame her
when she had more important things to worry about? As for
the savings, Bonnie figured it was Mum's money and Mum's

life. Truth be told, all three of them had been in denial. They never really believed Mum would die. She was fighting and even improving in the final months. It was all so sudden, there was no time to prepare.

The trouble was, Mum loved this house so much. Bonnie and Clara's grandfather had bought it for her when she was a struggling single mum and all she could afford was an inner-city flat with no garden. 'That's no place to raise my granddaughters,' he had told her. Mum once confided in Bonnie that she had no idea how he'd afforded it – he wasn't a wealthy man and she suspected he'd used his life savings to pay the deposit and a good chunk of his pension to fund the mortgage. He refused to take a penny from Mum until she had secured a decent job.

'It's our safe place,' Mum used to say when they cuddled up with her on the sofa as kids.

When Bonnie had suggested a few weeks earlier that it might be best to sell, Clara had been devastated. It's Mum's home, she'd insisted. All our memories are here; she died here. How can you sell that?

It wasn't like Bonnie wasn't trying. She had applied for a whole load of jobs to earn enough money to stay there. But apparently she was overqualified for the office job in the local accountancy firm and not qualified enough for the lecturing job at her university. Then there were the half dozen emails that had arrived thanking her for her interest but saying the standard of applicants had been particularly high. She could get a job at a bar, or on the tills of the local Tesco, but the salary would only just cover the mortgage, leaving her near to nothing to live on. And now they were almost out of time.

They could not keep this place without some kind of financial windfall and, with no other family to speak of, the chance of that coming from anywhere soon was zero. To give her sister credit, Clara had worked hard to win a place on this thing and come closer to saving them than Bonnie had.

This couldn't be their only option, though, could it? Reality TV. The thought of it made her feel a little sick.

'Bonnie?'

Clara was on the other side of Bonnie's bedroom door, her voice light and sweet. Bonnie knew what was coming now. Her sister was a master manipulator, always had been. Over the years, Bonnie had watched as Clara wrapped their mum around her little finger, not to mention the many babysitters and the odd 'uncle' Mum had brought home. Clara knew how to work people, which was ironic considering Bonnie was the one studying psychology. *Because I need all the help I can get,* she thought, not for the first time.

Bonnie imagined her sister was sitting on the landing floor with one palm pressed flat to the door. Even though no one could see her, Clara would still go all out for the emotive image. She'd be a TV producer's dream.

Bonnie looked up to the blue sky. It was midsummer and the day was bright. It was up to her to take care of Clara now.

Clara had always needed Mum more than Bonnie had. Bonnie was often happiest on her own but Clara craved constant support and reassurance, because she was one of life's worriers. This was why Mum had always had a ready hand for Clara to hold, a hug to envelop her in, or a cuppa and a chat to calm her down.

Was it true that Bonnie had never been there for Clara when she'd needed her? She hoped not. She hoped it was the anger talking because she didn't want to look back and really analyse things in case she was found to be wanting.

A truth that Bonnie had thus far refused to acknowledge settled in her mind: losing this place would hurt Clara so much more than it would hurt her.

And maybe a break from each other was not such a bad idea. She would certainly find it a relief to be away from all the reminders for a while.

Bonnie opened the door and Clara fell into the room from her position on the floor. Her newly cast broken leg was stretched out flat across the landing. She tried to lift herself up and was in obvious pain. Bonnie helped her back downstairs and on to the sofa before giving her some painkillers and sitting alongside her.

'OK, tell me more about it.'

'You'll do it?' Clara's damp eyes were full of hope.

'Maybe, if it's possible, yes.'

Clara took hold of Bonnie's hand and squeezed it so hard it almost hurt.

'I love you, sis.'

Bonnie swallowed back her own tears and nodded. 'I love you too.'

5

The Director

Even though the place was empty of any living presence but his own, it was never entirely silent. The structure creaked and groaned as if trying to communicate its secrets to anyone capable of deciphering them. The salty smell filled his nostrils, making him feel calm and at home. It made sense that he come here alone one last time to check everything was right before the whole spectacle began.

He turned the lighting throughout to its dimmest setting, enjoying the challenge of using all his senses to navigate his way around. He let his hand brush along the brick wall, feeling the slight, ever-present dampness as he checked each camera was positioned correctly. It had been a mammoth effort to get everything ready on time but the weeks of long hours had been worth it. It was sublime. A physical manifestation of his imagination. He had wanted something visually captivating and out of the ordinary to house what he knew in his core could be the greatest puzzle ever designed. It wasn't just that the various codes and tests were so clever, it was the whole illusion of it. A place that looks like a hotel but is in fact a locked box.

As he checked every room, he imagined the notoriety that would come afterwards. It would be his final 'F.U.' to anyone who'd ever written him off, to all the agents who had ignored his appeals for representation, to all the producers who had said his ideas weren't good enough. The excitement was palpable, he could almost taste it. He had heard it called 'wire in the blood' – the feeling of adrenaline coursing through your body. He hoped he'd done enough to recreate that sensation for the people who would arrive here soon; that they would feel more alive than they ever had as they rode the roller-coaster of fear and elation.

He opened the app on his phone and tested each lock in turn.

When he was a child his mother had won *Puzzle Me This*, a Channel 5 rival to *The Crystal Maze*. It was no doubt the reason he had wanted a job in TV. But now, in the days of *Survivor* and *The Hunted*, it wasn't enough to watch people playing fun games in teams. There needed to be more peril. More drama. More danger.

Without a doubt he was going to deliver on the danger front.

6

Bonnie sat in the boat with her suitcase resting against her legs. The sea air filled her head with memories of walks on the beach and ice creams. Their mum had loved the seaside and they had made frequent trips to Filey and Scarborough in their childhood. Her mum had been such a ball of energy, it was hard to imagine how they were going to exist without her. Everything had taken on a dullness. Food was tasteless, fun was redundant and even the sun above her now seemed less bright.

She watched the others selecting where to sit and chattering excitedly about what was to come. Bonnie smiled at a few of them and said hello but avoided holding eye contact. She wasn't ready to make friends just yet. She was still in shock at having agreed to take Clara's place.

'Grant Withenshaw, *University Challenge* winner and all round smart arse. Nice to meet you.'

Bonnie looked at the outstretched hand. The man who owned it was the kind of blond-haired, blue-eyed rugby player she imagined filling the halls of many a public school. His grin was wide and his cheeks flushed from the sea air but his eyes stared at her with more than a greeting. He was already trying to suss her out.

'Hi, Bon . . . err, Clara,' she said, feeling the embarrassment creep up her neck as she shook his hand.

'What's your story then, Bon-Clara?'

'It's just Clara, I was going to say . . . bonjour.' She shook her head. 'I don't know why.'

'Whatever.' Grant shrugged and moved closer, invading her space. 'What's your story, I asked?'

'I don't really have one.'

'Everyone has one. See that cowboy kid there.' Grant pointed at a slim, mousy-haired guy in a lumberjack shirt and Timberland boots. 'Calls himself Jacko. I mean what's that about? If your name's Jack just call yourself Jack, man.' He laughed loudly then pointed straight at the lady opposite. 'And Maria there reckons she was some chess champion as a kid, but I think it's more likely she was a cake-eating champion. Isn't that right, Maz?'

Bonnie cringed and was about to say how inappropriate that was when Maria spoke.

'Having the smartest mouth doesn't make you the smartest mind, you know.' Maria smiled at Grant but Bonnie detected a twitch that suggested this was not the first time she'd batted off such a hurtful comment.

'Hi, I'm Clara,' Bonnie said to Maria, realizing that taking on her sister's name was going to be much weirder than she'd imagined.

'I saw you on the train and wondered if you were one of us.'

Bonnie felt embarrassed knowing Maria must have spotted the book she had been reading. It was a GCHQ guide to codes and codebreaking, which wouldn't be so bad were it not intended for kids. Clara had bought it for her off Amazon as a joke. But it didn't seem so funny any more. How the hell would she hold her own with chess champions and *University Challenge* winners, never mind beat them to the prize?

26

Grant had moved away to interrogate the latest person to climb aboard; a girl more suited to *Love Island* than an escape room challenge. She wore denim shorts and a crop top under her lemon-yellow raincoat, and had a long black plait emerging from the very top of her head.

'This is all very odd, don't you think?' Bonnie said to Maria. 'I was expecting someone from the production company to meet us.' The instructions Clara had passed on simply said to arrive at Gunwharf Marina in Portsmouth Harbour for midday on 5 September and look out for the *Fortress* logo. Bonnie had found it on the end of a long pole in front of this boat. A member of the crew had then scanned her unique QR code and told her to find a seat as they'd be setting off in twenty minutes.

'I expect they'll be waiting for us there.'

'And where is there, do you know? I couldn't find any details.'

'Because there weren't any. It's the first secret, I suppose. All very exciting.' Maria's chuckle was that of a life-long geek. The kind of girl people at school flocked around when it came to homework help but ignored when it came to any social activities. She was probably in her late thirties but the soft slip-on shoes and beige slacks she wore would have been more at home on an old lady. Her jumper was baggy, which no doubt emphasized her larger figure, and her curly hair had been left untamed in a halo of frizz. Bonnie could see Maria's features were delicate and her eyes kind. If she made an effort . . . Bonnie stopped herself. How shallow and judgemental was that? Good for Maria if she didn't feel the need to conform to some social beauty standard. If she was a brainbox that was surely enough.

Grant's loud booming laugh made Bonnie look over. He was flirting with the young woman who was dressed like a contestant on *Love Island*. She clearly couldn't be that funny because Jacko the cowboy and the older man sitting near by were both looking a little bemused.

Bonnie watched the final contestants walk along the jetty to the boat and have their QR codes scanned before climbing aboard. The first was a red-haired man in a Superdry hoodie, followed shortly after by an intimidating-looking woman with multiple piercings in her nose, ears and tongue. She sat next to Maria and briefly met Bonnie's gaze with an expression of, *What?*, before taking out her phone and studying it. The woman wore black Doc Marten boots with her jeans rolled up above them. Her dark hair was plaited in two neat rows on either side of her head and she had multiple necklaces hanging over an impressive cleavage. Bonnie wondered what kind of bra you needed to wear to make your boobs look that good in a T-shirt. Hers always appeared kind of squidgy and round like half-deflated balloons. She felt self-conscious about the black eyeliner she had applied in an attempt to be more like Clara. It had taken her three attempts to get it right. She had also left her hair loose to match her sister. Bonnie was a throw-it-into-a-ponytail type of person, but she had to embrace her more glamorous side if she stood any chance of pulling off a convincing impression.

By the time they set sail there were eight of them all straining to see where they might be going. Bonnie wondered if the boat trip was something of a ruse to keep the filming location under wraps. They would sail down the coast for a short while then get dropped off somewhere to meet the production team. She imagined a large warehouse or an isolated TV set with multiple buildings, including some depressing-looking dormitory they'd all have to share.

That theory was soon debunked when, instead of sailing left or right along the coast, they headed straight out to sea. Bonnie took a deep breath. This was worse than she had feared.

There were a fair few boats around them, including a large car ferry, presumably on its way to France. She hadn't been told to bring her passport so they couldn't be going too far, plus this was a pretty small boat with no indoor space apart from the cab where the driver sat. The thing bounced and rolled as it moved and Bonnie focused on taking regular deep breaths to avoid any seasickness. That would be far too embarrassing with all these new people.

Most of the group were chatting and pointing out landmarks along the coast, but Bonnie, Maria and Doc Martens sat in silence, Doc Martens still studying her phone.

The nerves came on even stronger when they continued past the pleasure boats and into the darker water. Behind them, Portsmouth looked smaller and smaller and even the Spinnaker Tower began shrinking into the distance.

Maria pointed over Bonnie's shoulder and shouted, 'Isle of Wight.'

Bonnie twisted in her seat to look, hoping that's where they were going, but they moved no closer to it, continuing straight ahead and out to sea.

Maria sat sideways on the bench seat, leaning out over the opposite side of the boat. Her hair rose and fell with the wind and Bonnie could only imagine how hard it was going to be to brush through all those curls after this. Doc Martens glanced up and around with a deep frown then went back to her phone. Bonnie knew she should probably say hello and introduce herself but she was too concerned about where they were heading to do so.

Maria started to bounce up and down and make little squealing noises.

Bonnie leaned back in her seat to look past the cab of the boat and see what she'd seen.

What the hell?

The enormous cylinder rising from the waves was like nothing she had ever seen, a behemoth of algae-covered concrete topped with a ring of stone that towered high above them. Thin windows were spaced equally around the upper circumference making it look like part of an ancient castle – *a fortress.*

'What is that?' she asked.

'A Solent sea fort. There are four of them,' shouted Maria over the noise of the boat engine. 'Built in the war to defend attacks from the sea. It's perfect. There will literally be no escape!'

Bonnie faked a smile in response as she looked up at the thing. She had hoped for somewhere she could simply pack a bag and walk away from if she found the whole thing too ridiculous or humiliating.

Crap, crap, crappity, crap, she thought, realizing the only choice she had now was to play the stupid thing.

7

The boat moored on the far side of the fort next to a wide-framed scaffold that rose up to a doorway in the upper stone section. Above the door, on the rooftop level, sat a curved glass building shaped like a ship's stern and topped with a red and white lighthouse. A large sign had been strung across the scaffold, red letters on a black background, announcing, THE FORTRESS. The structure looked even more robust close up. It reminded Bonnie of the large gas storage cylinder they used to pass on the motorway when Mum took her and Clara to visit their grandfather as kids.

To reach the doorway they were told to take turns climbing a thin metal ladder and then zigzagging up the metal staircase. After climbing the ladder they would need to reach back to grab their suitcase from the person below. *Love Island Girl* kicked up a fuss at this point.

'Is there not another way in?' she asked the crew. 'I can't climb that.'

Bonnie could understand her concern. The water was choppy and the ladder looked wet and rusted in parts. The female crew member who had scanned their QR codes at the marina smiled and told them this was where their challenges began. And so the group did as they were instructed.

Bonnie was the last to climb.

'You go, I'll pass your case,' said the female crew member.

Bonnie wrapped her hands around the cold metal rung above her and began to climb. A gust of wind pasted her hair across her face and she let go with one hand to brush it away, only for a second gust to blow her whole body to the side. She gripped tighter to the ladder with her left hand, the metal feeling slick and slippy under her skin. *Good lord, this is awful.* Quickly pushing her hair behind her ear, she grabbed hold again with her right hand and climbed up to where her fellow contestants sounded like a gaggle of excited geese. She thanked the crew member for passing her case up, expecting the woman to follow her, but she didn't. She gave a quick smile and a half wave before untying the boat and using one leg to push it away from the wall.

Bye, then, thought Bonnie, watching her only means of escape sail away.

'They were built in the late 1800s as a defence against Napoleon, you know?' Maria looked far too excited. 'They had to make them out of iron and concrete because granite wasn't strong enough to withstand the waves but it took so long to do it that the threat from France was over. Cost a fortune as well.'

'I bet,' said Bonnie, trying to look interested. She sensed Maria needed a friend.

'Are we going in, then?' said Grant.

'Don't we need to wait for someone?' *Love Island* Girl looked windswept and her thick mascara had smudged around her left eye.

Grant strode towards the large white double doors and pushed against them. 'It's locked.'

'Of course it is. It's a fortress,' said the older guy, who had looked bemused at *Love Island* Girl and Grant's conversation on the boat.

The group all chuckled, which clearly irritated Grant. He said something under his breath before looking at the older guy. 'OK, then, Dennis, why don't you argue your way in, Mr Lawyer?'

'Oh, we have a smart alec. That'll be useful.' The sarcasm in Dennis's words had an edge to it. Bonnie guessed the man didn't suffer fools, which would make this whole experience a trial for him.

'Don't argue, they'll already be filming, I bet.'

You hope, thought Bonnie, watching *Love Island* Girl scanning the walls for cameras and adjusting her hair.

'This is so exciting. I love it.'

These people were going to be intolerable and Bonnie could be stuck with them for weeks. Failing early and going home was looking ever more appealing. Sod the prize money.

As the group continued to discuss whether they should find a different way in or wait for someone to greet them, Bonnie watched the woman in the Doc Martens study the area by the door. She felt around the edges of the door frame and then stooped down to look at the large metal doorknob, twisting it one way and then the other. After a while she stepped back to look up at the wall and then she looked down at her feet for a long moment.

'Hey, everyone,' said the woman. 'HEY!'

The group stopped talking and turned to face her.

'There's a pressure pad here under my foot. This has got to be how we open the door.'

'Let's see.' Grant strode over and crouched by her feet. 'There's another over there,' he said, moving a few steps away and standing on it.

'And one here,' said Maria, who walked to stand a little to Doc Martens's left.

Bonnie looked around where she stood for another of the round black discs.

'I bet there's eight of them,' said Doc Martens. 'One each.'

Love Island Girl and the lawyer called Dennis also found a disc each near to where they stood, leaving just Bonnie, the red-haired guy and the cowboy called Jacko still searching. When she could find nothing in the immediate area she began moving along the thin corridor that stretched away from their mooring point and around the fort's perimeter. She tried not to look over the side. All that separated her from the sea below was a set of thin white railings and a great height. She focused instead on the floor ahead.

'Have you found yours?' shouted someone.

Why is mine one of the last? she thought. *How come because you were all lucky enough to spot one near you, mine is the missing one? Like I'm letting the group down or something.* She knew the answer of course: the competition had already begun and she was falling behind.

When she had walked so far along that she couldn't see the group when she turned back, she returned to find Jacko coming from the opposite direction shaking his head. The red-haired guy still stood where they'd left him looking at his phone.

'Come on, you lot,' called Grant. 'They must be some-where. Does someone need to help you?'

Bonnie ignored him and moved towards Jacko.

'There isn't another one around there,' she said. 'I walked way along and there's nothing.'

'Same my way,' said Jacko.

'Wait,' said Doc Martens. 'Ours are all here in front of the door. It doesn't make sense that the others would be away and separate. Plus we're all standing in a neat shape, look.'

Bonnie turned to study the group's formation.

'It's a pentagon,' said Jacko. 'You're standing in the shape of a pentagon.'

'OK', said Maria, 'and this whole thing is a cylinder, so is the key to unlocking the door to do with shapes? The door isn't unlocked yet, is it, Jaide?'

Doc Martens tried to reach the door handle but she couldn't. She looked at Bonnie and Jacko. 'Go on then, you can move.'

Bonnie glanced at the redhead, who still stared at his phone, then she walked to the large metal doorknob and tried to turn it, but there was no give. She and Jacko tried pushing against the door but it didn't budge.

'There must be a key pad or a screen or something written over there to give us a clue to what to do,' said Dennis.

Jaide answered, 'There isn't. I checked.'

'Well, that's ridiculous,' said Dennis. 'How can they expect us to get in without a clue?'

'We found a clue,' said Maria. 'The pentagon.'

'Yes, but we have no idea how to use it,' Dennis replied.

'That's kind of the point of the game,' said Jacko under his breath. He glanced Bonnie's way and smiled. 'Jacko, hi.'

'Clara, nice to meet you. Do you think the fact we don't have a spot to stand on means we're already out?'

'Nah, it just means we're in control right now. None of them can move. Let's keep it that way for a while.' He winked and Bonnie smiled.

'There is absolutely no signal here,' said the red-haired guy in a soft Geordie accent. He looked around the group as if seeing them all for the first time. 'What's going on?'

Everyone began talking at once and the noise became a little unbearable. It was going to be an awful show to watch if they carried on like this. Bonnie walked away from the door and around the outside of the standing group, trying to memorize the various names. Dennis was the older guy and Grant had said he was a lawyer. Maria had called the woman wearing the Doc Martens Jaide. Jacko was the guy with the checked shirt and she was sure someone had called the red-haired man either Ross or Russ. That left *Love Island* Girl. The only one with no name yet. Bonnie was about to approach her to ask when Jacko called out.

'Clara, look here.'

Jacko stood staring up at the arch over the doorway.

'What am I looking at?' she said on joining him.

'There is another shape you can make from five equidistant points, right?' He pointed at a small wooden object attached to the ceiling.

'A star. A five-pointed star.'

'What's going on?' said Grant. 'Stop whispering.'

'We're not, we're just conferring. Jacko's solved it, I think. If he's right you're standing at the points of a star and there's some kind of button up here with a star on it.'

'We need a pole or something,' said Jacko.

'Just lift her up,' said Grant.

'I could?' Jacko looked at Bonnie and then up at the button.

'Or you could use that,' said Maria, pointing to a long broom lying on the ground.

'It's a star because we're going to become stars,' said *Love Island* Girl.

Bonnie exchanged a look with Jacko, who smiled before fetching the brush.

'Go ahead,' he said, handing it to her.

'No, it's your victory.'

'I insist, please. Then if I'm wrong you can take the blame.'

Bonnie shook her head a little but took the broom and reached up to push its end against the small wooden star. It depressed a little with a small clicking sound and then the double door swung wide in one smooth motion.

'We are going to smash this,' said Grant, barging past them.

'What did *you* do?' said Jaide to him as she also passed by.

Love Island Girl had come to stand next to Bonnie in the doorway.

'Hi, I'm Clara.'

'Charlie. Wow! Look at this place.'

The inside was totally at odds with the industrial exterior. The wide entrance hall they walked into had a huge Union flag covering one wall and two doorways leading left and right into curved rooms with highly polished wooden floors that stretched away from them in both directions. Ahead, another door opened on to an internal courtyard. Through the glass doorway Bonnie could see a central oval surrounded by iron railings, with steps down to the lower level and a set of iron stairs climbing up to the roof, presumably providing access to the glass building she had seen from the boat.

Bonnie and Charlie followed the rest of the group, who had turned left and walked under a red brick arch with the sign OFFICERS' MESS above it. The vaulted curves of the red brick ceiling reached down to encase floor-level arched windows and open fireplaces with stone surrounds. Two round tables, each with eight plush leather dining chairs, sat in each of the two window arches. Above one fireplace was a polished propellor from the front of an old-fashioned aircraft and against the opposite wall stood a line of six silver ice buckets on tall stands.

Charlie paused under one of the many cameras mounted on the walls. It had a small green light on and a long, foam-covered microphone attached to the top. 'How cool is this?' She faced it head-on. 'Hi, I'm Charlie, age twenty, and I am going to win this. You know why? I want it more than anyone else here.'

Because that's what it takes to win, wanting it most, thought

Bonnie, but she smiled when Charlie looked at her for approval.

'Your turn.'

'No thanks,' said Bonnie, walking swiftly away.

Charlie caught up, laughing. 'You know you're already on camera? Anything you say or do can end up making the edit.' Charlie took Bonnie's hand and gave it a squeeze before dragging her along to explore. Something about her enthusiasm reminded Bonnie of Clara and she wondered how her sister was feeling having been left at home. She recalled how excited Clara had been when she had told Bonnie she'd won a place. 'Don't look so surprised,' Clara had said, then she had laughed and skipped away to call her closest friends and tell them the news. It had been the first time Bonnie had heard Clara laugh since Mum had died.

Eventually they walked back via the entrance hall and through to the other side. The sign for this area read VICTORY BAR and its alcoves were furnished with plush leather chairs, velvet sofas and polished wooden tables. The candelabra lights and thick black chains and hoops crossing the ceiling made it feel like they were inside an ancient castle.

They entered the GUARDS' ROOM, which had a piano inside along with an old-fashioned desk and a large globe. When Charlie opened one of the desk drawers there was an old gas mask inside. 'Awesome.'

Bonnie wondered if she should point out that things that were awesome were supposed to fill you with awe. She wasn't sure a musty old war relic quite fitted the description, but she knew Clara would never do such a thing. In fact she felt sure Clara would adore Charlie. Bonnie ran her fingers through her hair. It was wind-swept and tangled from the trip over and the climb. She wanted to tie it back but knew Clara wouldn't do that.

When they caught up with the group, everyone was standing around a large wooden noticeboard edged in thick rope next to the bar. Pinned to its surface was a map of the floor showing an arc of bedrooms numbered one to eight. Down the side of it hung eight numbered keys.

'Do we just pick one?' Maria was saying as the TV screen attached to the wall buzzed with static, then displayed a single red dot blinking in its centre. After a few seconds a man began to speak and the red dot stretched into subtitles.

'Welcome to *The Fortress*. We start as we mean to go on. You are alone and stranded together to solve the ultimate puzzle. The public will be watching. Some may help you. All will be judging you.'

The man's voice was distorted and had a tinny element to it, presumably to make him sound mysterious or creepy.

'Oh, that's a bit cheesy, isn't it?' said Dennis to no one in particular.

The TV screen divided into three columns. The column on the right played images of the group entering the building and looking around in surprise. The one on the left displayed the show's Twitter feed, which announced that *The Fortress* was now live, and the one in the centre had the show's Instagram page, which displayed the application videos of all eight of them.

A wave of chatter and nervous laughter rippled across the group.

'Here we go, then,' said the redhead called Russ or Ross. 'How awful was your application vid?'

'Godawful,' Bonnie said and she meant it. Clara would no doubt have come over as bubbly and fun. Bonnie had to live up to that . . . somehow. She studied the silent image of Clara talking to the camera. Her hair was a shade or two lighter than Bonnie's natural colour, so Bonnie had visited the hairdresser two weeks ago and had blonde highlights put in. Clara's face was also a little longer but there was nothing Bonnie could do about that.

The tinny voice reminded them they had signed a disclaimer allowing the show to broadcast any footage it felt appropriate. 'If you don't want your loved ones to hear you swear, don't swear,' TV man said. 'If you want people to like you, be nice. If, on the other hand, you want to win, do whatever you please.'

The group laughed.

'The format of the show is simple. You are here to solve a series of challenges, each providing a clue to unlocking the secrets of the fortress. At regular intervals viewers will be asked to vote for who should complete an individual escape room, or even a two-person duel. In these cases, if you fail to escape you will remain locked in and your time on the show will be over. The rest will play another day.'

'And the winner is the one left at the end,' said Grant, grinning at the others.

'Or it's the one who solves the puzzle first. The whole point is to unlock the secrets of the fortress, isn't it?' said Maria.

The group looked at the screen. The red dot blinked back at them. After a few seconds, the voice said, 'Along the way you will uncover clues. Clues that will be critical to your survival. Pay attention. They are everywhere.'

Bonnie looked around the room at the photographs and information cards dotted on the walls, relics from the fort's past gathering dust on the various shelves and sideboards, and multiple rooms and cubbyholes stretching out from the corridor. The place was vast. She sensed they hadn't explored a quarter of it yet.

'Your first task is simple. Pick a room, unpack, then head

up to the sun deck on the top floor to get to know each other. You never know when you might need a friend.'

The red dot signed off with the text: GOOD LUCK, THE DIRECTOR.

As soon as the TV went black, Charlie took the initiative and grabbed one of the keys. The rest of the group followed, leaving Bonnie with the last one. *God's in heaven, lucky seven*, she thought, unhooking it. Her grandad had been an avid bingo player.

She checked the map and made her way along the corridor to find her room. She passed Dennis and Jaide – neither of whom glanced her way. There was a slight musty smell to the whole place but each room she passed was furnished with a grand-looking double bed covered in luxury bedding. When she came to her own room it was decorated in lilac and grey with an antique dressing table. Her French-style bed sat under a brick arch and at its base was a silver-coloured, velvet blanket box. Her bedside tables were silver-coloured wooden ovals with dainty drawers and curved legs. Opposite the bed was a white leather sofa and glass coffee table, and under the deep windowsill sat two grey armchairs with lilac cushions.

Wow, thought Bonnie. Not the dormitory accommodation she had been fearing.

She placed her wheely case on top of the blanket box and removed her toiletry bag before carrying it to the en suite. This was equally impressive with a large mirror above two his and hers sinks, an oval bathtub and a rain shower in the corner. She placed her bag between the sinks and ran the water until it felt warm. She washed her face, feeling instantly better. It already felt like it had been a long day and she had that grubby feeling that was particular to travel.

As she brushed through her tangled hair she walked to the

window in the bedroom to look out. The view stretched across the sea to Portsmouth. She had to admit this was pretty cool and one of the most luxurious rooms she'd ever stayed in. Plus that first test hadn't been too bad. She'd played a key role in it and that made her feel confident for the first time.

Relax and enjoy it. It might not be so bad, she thought, moments before the air was filled with a blood-curdling scream.

8

By the time Bonnie emerged into the brightness of the central courtyard the screaming had merged into shouting, and if she wasn't mistaken laughter. She found herself surrounded by high brick walls topped with black iron railings. Immediately ahead of her were steps up to the glass building with the red and white lighthouse on its roof that she had seen from the boat. Turning on the spot she saw two other iron staircases leading to different raised sections and at the top of one stood most of the group. Bonnie rushed to join them. The first thing she saw was Charlie sitting on the floor with her head between her knees and Jacko crouching by her side rubbing her back. The shouting was coming from Jaide and the laughter from Grant and Russ. These people could only have been moments ahead of her. What on earth had happened?

And then she saw it.

The woman's body was half naked and slumped over so that her head was fully submerged in the water of a hot tub. Her hair splayed out around her and her arms bobbed up and down. Bonnie's instant shock was diluted by the reactions around her; the laughter and the lack of panic. What she was seeing couldn't be true.

'You scared the bloody crap out of us,' Jaide was shouting.

Charlie lifted her head to reply. 'I told you, I thought it was real.'

'It's an escape room challenge, you know, a murder mystery!'

'I wasn't expecting a dead body.'

Grant and Russ dissolved into more fits of laughter and Charlie's head sank back between her knees.

'What's going on?' Maria arrived last and a little out of breath.

'Dead body,' said Dennis, who then waved the piece of A5 card he had been reading in the air. He had small brown reading glasses perched on the end of his nose. 'And a clue. It appears there will be no rest for the wicked in this place.'

Bonnie nearly asked him what he'd been expecting when he applied but then she remembered the cameras and the microphones. Best not to draw attention to herself.

'What have you got there?' Grant approached Dennis and attempted to take the card away, but Dennis moved it deftly out of reach.

'I'm perfectly capable of reading aloud, thank you.'

'What are you waiting for, then?' said Grant.

Had these people forgotten they were being filmed? Surely they wanted to present themselves in the best possible light. Perhaps it was a tactic to get noticed, or maybe they didn't realize how they were coming over, in which case they needed a helpful hint.

'Maybe we should try to work together and enjoy this thing,' Bonnie said.

Her words landed on total silence for a beat or two before Maria said, 'Hear, hear,' and patted her arm.

'OK, Mum, sorry, Mum,' said Grant, and Russ sniggered behind him.

'What's the clue, Dennis?' Charlie was blowing air up on to her face in an attempt to pretend she'd not been crying.

Dennis turned the card around so everyone could see how the words were laid out as he read them aloud.

> One day in may,
> Ann dashed away,
> A dot at sea,
> Who waved at me.

'Oh, that's easy,' said Maria. 'Morse code. Ann *dashed* away, a *dot* at sea.'

'Oh yeah,' said Charlie.

'And what about the rest of it? Why one day in May, why Ann and why did she wave?' said Jaide, sounding a touch irritated with Maria.

Bonnie thought for a moment. Something about waving from the sea triggered a memory. 'Is that a reference to the poem?' she said. 'The one about not waving but drowning.' She had studied it in English at school and it had always struck her as tragic.

'Hence the dead bird,' said Grant.

'It's a woman, not a bird. She doesn't have wings and feathers,' Dennis said.

Grant shrugged and smirked at Russ. They were quickly becoming a gang.

'And may isn't capitalized,' said Jacko. 'So it's not referencing the month of May or a person.'

'One day in may, one day in may, one day in . . . mayday. It's mayday!' said Jaide.

'Ha ha. OK,' said Dennis. 'We have a mayday call, Morse code and a drowned lady called Ann. What can we take from that?'

The group fell silent as everyone tried to work out what the rhyme was telling them.

'Well, S.O.S. is the most famous Morse code message and it essentially means mayday, which comes from the French *m'aider*, for help me,' said Maria.

'You are really good at this,' Charlie said, and Maria looked like she might burst with happiness.

'It's nothing. I like military stuff, history and things.'

'This is a dream come true for you, then,' said Russ with just a tinge of mickey-taking in his tone.

'We are smashing it again,' said Grant.

Jaide shook her head. 'We're far from solving this thing yet. What now?'

The group began looking around for more clues or instructions.

'Where did you find the card?' Maria asked Dennis.

'Pinned to the side of the hot tub.'

He went to show her as Charlie and Jacko followed Jaide back down the hot tub steps to the main rooftop level. Grant and Russ whispered something to each other and began laughing again.

Bonnie looked at the various cameras around them. She'd counted ten by the time Jaide spoke. They all had microphones attached. She had expected they would all be having to wear a lapel mic. Hopefully the fact they weren't meant they'd be afforded a degree of privacy.

'The lighthouse. That's where you'd signal for help or keep people from danger. Might there be something in there?'

'There's also an old comms room inside,' said Jacko. 'I bet that has a Morse code machine.'

'Great,' said Jaide. 'Let's divide and conquer. Ladies, come with me. Guys, you go check out the comms room, see if you can find anything useful.'

Maria and Dennis placed the dummy on the floor by the pool. They had been checking over its surface for clues.

'Who made you the boss?' said Grant.

'I did,' said Jaide.

'Well, I'm leading the men, then.'

'I sense he's a touch competitive,' Maria said to Jaide as they climbed the stairs up to the roof of the large glass building.

'I feel like I've met him many times before.'

The women shared a smile as they reached the AstroTurf roof. The small red and white lighthouse was situated right in the middle.

'I don't get what we're looking for. What are we supposed to be doing?' Charlie said as she joined them inside the small round room at the top of the lighthouse. It was a tight space for the four women so Bonnie squeezed up close to the wall.

'I think that's how the game goes. Like outside. We get one clue that leads to another and so on until we work out what to do with it,' said Maria. 'It's right up my alley. I'm as happy as Larry.'

'Who's Larry?' said Charlie.

Jaide smiled as she said, 'It's just a saying.'

Maria launched into another encyclopaedic answer. 'It comes from Australia. Some think Larry is a shortened form of Larrikin, which is a slang word to describe a troublesome character. Others say it comes from a famous Aussie boxer who never lost a fight.'

'Who needs Google when you have Maria?' said Jaide. 'Here we go. Check this out.' She was pointing to a black card attached to the front of a framed newspaper article standing on the small control table.

In the centre of the card was a string of dots and dashes.

.... / . / .-.. / .--.

'Anyone speak Morse code?' said Jaide. 'Maria?'

Maria shook her head. 'I know S.O.S., that's all.'

'Which is?'

'Dot, dot, dot, dash, dash, dash, dot, dot, dot.'

Bonnie looked at the symbols on the card. 'Doesn't help us.'

'There'll be a key somewhere, won't there? That's what most escape rooms have. The Morse code alphabet in a book or on a poster,' said Charlie.

Everything's a clue, thought Bonnie.

'Or scattered around the place one letter at a time,' said Jaide, pointing to a small sticker on one of the windows looking out to sea.

.‾

A

'We'd better get hunting then and go tell the guys. This could take a while,' said Maria.

'Wait,' said Bonnie. 'What about the article? Is that a clue?'

They all gathered round the framed newspaper article to which the code had been pinned and read it in silence.

'Whoa,' said Jaide.

'That's crazy,' said Charlie.

'Do you think it's true?' said Bonnie, aware of the little green light on the camera in front of her.

'I expect we'd have heard of it if it was,' said Maria. 'Don't you think?'

The women all looked at each other.

9

They found Jacko and Dennis heading back their way through the main floor. The two men were talking in low voices, possibly to avoid being heard by microphones.

'Find anything?' said Jaide. She held the small black card against her waist so the men wouldn't see it. Bonnie wondered at the game-playing nature of this. Winning was not only going to be about doing well yourself; it was about making sure the competition didn't.

Dennis held his own black card aloft. 'We sure did. It's Morse code as we thought.'

'We found one too. Can you decipher it?'

Dennis shook his head. 'Grant and Russ have stayed in the comms room. There's a load of books they're checking for a copy of the Morse code alphabet.'

'They're wasting their time. Look.' Jaide pointed to the white sticker on the wall behind the two men.

··−·

F

'We found A in the lighthouse then G and T on the sun deck.'

'G and T? Someone's got a sense of humour,' said Dennis.

'I'll show you mine if you show me yours.' Jaide tapped the little black card against her purple painted fingernails with a rhythmic clack, clack, clack. Bonnie realized she was tapping out the SOS rhythm.

Dennis and Jaide swapped cards and Bonnie leaned in to see what the men's looked like.

$$-. \ / \ --- \ / \ --- \ / \ -. \ / \ .$$

Maria said, 'Dash, dash, dash. That makes the second and third letters both O, with the same letter, dash dot, either side, like *noon*, but then there's another letter at the end. It can't be S as we know that's dot, dot, dot, so what other letter might go at the end?'

Bonnie mentally ran through the alphabet: toot and poop were the only other words she could think of. 'Y maybe, like tooty or poopy?'

Maria was biting her lip. 'That last dot on its own has to be a common letter, don't you think? Something that's used a lot as it's only one dot.'

'So a vowel?' said Bonnie. 'It's not A or O as we have their Morse codes, so could it be E? That has to be one of the most frequently used letters.'

'Wouldn't it be easier to just find the stickers?' said Charlie.

'Also, our card has numbers on the back. It says one of eight.' Dennis looked at the one Jaide had given him. 'This says one of eight also, so we have six more to find.'

'Where did you find yours?' asked Bonnie. 'Ours was pinned to a newspaper story about a pregnant woman who was stranded here alone after her family succumbed to carbon monoxide poisoning. It said the only reason she survived was because the foetus stored extra oxygen.'

'Is that true?' said Jacko.

'Don't be ridiculous, it's a game,' said Jaide. 'Everything is made up.'

'I'm not so sure,' said Dennis. 'Ours was tucked into the frame of an information sheet about the soldiers posted here in the First World War. Apparently they were specifically selected because they couldn't swim. So they couldn't go AWOL. That rings true to me. It's the kind of thing the bastards at the top would do.'

'That's awful,' said Charlie. 'What if the place was attacked and they needed to swim to survive?'

Dennis shrugged.

'There's probably some clues in these stories,' Maria said, 'but let's split up and see if we can find the other cards and letters first.'

'I'll go tell Grant and Russ,' said Jacko.

The group all moved away in different directions. It was a big space to cover. Bonnie fetched a pad of paper and pencil she'd spotted on the sideboard. She opened the first page and wrote down the letters and respective Morse codes that they'd already found on the stickers. Then she began searching for more. She discovered one of the black cards in the hallway opposite her bedroom. It was attached to a framed set of black and white drawings of the fort in various stages of construction. In the short description below the frame, one paragraph stood out to Bonnie. It said construction workers at the time had been spooked by stories of the ghost of the Solent who was rumoured to drag lone workers into the ocean for company.

This was no light-hearted escape room. Whatever secrets they were here to uncover, Bonnie guessed they were going to be dark.

She had to admit the whole thing was better than she had

expected, particularly the fact they were here alone. She had wondered how the production company would make it feel like an authentic escape room with lots of crew on set filming, so this was clever. And the fact that the theme was a little dark only added to the mood. Who didn't love a good spooky story? For the first time she felt grateful to Clara, but also sorry for her. Her sister would have been in her element here. Bonnie could imagine Clara's excitement infecting the group with a sense of fun. She was so much more colourful and warm than Bonnie. Everyone would have loved her. Bonnie had intended to be more Clara-like in this thing, but it was harder than she'd expected. Maybe it was all the cameras, or the fact these people were so smart. Faking it simply didn't feel like a viable option. The only tactic that made sense was to be unobtrusive and avoid attracting too much attention.

Twenty minutes later the group were all back on the sun deck. Between them they had found all of the eight black cards and everyone had either noted down the various stickers they had found or photographed them on their phones.

'Let's start with this one,' Maria said, picking out the card Dennis had found with the double Os.

$$-. / --- / --- / -. / .$$

'The single dot is E, like you thought, Clara, so what's "dash, dot"?' After a few seconds of checking her notes, she said, 'It's NO ONE. "Dash, dot" is an N.'

Bonnie checked the five symbols against her list and nodded.

'Let's do the one we found,' Maria said, placing the card from the lighthouse in front of her. They were standing in the lower deck area of the roof terrace, shaded from the breeze and using the wall of the hot tub deck as a table.

. . . . / . / .-.. / .--.

'The four dots are an H, the dot on its own is E,' said Maria.

'It's HELP,' cut in Bonnie, scanning her alphabet codes for the other two letters.

'HELP NO ONE,' said Jacko. 'Is that an instruction?'

'Or a tip,' said Bonnie, looking over at Jaide and Dennis, who were engaged in a discussion about the accuracy of the information.

'I'm telling you, it's not all true,' Jaide was saying. 'These games are all fantasy.'

'No, not always, some of the online escape rooms like Red Eye and Cipher-Ville use real historical facts to build their puzzles.'

'OK, that might be true, but Russ found one of the cards pinned to a newspaper story about some eighties celebrity who was locked in the basement here for a TV show. You can't believe that's true?'

'What do you think *we* are here for?'

'Are you talking about Jeremy Beadle?' Maria said as she carried on noting down letters for their next word. 'I remember that, Ant and Dec, *Saturday Night Takeaway*, first broadcast in 2002.'

'See?' said Dennis. 'And I bet the selection of soldiers who can't swim was true, and the fact the finance guy who turned this into a hotel holed himself up here for months to avoid his debtors.'

'COMING and FOR are the next two,' said Maria, 'and then we have two words that are the same. Two dots followed by three dots.'

'That's IS,' said Bonnie.

The others started to gather around them.

'HELP IS COMING,' said Charlie, reading the deciphered words.

'Or NO ONE IS COMING,' said Jaide.

'USELESS is the next one,' said Maria.

'And CALLING is the last,' said Bonnie.

'HELP IS COMING,' Charlie repeated. 'NO ONE IS USELESS FOR CALLING. That fits with the S.O.S. and mayday in the rhyme.'

'That's sweet but I don't think that's it,' said Dennis, narrowing his eyes and biting his bottom lip.

'Me neither,' said Bonnie. 'I think all those stories about people being trapped here are a clue to this sentence.' She moved the words Maria had written on separate scraps of paper into a line then stood back to let everyone see.

CALLING FOR HELP IS USELESS, NO ONE IS COMING.

10

Chardonnay @Chardonnay84

Does anyone else think this is totally lame? Who are these people? Total dullards. How long did it take them to open a door FFS?!!

LaLa Boyes @Laboy

Like you could do any better sweetheart. I'll certainly be watching again, if only to check out Grant's hot bod. #THEFORTRESS #Secrets

---

Katy Sky @Katysky

What is going on with Maria's hair. Seriously, girl, brush it. You're on TV!

P Foulds @PFoulds345

She is rocking that frizz bomb. Love it. Plus she's a mega brain. #humangoogle #unlockthefortress

Heather @Heather_Trent2

Loving the Maria, Jaide girl power. Their little asides and amused looks are cracking me up. #TheFortress #Girlpower

---

Paul Brunson @PaulBrunson4

Loving this. Finally we have reality TV for the grown-ups. I'll be racing you to every clue. #thefortress #channel5

Gabe @GRiel

CALLING FOR HELP IS USELESS, NO ONE IS COMING. This gave me goosebumps. #Thefortress

11

'Speaking of calling for help, you do know we have no WiFi as well as no phone signal on this place?' said Grant, holding up his huge phone.

'They can't have us contacting people for clues,' Jaide said. 'Hey, the doll is gone.'

Bonnie looked at Russ, who was standing above them by the hot tub.

'Are you sure?' Dennis went to look. He and Maria had placed the dummy on the floor before they all went on a hunt for the Morse code cards. 'Who moved it?' Dennis stood with his hands on his hips and stared at the group below like a school headmaster.

Bonnie looked around and saw the same confused expression on everyone's face. Everyone except Grant, that is, who had a slight smirk on his lips. *What are you up to?* she thought. He seemed the type for practical jokes and she could imagine him getting a kick out of spooking people; it was no surprise his partner in crime Russ was the one who spotted the missing dummy.

'Someone must be here with us,' said Charlie. 'It makes sense they wouldn't leave us completely alone. Wouldn't it be a health and safety thing?'

'Or insurance,' said Grant.

'Well, I don't bloody like it,' said Dennis. 'Show yourself. Don't be creeping around the place. We're all grown-ups. There's no need for stupidity.'

There was a moment of quiet as the group waited to see if any response would come.

'More importantly,' said Maria, 'what are we supposed to do with this Morse code clue?'

'Log it. Remember it. What did the Director say? "You are alone and stranded together to solve the ultimate puzzle." You can't cheat, you can't get help, you have to just do the work.' Jaide didn't meet Maria's eye as she answered.

'Maybe there's something from the Director on the screen in here. It looks to be on,' said Grant, who had moved to the upper deck and now stood at the entrance to the glass building with the lighthouse on top.

As Bonnie followed the others, she noted that the sign above the doorway read PARADISO.

Inside, the TV embedded in the wall was much larger than the one downstairs and it was populated by a stream of Twitter comments.

'Brace yourselves,' Grant said as they all filed in. 'It's not all pretty.'

The comments scrolled in a stream of consciousness from what looked to be hundreds of people. Bonnie wasn't sure how she felt about that. Clara's name was not mentioned in any of the tweets she read, which she was more than happy about. She watched Maria pretending to laugh at the various attacks on her looks and could not miss Grant's smug expression at seeing the odd comment about him. Even Dennis and Jaide were transfixed. These people had not only wanted to test their brains in this thing; they actually wanted to be on TV. She knew this had been true of Clara too. Her sister was always the school show-off, auditioning for all the productions, or singing and dancing on tables at parties. She loved nothing more than knowing the room was looking at her, so this would have been intoxicating. Bonnie sank back towards the wall and joined Russ, who looked as uninterested as she was.

'What do you think of it so far?' she asked.

He raised his eyebrows and moved his head from side to side. 'It's something to do.'

'You and Grant seem pally.'

'He's a good guy.'

'Are you not interested in what people are saying about us?'

'You have a lot of questions.'

'Just trying to be nice.'

'You're all trying too hard. Everyone's too keen to get stuck in.' Russ's tone sounded judgemental, like he was somehow better than the rest of them.

'So we should stand by and let everyone else do the work, like you do?'

'I'm just saying. Don't be so . . . enthusiastic. Be cool. Take it in. Let the others fail first.'

'Do you think you're cool, Russ?' Bonnie was aware of her heart beating fast. She didn't like conflict but she couldn't help but call out his bullshit. He was clearly holding back because he had nothing to contribute, not because he was some cool tactician waiting patiently to take the glory. The guy was out of his depth.

His smile had a bitterness to it as he pushed away from the wall and walked off.

Bonnie moved outside. Dusk was upon them and as she looked down on to the top deck with its unfamiliar shapes and dark corners, the structure felt eerie. A shiver ran across her skin. *Was* someone else here with them, or were Grant and Russ making mischief?

She could smell the ocean even though it was hard to see it now the light was dimming. Looking out towards it, she thought of the Solent ghost. She didn't believe in ghosts, or any spiritual ideas actually. Once you'd studied the brain and knew how powerfully it could trick you into seeing things that weren't there, or finding evidence for what you wanted to believe, it made you question every extraordinary claim people made. It was more likely that the construction workers had felt this same chill in the air and thought some ghostly sea creature was watching them. She felt the same about a mass of Twitter users.

'Howdy, partner.' Jacko had followed her out into the fresh air.

'Fully embracing the cowboy title, I see.'

'What choice do I have?'

'You could have got changed.'

'Ouch. That hurts.' His lopsided smile suggested he might not be joking.

'Sorry. You look very nice.'

Jacko hung his head low over the railing with a small laugh. 'Wanna know a secret? I saw this whole outfit in a shop window last week and thought, "That fella looks confident, like the kind of guy people slap on the back and invite to drinks."'

He picked at some chipped paint on the railing. Bonnie studied his profile. He had light freckles covering his skin and what her mum would have called good bone structure.

'So you came in camouflage?' she said.

'Tragic, isn't it?'

'No.' She smiled when he looked her way because she was in camouflage too, only she couldn't admit it without getting thrown off the show and losing a shot at that money.

'You were good today. You solved both challenges.' He nudged her arm as he spoke and she felt a tingle rush across her skin.

'I helped you and Maria solve them. I'm an effective side-kick. I can be the Sundance Kid to your Butch Cassidy any day.'

Jacko laughed deeply, which made her laugh too. It felt good to properly laugh. The tension and weirdness of being thrust into the company of these people in this place had been intense. It was nice to release some of that.

'Where do you think the food is in this place?' she said eventually.

'Oh yeah, didn't you see? The Director put a message on the TV. Not only is there food in the kitchen but we won the code to unlock the wine store when we decoded that message.'

'Well, what the heck are we doing standing out here?'

12

Bonnie awoke to the sound of a low buzzing siren. For a moment she had no idea where she was. Her head hurt and she placed a pillow over it to try and drown out the noise. Then she remembered. She was on a reality show, trapped on a hunk of concrete in the sea and, to make matters worse, she'd downed at least a bottle of wine the night before. *What did I say? What did I do?* The usual hangover questions bounced around her brain as the sick feeling of dread spread across her stomach. She wasn't a big drinker. It didn't take much to get her tipsy and make her stumble about and mumble incoherently. Had she embarrassed herself? Upset anyone?

She sat upright in bed. *Did I reveal the truth about not being Clara?*

The siren stopped.

She climbed out of bed and made her way into the bathroom to turn on the shower. The water was lukewarm and no matter how high she turned the hot tap it did not get any warmer. *Not so luxury*, she thought as she washed her hair as quickly as possible before the water cooled even more.

Afterwards her head felt a little clearer. She remembered laughing a lot at Jacko's stories as they sat slightly away from the group. They had all selected microwavable meals from the rows and rows of them stacked in the fridge. The choices were rice dishes, pasta or noodles. She had gone for tomato pasta, which was surprisingly OK – well, washed down with red wine it was. It had been a pleasant evening. The tensions of the day had settled into a kind of merriment where everyone relaxed, perhaps because for the first time since they had arrived, the camera lights were all off. Charlie turned out to be quite the party girl, making cocktails and even encouraging a drinking game. Once again, Bonnie had been reminded of Clara, who would have done exactly the same. She and Charlie would have had a blast here together.

Bonnie dressed quickly after towel drying her hair and brushing her teeth. The siren was sounding again so she assumed she was being summoned somewhere for something.

'We didn't think you were coming,' said Maria as Bonnie entered the main dining area.

Jacko briefly caught her eye and smiled before looking quickly away.

'Sorry. What's going on?'

'It's nominations,' announced Grant, who had chosen to wear shorts and flip-flops with a muscle T-shirt. 'The selected two have to duel . . . in the basement.' He said the last words in the style of a movie voice-over.

'Someone's going today?'

Bonnie noticed that Charlie had both her fingers crossed behind her back.

The TV displayed a bar chart with each of their names along the bottom and a clock above that was counting down. Only a couple of minutes left.

Maria had the most votes, which struck Bonnie as entirely unfair. She was most definitely their strongest contender. Did the public not like her? Dennis, Grant and Russ also had a good few votes but thankfully she, Charlie, Jaide and Jacko had very few.

As the timer ticked down the final few seconds, Russ's column rose up a couple of points towards Maria's. Bonnie looked at him. The public had spoken. They disliked him as much as she did.

'That's disgusting,' said Charlie. 'Maria was amazing yesterday.'

The siren finally stopped, much to Bonnie's relief, and people started to fetch breakfast from the kitchen.

'How's the head?' Jacko asked, handing her a mug of coffee.

'Was I really embarrassing?' She smoothed down her hair and tried to channel Clara.

'Not at all – you were lovely. Company, I mean,' he said when she raised her eyebrows.

The coffee tasted amazing and she grabbed a croissant out of the bag someone had placed on the side. 'I'm not a good drinker. At least they weren't filming that bit.'

'How can you be sure?'

'The camera lights were off.'

'Wouldn't you do that to catch people out if you were filming this thing?'

'A conspiracy theorist as well as a cowboy. You're the all-American guy, aren't you?'

'Made you think, though, didn't I?' Jacko took his own croissant from the bag and wandered off.

He was right. She was now paranoid that the whole evening had been recorded too. She hoped she hadn't come over as some giggly airhead. She hated the thought of her colleagues seeing that. She knew she was here as Clara, but Clara and her friends knew it was really Bonnie and, once this thing was done, how long would that stay a secret? It wasn't until that moment that Bonnie realized that if by some slim chance she won, the TV company might be able to deny her the prize on the basis of her being here fraudulently. Then this whole thing would have been for nothing. Bonnie threw the remainder of her breakfast in the bin. Her appetite was gone.

In every communal space around the building there was a TV screen and today they all displayed the same message, instructing them to gather by Basement Door One at ten a.m. She checked her watch: it was quarter to. Just enough time to pop back to her room. She passed Basement Door One on the way and pushed a hand against it – a quick look wouldn't hurt – but it was locked.

By the time she returned ten minutes later, her hair was pinned on one side with one of Clara's sparkly clips and her eyeliner and lip gloss were successfully applied. Maria, Jaide, Dennis and Charlie were already gathered.

'This is very unfair,' Bonnie said to Maria.

'I always knew I wouldn't win any popularity contests.'

Bonnie wanted to say something reassuring but couldn't figure out what that might be.

'The basement awaits,' said Grant in his movie voice again. 'Only the strongest will survive.' He patted his mate Russ on the back. 'How ya feeling, Maz?'

'It's Maria,' said Dennis.

'It's fine,' said Maria. 'I don't mind.'

At that moment the basement door swung open.

'Cool,' said Russ, looking a little nervous.

Is it? thought Bonnie. Wasn't there something unnerving about the whole place being remote controlled? It reminded her of movies where the computers take over. She shook the feeling away. Her hangover was giving her the blues.

Cool, damp air wafted out of the doorway. It smelled of dust and salt and something metallic.

'Ladies first,' said Grant.

Jaide pushed past him and walked down the stone steps. Bonnie wished she had half of that woman's bravado.

Bonnie was third to walk down after Maria. On the wall inside the doorway a sign read, DEDUCE NOT. What was that about? Was deduction not the whole point of this place?

The way ahead was lit by low-level LED lights and the steps taking them down into all that concrete were worn in the middle where many boots had trodden. Bonnie tried to imagine what it was like to be here in the midst of war when under attack. Would you feel safer going down these stairs, or fearful that the enemy's bombs would collapse the structure above you and leave you trapped in a concrete prison?

She shook the thought away. At the bottom of the steps they stopped to wait for the others. The passage moving away from them in both directions was dark. The curved walls of the corridor were whitewashed brick, the floor cold stone and the ceiling above so low Bonnie could reach up and touch it. She wished she'd put on an extra layer.

'I don't like this. It's cold and it smells funny,' said Charlie.

'Don't worry, I'll protect you.' Grant put an arm over Charlie's shoulders. She shrugged it away but only after she'd giggled.

Women's lib lives on, thought Bonnie.

'Which way?' said Jaide. 'I'll check this one, someone else go that way.' She began walking away to their left and Dennis did the same on their right. After a few steps the lights above Jaide flickered on. Dennis took a few more steps in the dark.

'I guess we go your way,' he said to Jaide, and the group followed her away from the warmth and light of upstairs into the dark unknown.

13

'This must be it,' said Jaide.

The two rooms in front of them were fully lit and open, unlike others they had passed along the way. Bonnie looked inside the first one. It was narrow and long. There was a small piano keyboard to the left of the door and on the wall above were what looked to be sections of a music score. In the middle of the room was a small table with paper and a pencil. Against the back wall was a cupboard on top of which sat some old-fashioned weighing scales and a bowl of apples. Hanging above that was a cuckoo clock. The rest of the room was empty apart from a couple of battered posters stuck to the walls.

'Here are your instructions, guys,' Jaide said, looking at a small screen, the size of an iPad, that was positioned between the two doors. 'It says you can pick one person each to assist you but they must stay outside. You will be given one minute to read the instructions then you enter each room and close the door. The first to enter the right code and escape will win. The loser remains locked in, their time on *The Fortress* finished. OK. Shall I press enter?'

'Wait, who's helping you?' said Grant to Russ.

'No brainer,' said Russ and the guys high-fived.

Maria looked back at Bonnie. 'Will you help me, please?'

'Of course.'

When Bonnie glanced at Jaide, she caught a frown before the other woman looked quickly away and said, 'Ready?'

Russ and Maria stood side by side in front of the screen. When Jaide touched the word ENTER, a new message appeared with a countdown clock above. Bonnie and Grant moved closer to read it too.

Every Good Boy Does Fine on the line
A FACE within the space will show
The notes you need
To set you free
May be funny or saintly

'I hope you're musical, man,' said Grant.

Russ didn't reply.

When the countdown reached zero the screen became blank. Maria and Russ entered their rooms. As the doors automatically swung closed behind them, blaring music began to play. Bonnie could only see in through a small letterbox opening halfway down the door. She knelt on the floor and lifted the flap inwards with her thumb.

'You OK?' she said loudly to make herself heard over the music.

Maria came closer, 'What?'

'You OK? Do you know what you're doing?'

Maria moved to the table and began writing quickly. Then she looked around at the room before focusing on some music scores on the wall. There were three separate pages each displaying musical notes on a set of five horizontal lines.

68

Underneath them a partially written phrase was written in chalk on the wall.

I ____ you to ____ the ____ bird

Maria came over to Bonnie.

'I think I have to decode these notes into three words to finish the sentence.' She pointed at the music scores.

'Can you read music?'

'No, but I think the instructions told us how.' She read from the piece of paper she had scribbled on. '*Every Good Boy Does Fine on the line. A FACE within the space will show.* The phrase Every Good Boy Does Fine has capitals at the start of each word and FACE is entirely in capitals so I'm thinking, E, G, B, D, F are the notes on the lines and F, A, C, E are those in the spaces.'

'Oh my gosh, I think that's right, yes. I remember something similar from playing the recorder in school. Try it,' said Bonnie, impressed as ever by the speed of Maria's intellect.

'Do you think the letters start at the top and go down or vice versa?'

Bonnie had no idea.

Maria shook her head. 'I'll try both ways.'

Maria ran back to the wall and, using her pencil, began writing letters under the notes on the music scores. After a while she moved back to the beginning, scribbled out what she had written, and started over. Bonnie made out a B, E and G under the first set of notes. *BEG*.

She looked back at the sentence I *BEG* you to *something* the *something* bird. No inspiration came to her for what the other two words could be. She felt entirely helpless. She looked over at Grant, who stood bent forward to look through Russ's door. Every now and then he'd say something into the hole but Bonnie couldn't hear it over the music. That was clever; there would be no cheating and no way of knowing who was faring better.

Come on, Maria. She wanted her to win for many reasons but mainly because the woman deserved to be here more than any of them.

'How's she doing?' mouthed Dennis from beside Grant. The men and women had naturally divided to support their own. People were weird.

Bonnie put her thumbs up and mouthed. 'Russ?'

Dennis waved his hand up and down.

Did that mean OK or not OK? Bonnie wasn't sure.

She focused back on Maria, who was on the final word. When she'd finished she looked around the space then walked over to the cupboard with the scales on top and reached up to the cuckoo clock. After a moment she came to Bonnie.

'The notes spelled out BEGGED, FEED and CAGED, so the sentence is, "I *begged* you to *feed* the *caged* bird." It must be something to do with the cuckoo clock but I can't see any buttons or gadgets.'

Bonnie studied the cabinet and the items on top. 'How about the apples and the scales below? Might the scales be connected to the clock?'

'Why apples? Do birds eat apples?' Maria shouted.

Bonnie shrugged. *Possibly? Maybe?* She wasn't sure. 'It's the only food in there.'

A cheer erupted from the men.

'Quickly,' Bonnie shouted, and Maria ran.

Maria placed an apple in the bowl on one side of the scales, then another. Nothing happened. She placed more apples on the opposite flat side of the scales, again nothing.

'Balance it,' shouted Bonnie through the hole.

'What?' Maria came over.

'Balance the scales with the weights to weigh out the food.'

Maria looked back at the scales then went to remove all the apples before putting just one in the bowl. On the flat side of the scale she began placing various weights from the pile on the table. The apple in the bowl sank low, then rose up high before finally levelling out as she found the right combination. The cuckoo clock sprang to life and out popped the bird with a piece of something attached to its beak.

Maria removed it and unrolled a long piece of card in the shape of a key.

'Do you have it?' Bonnie glanced at Grant, who was still watching Russ.

For the first time Maria looked worried.

'Bring it here and show me.'

'YES!' shouted Grant.

'I don't get it,' said Maria, holding up the key-shaped card.

Bonnie studied the writing along it.

_ IVIN_ _OM_ _Y

Maria's eyes scanned the room frantically. Bonnie could see the woman was starting to panic. Bonnie also looked around the room, pausing for the first time on the posters.

One showed a large bonfire, the other a desert island. She studied the letters on the card again. *Bonfire, alight, fire, island, holiday, paradise.* Nothing fitted. The first word could be living, but what was the second? Homely was the only thing that sprang to mind and she wasn't sure that was a real word. She studied the room again and the closed cupboard. Could there be something inside that?

The song chorus kicked in and Bonnie had a moment of recognition. It was one of Mum's favourites.

Don't get distracted, Maria needs you.

'Maria?' she called, focusing on the task at hand. 'How about the cupboard underneath?'

Maria went to check.

'I can't open it. There's no handle. I think it's locked.' She came back to Bonnie. 'I can't do this. I don't know what I was thinking. I'm going to let you all down. I'm so sorry.'

'OK, so what did it say in your instructions again? Might that be a clue?'

Maria went back to the table to check her scribbles. Another cheer went up from the men. Maria came back to the door.

'The instructions say, "The notes you need to set you free may be funny or saintly." '

When Maria held up the key-shaped card to show Bonnie, her hand was shaking.

_ IVIN_ _OM_ _ Y

'Breathe, we can do this,' Bonnie said, looking Maria in the eye. *Funny, funny, funny – what are other words for funny?* 'Oh! Could the second word be comedy? Living comedy?'

'Yes! Comedy. Thank you.'

Bonnie's attention was drawn once more to the song blaring out. This was a funny song, wasn't it? Mum had liked the

72

band because all their songs were witty. There had been one about a bus journey and another about a woodshed. She recalled that her mum would sing along to them at the top of her voice.

'Stop it, Mum, you're embarrassing,' she remembered pleading one day when she had a schoolfriend over.

'But, darling, it's divine,' her mum had responded over the music with her arms outstretched. 'Divine Comedy.'

'Maria, it's Divine Comedy,' said Bonnie. 'Funny and saintly. It's the name of the band playing now.'

'Divine Comedy. That works!' Maria wrote the missing letters in the spaces on the key-shaped card. 'So D, E, C, E, D are the missing letters.'

'Type them into the lock.'

Maria looked at her blankly. 'There is no lock.'

'What do you mean?' Bonnie looked at her side of the door. There was no handle, no keyhole, no electronic lock – just smooth metal. 'What is there?'

'Nothing. There's nothing.' Maria looked panicked again. 'What do I do? What do I do?'

'COME ON!' shouted Grant over the music.

Bonnie's eyes rested on the only unused item in the room.

'The keyboard,' she said to Maria. 'Maybe you have to play those notes on it?'

Maria's eyes widened. 'But I can't play.'

Bonnie glanced at Grant, who was laughing. This did not look good. Russ was clearly doing well.

Maria walked to the keyboard and studied it. After what seemed like an age she placed her thumb on one of the central keys followed by her index and middle finger on the next two. She took a couple of deep breaths then depressed her index finger, middle finger and thumb one after another and then her middle finger and index finger in reverse.

73

As soon as Maria lifted her finger from the final note the loud music came to an abrupt end. From her very basic music lessons at school, Bonnie realized Maria had somehow found middle C, making D and E the next two notes along.

Bonnie was leaning her weight on the door and as it unlocked she stumbled forward. It reminded her of Clara falling into her room. Was that only last week? It felt like a lifetime ago.

'Yes! Yes! Yes! You total legend,' Jaide was shouting, and beside her Charlie was squealing with delight.

Maria grabbed Bonnie in a tight hug.

Along the corridor the men looked on silently from outside Russ's locked door.

14

The Director

Why an escape room? He expected people might want to know that. It wasn't just that they were fashionable these days. Quite the opposite, actually. It was the history of the things: the fact they had been around since the dawn of mankind. Look at the Garden of Eden – was that not the first escape room ever designed? Two people restricted from leaving their garden paradise because certain truths were hidden from them.

Secrets have always been a tool of power by which the strong become stronger and the weak lose out. The original cipher was invented by none other than Julius Caesar in 100 BC. His simple system of lining up two sets of the alphabet, one above the other, and then moving one set three places to the right so that A becomes D and so on allowed Caesar to send coded messages to his generals in the field. And as a result he became one of Rome's most successful generals and ultimately its dictator.

After that, everything from the Knights Templar to the Illuminati, the Nazis to Bletchley Park led us all here; to a world of spy craft, computers and escape rooms.

He watched the women celebrating their win as the men commiserated with their locked-in teammate. It was indeed a Divine Comedy. How oblivious they were to the truth of things and the reality of what was to come.

For now he would let them enjoy it. He had to admit they were doing well.

15

P Foulds @PFoulds345

I frickin love Maria. She's like a mad professor.
#whoneedsgoogle #frizzfantastic #Thefortressrocks

Amy @Amypeters2

Is anyone else wondering how Charlie made it on The
Fortress? Talk about dumb. Has she said anything useful
yet? #Charlietogo

LaLa Boyes @Laboy

How I would love to be Grant's shorts right now.
#grantsnumberonefan

Freddie @FRBrown5

Russ was cheated. He clearly had the better skills for the
challenge. #thefortressisafix

P Foulds @PFoulds345

No way. He missed the point. It's like he'd never done an escape room before.

Chardonnay @Chardonnay84

Did you see the way Jaide looked at Clara when Maria picked her? Pure jealous hatred. Watch your back Clara. She's out for blood. #Jaidetowin #thefortress

16

'He looked so disappointed,' said Maria, sipping from her champagne flute.

'He deserved to go. He was the weakest link,' said Jaide.

'I think that's a different game,' Bonnie said and the girls all laughed.

They were sitting in the glass building below the lighthouse. The inside fitted perfectly the label of PARADISO. It was furnished in light grey and white with soft comfortable chairs, glass tables and floor to ceiling windows that provided an impressive view of the sea and Portsmouth Harbour beyond.

Maria's congratulatory message on the TV had given her the four-digit code to open one of the padlocked cupboards underneath the glass-topped bar in the corner where they found a fridge stocked with fizz, cheese and meats plus a drawer full of crackers, crisps and cakes. There were also instructions for turning on the hot tub, which Charlie and Grant had set about doing immediately before changing into swimwear.

'I did enjoy it, although it was hard. Harder than when you do a standard escape room just because you know *everyone* is watching.'

'You have to try and block that out,' said Jaide, as if ignoring the cameras was the easiest thing in the world.

'How did you work out where the notes were on the key-board?' Bonnie said. 'I never would have done that under pressure.'

'No idea!' Maria took a long swig of fizz.

'Well, cheers to that,' said Jacko. 'If all it takes to win is to have no idea, I am home and dry.'

Laughter rippled around the group as they all chinked glasses and selected more nibbles to eat.

'No, really, how did you work it out?' said Bonnie as Maria topped up her glass.

'There was a note on the keyboard that said, "In the middle you will see." A few of the keys had stickers on them and I found a central one with a picture of a wave on it. I figured the sea has waves, so that must be C.'

Bonnie was relieved to hear that even if you weren't musical it had been possible to follow the clues and escape. It gave her hope for when it came to her turn.

Bonnie looked at the Instagram feed displayed on the TV. It showed a still of Russ alone in his room. He stood by the table with both hands flat on its surface and his head bowed. An image of defeat. She wasn't sure if she felt sorry for him or envious that he could now leave this concrete prison and go home.

'It was a fix,' Grant was saying for the umpteenth time. 'Anyone who can read music would automatically play the notes on the staves on the piano because the piano was there. They would know Russ could play from the questionnaires we did so it was designed to send him off track. This whole bloody thing is skewed to favour the women. It's a MeToo conspiracy.'

'Whenever you men feel threatened why does it have to be a conspiracy?' said Jaide. 'Why is it so hard to believe that sometimes women are better? Maria beat him fair and square.'

Bonnie left the brewing argument to head back to the

bathroom in her room. There were toilets on the top deck but she didn't like the draughts. She passed by the door to the basement en route. It was ajar, but the lights on the stairway were out. She paused and checked her watch. It had been nearly three hours since the duel had finished – Russ was most likely on his train back to the north-east by now. It was clever how the rest of them had been given access to champagne and the hot tub. It meant they'd been too distracted to notice Russ being escorted away, which ensured that sense of being isolated and alone remained.

She stepped through the doorway and stood at the top of the stairs. That cold, damp air filled her nostrils again and she felt something crawl across her skin; some physiological warning. She stared down into the darkness. She knew the brain's fight or flight system was wired to alert you to danger, but this was just a basement, one she had been in only hours before and nothing to be afraid of.

So why couldn't she walk down the steps?

For a moment or two she tried to will herself to do it. She knew the lights would come on once she got to the bottom and yet she couldn't walk down. Not even one step.

Weird, she thought as she continued on to her room.

After using the bathroom she checked her phone on the bedside table. This was simply habit. She knew there was no signal here so no chance of any messages. Sure enough, her screen shone back bright but empty of notifications. She wished she could call Clara and see how she was doing. Had she been to her hospital appointment? Was her leg healing OK? Bonnie had arranged for their neighbour Shelley to drive Clara. She knew this would annoy Clara and she could almost hear her protesting that she was perfectly capable of calling a taxi, but Clara needed someone to lean on. She had been even needier since Mum had died, and she'd always been needy: asking Mum for help with school work, crying on her shoulder when friends were mean or life didn't go her way, demanding to be ferried from place to place because she didn't like travelling alone. In fact there were many mornings when they were kids when Bonnie would wake to find Clara curled up in Mum's bed. Sometimes she would stand in the doorway looking at them both cuddled together and feel horribly left out and lonely, but mostly she just got on with things because Mum couldn't cope with two babies.

Bonnie returned to the sun deck to join the others, noting that the basement door was closed again when she passed by.

'Did anyone head downstairs while I was gone?' she asked Maria, who shook her head.

'That's odd.'

'What is?' Jaide joined them with a half-bottle of champagne clutched in one hand.

'I noticed the basement door was open on my way to my room but on the way back it was shut.'

'So?' said Jaide, taking a long swig from the bottle like it was beer.

'So, who shut it?'

Jaide looked over at Grant. 'If he doesn't quit moaning, I swear to God,' she said in response to something he'd said. Her words were slightly slurred.

'He can't cope that a fat woman beat his mate.' Maria was swaying a little on her chair.

'Don't call yourself that,' said Bonnie, retrieving her glass from the side and letting Jaide fill it. These people were in no fit state to have a serious discussion.

On the screen the social media feeds were continually updating. Bonnie scanned them as she half listened to Jaide and Maria's drunken nonsense.

'Don't worry about it,' said Maria, squeezing Jaide's hand.

82

'It's nothing we haven't seen or heard before. Don't let it upset you.'

'I'm not upset, I'm irritated. It's the same old crap, from the same old misogynistic Neanderthals.'

'They're not that bad. They just want to win and today they lost a teammate. Let them vent.'

Bonnie watched Jaide down the remainder of the champagne.

'What's up with you?' Jaide said, swinging the now empty bottle in Bonnie's direction.

'Nothing?'

'Well, tell your face that.' Jaide staggered off to find more booze.

'Hey, gorgeous lady.' Charlie enveloped Bonnie in a hug. 'Where did you go? We need to get drunk.' She handed Bonnie a full glass of red wine.

Bonnie sensed Charlie would not be taking no for an answer; she had the same look of mischievous challenge in her eye that Clara often had on nights out. Bonnie placed her half-drunk champagne down and took the wine, but before she let Charlie drag her away she leaned towards Maria, who was staring at a spot on the floor.

'You did fab today. You should be proud.'

Maria blinked at her as if she was struggling to focus. 'I can't win it.'

'Why would you say that?'

Maria slowly looked around the room. Grant and Jacko were laughing about something, Dennis was reading the Twitter comments with a frown on his forehead, and Jaide was trying to open the other locked cupboards. 'Because it's already decided.'

Bonnie started to ask what she meant but Maria suddenly stood with her hand over her mouth and rushed from the room.

17

Expect the Unexpected Podcast
Season 2, Episode 1: 'The Fortress'

'Can I stop you at that point, Bonnie? This is fascinating. Sorry if that's the wrong word to use considering what you went through, but I never realized it all started so . . . well. I mean other than some competitive banter it sounds like you were having fun.'

'Yeah, definitely. We were doing well, we thought. We were winning rewards and getting to know each other. It was nice.'

'You said you thought the game was spooky but other than feeling weird at the top of the basement steps you didn't think anything was amiss?'

'I'm not sure that's true. I think I always knew on some level. I only wish I'd paid more attention. If we'd done that then maybe things might have been different.'

'But that would have required that you work on the game rather than in it and it was designed to keep you busy.'

'My gosh, yes. I'd not thought of it like that.'

'I don't think that was accidental. I think it was strategic, which starts to give us some insight into how well put together this thing was. How about your relationship with the others? It

sounds like friendships were forming and divisions were emerging and you were, what, only a few days in?'

'This was day two.'

'Russ was out on the second day? That must have been tough to take.'

'Yeah, I remember thinking this was a different kind of show. More brutal. Little did I know, hey? As for what I thought of the others, I was definitely worried before I got there that they'd be either really intelligent and intimidating or totally annoying, you know?'

'Your typical reality show egos and wannabes?'

'Exactly, but on the whole it was a lovely bunch of people. I instantly liked Maria and Charlie. They were total opposites in so many ways, but at the same time both so warm and humble. They were there to enjoy the experience and they threw themselves into it straight away. I admired that.'

'It sounds like you were pretty involved in things, too.'

'Not like them, I was more . . . self-conscious, I think, more worried about the cameras. Whereas Charlie loved them and Maria didn't care one jot about them.'

'How about the others? You said Russ had annoyed you by holding back and you don't seem impressed by Grant and Dennis so far.'

'I won't have a word said against Dennis. I have huge respect for the guy. If I've made it sound like he was annoying me, that's not quite accurate. I think he was just out of his depth. For such a smart person he was incredibly naive about how these TV shows work. It was like he'd never even watched reality TV. He read every tweet, getting wound up by any apparent injustice in how he was perceived.'

'A proud man.'

'That's very perceptive. I sensed he wanted to be seen a certain way but he didn't help himself. He thought viewers were taking his tuts and eye rolls out of context, but they were still his tuts and eye rolls.'

'*It would certainly put me off going on a show like that, the idea that those annoying little things we all unconsciously do might get exaggerated and ridiculed. So how about Grant?*'

'Grant was always cracking jokes but they were kind of hurtful at times and I don't think he was sensitive to that. He also seemed to need a sidekick to adore him. There were a couple of moments when he let his guard down and I think we saw the real Grant, but not many.'

'*He was the opposite of Dennis.*'

'He'd done TV before, he knew a lot about reality shows and he was savvy about how to portray himself.'

'*Was anyone able to be a hundred per cent real in there?*'

'It's not like normal life. The cameras make you really self-conscious. But I think it's a range, isn't it? Maria seemed less concerned with how she looked versus how she performed, whereas Dennis wanted to be rated well by viewers but didn't know how to court that. Then there was Charlie and Grant, who I think caricatured themselves a bit, and as for Jaide, I've no idea. She was hard to read. Her whole persona kinda screamed *back off*. The piercings, the tattoos, the attitude.'

'*OK, so now we're getting somewhere. It sounds like you guys didn't get on. Why was that?*'

'She just didn't like me. Right from the start, that first look on the boat made it obvious. I don't know why and I wasn't about to ask her because I reckon she'd have told me, so I kept out of her way as much as possible. It bugged me for a while that she knew things. Like when we arrived and we didn't know how to get in, it was Jaide who found the pressure points and the pattern that eventually led us to identifying the star shape.'

'You were suspicious of her?'

'I thought at one stage that she might have been tipped off by the production company. It wouldn't make good TV if we were clueless about how to get inside the fort. Then when things got dark, I wondered if she was more than that, but I was tired and scared and probably delirious. I think Jaide was a complicated person. Every single one of us suffered in there. We were all victims in some way.'

'*This is* Expect the Unexpected, *the podcast that blows your mind with crimes that beggar belief. We'll be back with Bonnie in one moment as I'd like to take a minute to mention our show sponsor this month. As regular listeners will know, I'm a huge advocate of effective home security and the importance of keeping yourselves and your families safe. SecureIT is a digital home security system that gives you peace of mind at the touch of your fingertips. Through their app you can secure your home from wherever you are and even see who's calling. I have it at my house and I have to say it was so easy to install and very easy to use. Check out SecureIT today so you can feel safe at home, every day.*

'*And now back to our conversation with Bonnie Drake.*'

18

In this fortress made for war
The buried clues you're searching for
Continue to hide
At loss a pride

'What does that mean?' Jaide looked at Maria and then the rest of the gathered group.

'That we have to find some hidden clues, somewhere in the fortress,' said Dennis.

Grant laughed loudly but no one joined in.

Both Maria and Charlie looked a little worse for wear today after their night of drinking and celebrating. Thankfully Bonnie felt OK, having managed to dodge Charlie's continued attempts to ply her with alcohol by placing various half-drunk glasses down around the room. Jaide also looked surprisingly fresh-faced, although it was hard to really tell under all that black eyeliner. The boys had been far less exuberant, given they were the losing team. Grant had even boasted that he'd been up at the crack of dawn doing press-ups on the top deck – of course he had.

It was a sunny September day and despite the ever-present breeze on the upper deck it felt warm. Earlier, Bonnie had sat there with her morning coffee enjoying the sound of the sea-gulls swooping overhead. That was until Jacko and Maria convinced her to help uncover as many clues as possible from around the fort. They thought the Director's tip that the clues were everywhere was probably critical to success in the game. And so, while Grant, Dennis, Jaide and Charlie discussed the Twitter feeds, dissecting everything that was being said about them, she, Maria and Jacko studied each room in turn.

'Watcha got?' Jacko said on finding her in the guards' room checking out the pictures of various ships on the wall.

The little spark of pleasure Bonnie felt each time Jacko spoke to her was intriguing. He wasn't her usual type. Not that she had much of a romantic history. She'd had a couple of boy-friends in high school but nothing significant, followed by her only real relationship with a medical student at university. He had been clever and confident but ultimately a bit boring.

She walked towards where Jacko stood in the doorway. He wore a simple green T-shirt with jeans and pumps today. The cowboy look was gone and he seemed far more comfort-able in what she guessed were his usual clothes.

'There are a whole load of naval items scattered around as you'd expect, so I took a note of things like the ship's steering wheel and the brass telegraph ring. There's also a large spot-light on a brass stand and a couple of world globes.' She had agreed to note down the key items displayed while Jacko checked out the books and Maria visited the staff sections.

'Nice.' He held her gaze for a moment before smiling and looking at his notes. 'I found a whole load of sea maps, along with an old-style *Encyclopaedia Britannica*, the Bible and a stack of novels.'

'It's got to be something to do with the Second World War, don't you think?'

'I don't know. Would people really be interested in something about World War Two these days? Most people watching would be too young to care.'

'What's this?' asked Maria from the corridor outside.

'Would viewers want to watch an escape room based on World War Two?'

'You're asking the wrong person.'

'Course we are,' said Jacko with a grin. 'What did you find?'

Maria filled them in on the produce in the larder – which included tins of spam, beans and tomatoes, packets of rice and bags of flour – and had just started describing the kitchen area when someone gave a long, high-pitched whistle.

Bonnie and the others found Grant, Jaide, Dennis and Charlie by the screen in the officers' mess.

In this fortress made for war . . . Bonnie read.

'There's lots of military memorabilia scattered around the place,' she said. 'There's a soldier's helmet, the propeller from the front of an aircraft, telescopes, diving gear, pictures of rifles and the like.'

'This whole place is also labelled with military terminology,' said Maria. 'I've seen a guards' room, the comms room and even our bedrooms have names above the door such as Churchill, Captain Cook and Admiral Nelson.'

'Do they?' said Grant. 'I never spotted that. What's mine called?'

'General Crew,' said Dennis, which brought a big laugh from the group.

'In this fortress made for war, the buried clues you're searching for, continue to hide, at loss a pride,' Jacko said. ' "At loss a pride" is the only phrase that doesn't make sense. Is it an anagram, do you think?' He spoke quietly as if expecting everyone to judge his suggestion, but there were only appreciative murmurs.

A few moments later, Jaide said, 'I can get LAST, RISE or RISE LAST but then that leaves . . . D, O, P, A?'

'I have POSTED and SAIL, A POSTED SAIL? No. That still leaves an R,' said Dennis.

'I need a piece of paper,' said Grant, heading off.

'I feel like we should have some *Countdown* music,' said Maria. 'Dum, da, dum, da, dum. Dum, da, dum da, dum.' She looked around at the others. 'Sorry.'

Bonnie smiled and touched Maria's arm briefly. Why couldn't she focus on the task at hand? She hadn't even started to try and work it out. She glanced up at the small green light above and imagined all those people watching her every move. How were the others speaking and moving as if the cameras weren't there? Did that mean there was something wrong with her or them?

'PARADE, could it be LOST PARADE?' said Dennis. 'That could have a military meaning. It leaves I and S. PARADE IS LOST? Wait! Of course.' Dennis looked around the group with a smile. 'Oh, come on,' he said after a moment. 'It's PARADISE LOST.'

'Of course,' said Maria. 'The John Milton poem.'

'Is that a poem about World War Two?' said Bonnie, thinking of the word PARADISO above the entrance to the glass building on the sun deck.

'It was published in 1667,' said Dennis, looking a touch exasperated.

'In this fortress made for war, the buried clues you're searching for, continue to hide, paradise lost?' said Charlie. 'That makes no sense.'

'Come with me, people,' said Jacko, looking excited.

Grant raced to catch up clutching a piece of paper but no pen.

Jacko led them out to the courtyard and straight across to the opposite door.

'The library,' he said, glancing back before going in.

When Bonnie entered, she saw that books lined both of the side walls, many of them worn and well read. There was a whole shelf of leatherbound encyclopaedias and what looked like rolled-up maps stacked in baskets at the bottom. Jacko was studying the books along the left-hand wall.

'I'm sure I saw it earlier somewhere here . . . here, maybe? Here it is.' Jacko prised a Penguin paperback off the shelf and placed it flat in one hand. '*Paradise Lost*.'

The front of the book had an image of a naked woman reaching up to take an apple from a tree while a large serpent looked on. *Eve in the Garden of Eden*, thought Bonnie. What did that have to do with a fortress made for war?

'Good work,' said Dennis.

'Not bad,' said Grant.

Jacko opened the book to find its centre had been hollowed out. In the space remaining lay a rolled-up note tied with red ribbon. Jacko slid the note free and unravelled it before reading it aloud.

> *The truth of things is a bitter pill*
> *But Mr Darwin meant no ill*
> *The origin is what you seek*
> *To separate the strong from the weak.*

'Right,' said Dennis. 'Did you see Darwin's *Origin of Species* by any chance?'

'I'm afraid not,' said Jacko. 'We'd better get hunting.'

Everyone took a section of books to check. Bonnie and Charlie looked behind the door on the right of the room, Bonnie taking the top three shelves and Charlie the bottom three. After five minutes or so it was clear no one had found it.

'How about in the other rooms?' suggested Maria. 'Let's divide and conquer.'

'Check the walls as well,' said Bonnie. 'It might not be a book. There's lots of art, too.' She had looked at most of it earlier and although nothing struck her as Darwin-related, it was worth checking again just in case.

Jacko made Bonnie jump a little as he came to her side in a small room with large comfy chairs and an open fireplace. Was he following her?

'Some people are weirdly intelligent, don't you think?'

'Thanks, I don't like to show off about it.'

Jacko chuckled.

'You mean Dennis and Maria.'

'It was published in 1667,' he said in a pretty good impression of Dennis. 'They're like walking computers. They need to get a life!'

'They are. They're showing off their super power on the telly. What's your excuse?'

Jacko sniggered again. Bonnie liked the sound. It was almost boyish.

'Boredom.'

'Yeah, well, I'm just here for the money.'

'Course you are. There's no desire for B-list fame at all.'

'B-list? You're optimistic. I'm guessing it'll be more like Z-list.'

'We can have reunions at naff opening ceremonies for local escape rooms.'

'Oh God, that is what's going to happen, isn't it?'

They both laughed before continuing their hunt around the place for any books.

'Got it! Got it!' came Grant's shout from outside.

'Sounds like Grant has had his first breakthrough – he'll be insufferable now,' said Jacko.

'Don't you mean more insufferable? I saw him flexing in front of his reflection earlier. I expect he'll be doing lunges in his short shorts next.'

The two of them exchanged an amused look as they walked to join the others in the entrance hall. It was chillier than the rest of the building as there were no windows to capture the heat of the sun. Bonnie shivered and folded her arms.

'I figured it might not be a book we were looking for so I checked out the artwork and voila!'

'Wasn't that your suggestion?' Jacko said under his breath.

Bonnie nudged him to keep quiet. It would be all over the final footage. Let Grant play his own game and she would play hers.

The brightly coloured A3 poster on the wall opposite the giant Union Flag was full of animals and plants grouped into clusters. They were labelled as monocots, crustaceans, primates and the like. On the left-hand side was a pencil sketch of a bearded man above the title, 'Origin of Species by Charles Darwin, 1809–1882'. Below that were a few paragraphs describing his work. Bonnie was amazed she'd not spotted this earlier. She must have completely bypassed this section.

'And look here,' said Grant, puffing his chest out as he kicked a large trunk sitting below the picture. 'It's padlocked and needs a four-digit code to be opened.'

'Try his date of birth and death,' said Charlie, pointing to them in the image.

Grant tried both 1809 and 1882 but the lock remained shut.

'What was the clue?' asked Dennis.

'The origin is what you seek,' Jaide said.

Jacko read from the note he still held. 'The truth of things is a bitter pill, but Mr Darwin meant no ill, the origin is what you seek, to separate the strong from the weak.'

'The truth of things,' said Dennis under his breath. 'Does it say here when he published the *Origin of Species*? That would be when the truth of evolution came out.'

'1859,' said Charlie, reading it from one of the paragraphs.

'Try that,' said Dennis, but Grant was ahead of him and already opening the padlock.

He lifted the lid and everyone stepped forward to look inside.

19

'Are they wooden animals?' said Dennis.

The chest was full of brightly coloured carved toys. Bonnie made out a long green snake, a large pink pig and a yellow frog. Stuck to the underside of the lid was a sheet of A4 paper with details of their challenge.

SURVIVAL OF THE FITTEST
In the struggle for life the strongest are
favoured over the weak.
Select your animal.
Your animal will determine your struggle.
Choose carefully.

Before anyone else had an opportunity to study the selection, Grant snatched the long green snake from the pile. Dennis and Jaide voiced their objections but these went largely unheard as Charlie selected a peacock and Maria a black and white cow.

'Interesting,' Bonnie said as Jacko selected the pink pig.

'The instructions say your animal determines your struggle so I'm hoping for an eating challenge.'

'Or getting processed into bacon.'

Jacko smiled. 'Are you picking one?'

Bonnie looked at the remaining items. There was the frog, along with an orange and blue snail and a white polar bear.

'Any preference, guys?' she said to Dennis and Jaide.

'Ladies first,' said Dennis.

'Er, age before beauty,' replied Jaide.

When neither of them moved to select, Bonnie reached in and took the polar bear. The instructions said the strongest will survive and the bear was no doubt stronger than all the rest.

'What now?' said Grant, holding up his snake as if to kiss its face.

'We roll the dice?' said Maria, taking a seven-sided die from the bottom of the box. On each face was a picture of their respective animals.

'Try it,' said Jacko.

Maria rolled the die across the floor. It landed on the picture of a frog.

The group all looked at Dennis, who was holding the yellow frog by its head. He gave a deep sigh. 'Fine, what do I do?'

'Is there anything else in the box?' said Jaide.

Maria bent to check before shaking her head.

'It is not enough to live only on land,' said the Director's tinny voice from a loudspeaker, making Bonnie jump. 'The greedy frog lives in water too. Your task is to solve the puzzle on the floor of the hot tub. Each time you return to the surface to take a breath, the clock will add a thirty-second forfeit.'

The group walked through the inner door into the court-yard and then up the curved stairs to the sun deck. The sun felt even warmer on Bonnie's face than it had this morning. The breeze had dropped a touch and the fresh air felt light and clean in her lungs. When they gathered on the hot tub platform and studied the water, Bonnie saw a square object stuck to the floor in one of the corners with a set of small tiles on top.

'It's a slide puzzle, like kids have. That's too easy,' said Grant.

'The images are pretty small – I don't think you can do that from the surface,' said Maria.

'Which is why the Director said Dennis will have a time forfeit for every breath he takes,' said Jaide. 'Not a smoker, are you, Dennis? You'll need good lungs for this.'

'I'm not getting in that thing.' Dennis took a step away.

'You have to,' said Grant.

'What's the problem? Come on, Dennis. You came here to do this; you said you'd do every task,' Jaide said.

'I. Am. Not. Going. In. Do you hear me? No way.'

Bonnie could see his point. He wasn't in the best shape and the cameras would be on his backside as he bent under the surface. It was a recipe for ridicule.

'Really?' said Maria.

'No. I can't read without my glasses anyway so it would be pointless.'

'Leave him,' said Grant. 'Let him drop out, makes life easier. He's only going to slow us down.'

'Says Mr Sit Back and Take the Credit,' said Jaide.

'I've done my bit in every challenge.'

'Have you? I can't have been paying attention,' Jaide said.

'I didn't see *you* helping Russ or Maria yesterday. Did anyone else? I mean what the f—'

'Grant!' Maria put a hand on his chest. 'No swearing. Kids might be watching.'

'Who gives a fuck?' he said, pushing past Maria's hand and squaring up to Jaide. 'You got a problem?'

'Yes. You.'

'You don't have to stick up for me,' Dennis said to Jaide.

Then, rounding on Grant, 'I'll have you know I've done more in my life deserving of respect than you ever will, sounding your mouth off every chance you get. I've met your type in my professional life and it's rarely a happy ending.'

'Yeah? Well, my old man's a barrister and he says you lot are a waste of fresh air. Bloody civil servants.'

Dennis held a shaking finger towards Grant's face. 'And what have you done to make your father proud? This? It sounds like he worked hard but can you say the same? Have you done anything whatsoever to make anyone proud of your pathetic existence?' Dennis was almost frothing at the mouth and the venom in his face was hard to look at.

'Don't give yourself a heart attack on my account.' Grant's jaw twitched as he spoke and his tone was that of a petulant child.

'Right, anyway,' said Jacko. 'Shall we focus? There's a challenge to be done and, Dennis, you either have to do it or drop out.'

Dennis's face and neck were red and blotchy as he stood with his back to the wall, gripping the yellow frog as if to squeeze the life out of it.

'We can swap,' said Charlie, who was sitting on the steps to the hot tub platform. 'I don't mind.'

You don't mind getting your bikini body on TV, thought Bonnie. That girl really was on the wrong show.

'It's fine,' said Dennis.

'Dennis. Here, have my peacock.' Charlie held out the carved animal until Maria took it from her and gave it to Dennis.

After a few moments, Dennis handed Charlie the frog in return.

'Don't bother saying thank you or anything,' Grant said to Dennis, who remained with his back to the wall, and his face flushed as the group surrounded the hot tub platform with Charlie.

As Bonnie predicted, Charlie stripped off to reveal a white bikini under her clothes, before stepping into the hot tub.

'Ooh, it's cold today.'

'Safer that way,' said Jacko.

Charlie looked at him for a long moment and then nodded with understanding.

'Shall I just start?'

A red timer clock was now displayed across the sun-deck floor. Bonnie scanned the side of the lighthouse building until she found the small projector attached to the wall.

Charlie took a deep breath and submerged her head.

The clock on the floor began its count.

After thirty-four seconds, Charlie resurfaced and took a gulp of air. 'There's too many pieces.'

Bonnie watched the clock reset to 1.04.

'Take a few breaths,' said Grant. 'You've made a start so try and finish on this go.'

Charlie resurfaced once more before her final attempt gave her a time of two minutes and twelve seconds.

The group all congratulated her, apart from Dennis, who remained on the lower section of the sun deck.

Maria rolled the die again. It landed on the snake. The next to go was Grant.

'The serpent envies those with more since he was banished to crawl on the floor,' said the Director. 'Your task is to retrieve the flag strung up high. Any aborted attempts will incur a thirty-second penalty.'

'Is that a reference to the Union Flag?' said Jacko.

'That isn't really strung up high; it's just pinned to the wall – but maybe,' said Grant, looking up above them for any sign of another flag.

'Shall I go and check the Union Flag?' said Charlie.

'Oh no,' said Maria.

Bonnie's eyes followed to where Maria pointed. The section of railings bordering the lighthouse level had a horizontal bar attached to it that stretched out over the sea. Tied to its end was a red flag.

'That can't be it,' said Dennis. 'That's dangerous.'

Bonnie and the others walked up to the higher deck to take a closer look. As they neared she could see that the bar was part of an A-frame anchored to a lower part of the building by two diagonal bars. Both bars were smooth black metal and the flag at the end was tied with a thin white string. She looked down at the sea below and felt her knees buckle. The murky green water smashed against the concrete sides in an explosion of white foam.

'That's ridiculous,' said Maria.

'There must be something he can reach it with,' said Bonnie.

'Bet you're glad you didn't pick the snake, old man,' said Grant.

'What about a long grabby tool? You know – like the ones for picking litter. Might that work?' said Maria. 'He could grab the string and slide the flag back towards him.'

'Have you seen something like that?' asked Bonnie, but before Maria could answer, the others started shouting Grant's name.

'Start the clock,' Grant said.

Bonnie looked back to see him sitting astride the railings and reaching out to grab the pole.

'Don't be an idiot,' said Dennis.

Grant leaned forward, grabbed the pole with both hands and then slid his body along to wrap his legs around it too.

'Get down,' said Jaide.

Grant shinned forwards along the top of the pole. The guy was reckless. The sea below continued to smash against the fort and Bonnie felt sure the breeze was picking up again.

The group gasped and Charlie screamed as Grant suddenly rolled so he no longer lay on top of the bar but hung underneath it. Dennis shouted again for Grant to come back and get down.

'Oh God,' said Charlie, covering her eyes.

Grant laughed loudly as he began to walk his hands backwards and pull himself out over the sea bit by bit. The flag was maybe 12 feet ahead of him. Below that was a 30-foot drop into the water. If he fell they would not be able to get to him.

Calling for help is useless, no one is coming.

'Come back, Grant,' Bonnie said but her voice came out raspy and quiet. 'Get down,' she called a little louder as Grant walked his hands backwards along the pole then dragged his feet behind him. 'COME BACK!' she shouted.

'You're an idiot,' shouted Jaide.

'It's fine. I'm fine,' Grant said a split second before his legs slipped from the pole.

20

Charlie's scream was whisked away by the wind.

'It's all cool, baby,' Grant called. He now clung to the pole by his hands alone.

'It's not cool, you'll get hurt. Please come back,' said Charlie.

Grant began doing pull-ups on the pole.

'I don't know who's more tragic, muscle man out there or his bawling bimbo,' said Jaide.

'Definitely muscle man. If he falls he's gonna mess up that expertly coiffed hair,' said Jacko, which raised a rare smile from Jaide.

'How can you be so cold? He could really hurt himself.' Charlie looked like she might cry.

'And it would be his own damned fault. I'm not cold, I'm intelligent. You should try it,' said Jaide.

'I can't watch this,' said Charlie, retreating down the staircase.

Maria stepped towards the railings. 'Grant, when you get to the flag are you going to detach it or slide it?'

'What are you doing?' said Jaide.

'Helping him. If he says he can do it, I believe him.' Maria turned her attention back to Grant. 'I think it's intended to be slid backwards so try that first. If it won't move, and the string is thin enough, you could try biting it. Otherwise you'll have to let go with one hand to untie it.'

'Sure thing, Mazza.' Grant continued to make slow progress. He was now halfway to the flag, which was flapping in the breeze.

Jaide scoffed.

'Do you think he can do it?' said Bonnie to Jacko and Dennis, who stood to one side, watching.

Each time Grant let go with one hand to move forward, Bonnie expected him to fall. The timer on the floor of the deck below them clicked on.

1.27, 1.28, 1.29.

'I couldn't hold my body weight up there for long, I know that for sure, but I'm no body builder,' said Jacko.

'I could have,' said Dennis. 'When I was younger. I did a bit of boxing.'

1.36, 1.37, 1.38.

Grant was nearly at the flag and terrifyingly high in Bonnie's opinion. She wanted to join Charlie below but couldn't drag herself away from the impending disaster. This couldn't have been what Grant was supposed to do. It was far too dangerous. She'd heard once that hitting water from height was like hitting concrete.

Just then, one of Grant's hands slipped from the pole and his body swung violently to the right. Jacko swore and Bonnie hid her face behind his back.

'Oh, you are more of a dickhead than we could have imagined,' said Jaide, causing Bonnie to peek out from behind Jacko to see Grant laughing and doing one-handed pull-ups on the pole.

'Just get the flag,' shouted Maria.

Grant swung his free arm back up on to the pole and

studied the flag. He hooked one finger through the string and started to pull it backwards with him. When it snagged against the metal, he lifted his head up, grabbed the material in his mouth and tore it free. Then he rotated on the pole to face the group on the deck and came back to them hand over hand with the flag between his teeth. He climbed over the railings and jumped down with a theatrical bow.

'Two minutes forty-seven seconds,' said Maria. 'Very impressive, although I think you need to apologize to Charlie.'

A stunt like that may have looked idiotic and dangerous to them but Bonnie could imagine how thrilling it would be on TV, and how much of a hero Grant would now be to macho men and swooning women everywhere.

'Well done, Charlie and Grant,' said the Director's tinny voice. 'You have set a strong example for your team. You are now men versus women. Your times will be added together and divided by the group's number. The lowest-scoring team will win amnesty against the next duel.'

'He could have mentioned that earlier,' said Dennis.

'Thanks, Grant,' said Jaide. 'If you hadn't been messing around, you might have won.'

'There are four of you and only three of us, so you are already at an advantage,' said Grant.

'Our scores will be averaged,' said Jacko, patting Grant on the back as he passed.

'Don't worry, lad, we'll do our best to compensate,' said Dennis.

Maria handed the die to Charlie. 'I shouldn't be the only one to roll it.'

Charlie rolled a frog first so rolled again. It was the snail. Jaide was up.

'The sluggish snail misses much by taking things so slow,' said the Director. 'Go to the snug. Your task is to finish the game as fast as you can. Each error incurs a thirty-second penalty and requires that you start over.'

Jaide found the game in question on a corner table in the snug. It consisted of a long wavy wire full of loops and dips along which Jaide had to track a circle of metal on the end of a stick without touching metal to metal. Bonnie's grandad had bought a similar game for her and Clara when they were kids. This had led to many tears on Clara's part as she did not have Bonnie's patience. She would frequently scream and shout every time the loud buzzer indicated a failure and she had to start again.

Jaide finished in three minutes fifty-two seconds, after hitting the wire four times and incurring a two-minute penalty.

'Sorry, girls,' said Grant as Jaide finished. 'I beat Jaide by over a minute.'

'And I beat you by over thirty seconds,' said Charlie, handing him the die to throw. 'I wouldn't celebrate too soon.'

Grant rolled the snake twice and then the snail again before finally landing on the pig. The Director's voice boomed aloud.

'The gluttonous pig doesn't know when to stop. Your task is to eat all the items in galley cupboard number two. Any sips of water will incur a thirty-second penalty.'

'Yes!' said Jacko. 'I was hoping for an eating task. Watch and learn, ladies.'

'Where's the galley?' said Dennis.

'I know,' said Maria. 'I found it earlier.'

'You're a diamond. Let's go,' said Jacko.

Maria led them behind the bar and into an industrial kitchen with stainless-steel work surfaces and large ovens.

'How did you know this was here?' said Charlie.

'Those of us who avoided staring at our Twitter fans got some work done,' said Jacko with a wink.

On the wall above the sinks a row of cupboards were numbered one, two and three. Jacko opened number two then hung his head low and gave a laugh before reaching in and bringing out a full packet of cream crackers.

'I'll be needing that water,' he said.

'I don't get it,' Charlie said.

'It's impossible without water,' said Grant. 'Honestly, they, like, suck all the saliva out of your mouth.'

Another projector that was attached to the kitchen ceiling displayed the timer on the floor.

Jacko began with two crackers at a time but soon struggled to chew the dusty mass filling his mouth. His head bounced up and down and side to side as he forcefully chewed and tried to swallow. It wasn't long before he was reaching for the water glass and his timer was jumping forward by thirty seconds. He began to take the crackers one at a time, nibbling them in small bites as quickly as he could. But before long his efforts slowed again, his face contorted and he reached for the water.

'This is bloody awful,' he said at the halfway point, but there was no denying the rest of them were finding the whole thing pretty amusing, apart from Grant, who became more agitated every time Jacko took a sip.

Bonnie wasn't sure if Dennis's smiles were at Jacko's attempts or Grant's fury.

Four minutes, fifty-five seconds and five glugs of water later, Jacko finished with crumbs scattered down the front of his T-shirt and pasted around his lips.

'Teamwork makes the dream work,' said Jacko, wiping his mouth.

After that, Dennis was true to his word, smashing his peacock task with the fastest time so far.

'Mirror, mirror on the wall, the peacock thinks he's the

fairest of all,' said the Director. 'Your task is to decipher the writing on the screen. It will display for ten seconds at a time. Each requested repeat will incur a thirty-second penalty.'

Dennis found the nearest screen outside the officers' mess and touched the image of a peacock with his finger after removing his glasses from his shirt pocket and putting them on. He was faced with a page of mirror writing: each letter back to front, each word spelled backwards, each sentence running from right to left instead of left to right. It looked like nonsense to Bonnie but Dennis deciphered it in under a minute.

'It's the lyrics to "You're So Vain" by Carly Simon,' he said.

'Oh yeah! Come on the D-man.' Grant slapped Dennis on the back.

'I thought you said he would slow you down?' said Bonnie.

'That was before we were teammates. Come on, the boys!'

Only Bonnie and Maria were left to go now. It took a while to throw their animals. Bonnie's polar bear came first and she was sent back to the kitchen and specifically the freezer.

'The mama bear knows fury like no other. Your task is to smash the ice and free her cub. Each time you use the chisel to help you'll incur a thirty-second penalty.'

The block of ice was not insignificant, almost the size of the freezer drawer. Jaide helped her to lift it out and place it on the floor. Underneath where it had sat in the freezer drawer lay a small hammer and a thin chisel.

'The boys finished in two minutes forty-seven, fifty-seven seconds and four minutes fifty-five,' Jaide said to the gathered women. 'That gives them an average of just under three minutes. We need to beat that.'

'What's our average?' asked Bonnie.

'Just over,' said Jaide.

Bonnie picked up the hammer and knelt by the ice. She

didn't look over to the men but she could feel the weight of their gaze. Her first swing missed the ice completely and jarred her arm as the hammer slammed into the stone floor. Grant snorted. She widened her knees to strengthen her frame, lifted the hammer high above her head with both hands and hit the ice with all the strength she could muster. Perhaps it was the pressure of Jaide's gaze or the added adrenaline of wanting to impress Jacko and annoy Grant but to her amazement a large fracture appeared right through the block. Encouraged by her success Bonnie hit it again and again, to the sound of Charlie's whoops and cheers, until the whole thing shattered into fragments that skittered across the floor.

'Competitive much?' said Jacko.

Charlie was bouncing on the spot with whoops of delight and singing, 'One twenty-two, one twenty-two.'

'Second fastest to finish. Well done,' said Jacko, ignoring Grant and Dennis's sulky expressions.

Bonnie lifted a small carving of a polar bear cub out of the remaining ice block. 'Here you go, mama bear. Your baby's safe,' she said, showing the toy to the polar bear Maria was holding for her.

'Just me to go now, then,' said Maria.

'You'll be fine. You win everything,' said Bonnie with a wink.

But she was wrong.

Maria's bizarre cow challenge required her to stand in front of a large electric fan they found under a tarpaulin on the sun deck while holding a lit candle. Her task was to shield the flame for a continuous minute. Each time it blew out and she had to re-light it, she incurred the thirty-second penalty. She never managed a full minute and gave up after five.

The moment she quit the men let out a loud cheer and to Bonnie's surprise high-fived each other.

'Since when were they all so chummy?' she said.

'I'm so sorry,' said Maria.

'Hey, it's just a silly game,' said Jaide, giving Maria a quick hug, before looking at Bonnie and saying, 'What?'

Why are you being so nice? What are you up to? Bonnie was thinking but said, 'Just wondering which of us the public will choose to go next.'

The four women all silently looked at each other while the men continued to congratulate themselves.

21

Bonnie woke to a sound. She lay still for a moment to see if it would happen again. Their third evening had been much more sedate. Charlie and Maria had excused themselves early, presumably still nursing their hangovers from the night before. Bonnie had sat with the others to eat and then found a quiet corner to read, having selected a dog-eared copy of *Harry Potter and the Philosopher's Stone* from a shelf in the library.

After a few hours she had made her way to bed without seeing anyone else and fallen quickly into a deep sleep.

When the scraping noise happened again, she knew she wouldn't get back to sleep so she grabbed her sweatshirt and went to investigate. The hallway outside was pitch black and she ran her right hand along the curved wall opposite to guide her.

The temperature had dropped significantly overnight and she could feel the chill on her face. As she rounded the corner towards the communal area, she heard a man cough and stopped walking. She listened, straining to hear any movement so she could gauge who the person was and how far away they were. There was nothing but silence. After a few moments she slowly began to move again.

When she saw Dennis sitting in the kitchen with a hot drink, she let out a long breath.

'Couldn't sleep?' she said.

'Rarely can these days, I'm sad to say.' He held his glasses in both hands and twisted them back and forth on the table top.

'Can I join you?' When he nodded she took a seat opposite him. 'It's an odd experience, isn't it?' When he didn't answer she continued, 'How are you finding it? You don't seem overly happy to be here.'

'Neither do you.'

It was a fair point. She checked the cameras on the walls. They were all off.

'Well, I'm here more for my sister than myself. We lost our mum earlier this year. She'd spent all her money on various treatments and had limited life insurance so we can't afford to stay in the family home, but my sister wants to.'

'So you thought the prize money would come in handy?'

'Stupid, isn't it?'

Dennis scratched his forehead and rubbed his eyes before saying, 'Not if you win.'

'I don't think that's likely. I'm hardly setting the puzzle world alight with my brilliance.'

Dennis smiled warmly and it made him look like a kindly grandad instead of a grump.

'Can I ask why you're here? It strikes me you're not enjoying the experience.'

Dennis shrugged and took a sip of his drink.

When it was clear he didn't plan to answer, Bonnie changed the subject. She didn't want to make him feel uncomfortable.

'Don't you wish you were Russ right now? At home in your own bed with all this nonsense behind you?'

A strange look passed across Dennis's face.

'So you were a lawyer before you retired. In what field?'

'Criminal law. I was a prosecutor for thirty-two years.'

'Wow. I bet you saw some things.'

Dennis pursed his lips and stared at the wall. He was not an easy man to chat to.

'Anyway, perhaps I'll see if I can get some more sleep,' Bonnie said, starting to stand.

'Thirty-two years of putting away rapists, murderers and child abusers and I was bloody good at it. Before I knew it, I was twenty-five years in and they were bringing in all these young managers who didn't have a clue. They changed this and changed that with no thought of the consequences and spent more time worrying about their careers than serving justice, and I wasn't afraid to tell them. I became the dinosaur, the problem child they'd put on performance plans and send for mediation sessions with a psychologist. But you know the worst thing? Eventually my colleagues started to believe it too. When they began dismissing my ideas, I left.' He looked up at the ceiling. 'My marriage had fallen apart years earlier because I was always at work and we had no kids so there I was sitting at home with nothing to do and nowhere to go.'

Dennis's anger at being berated by Grant on the first day made sense now.

'Is that why you applied?'

'I thought I'd show them all I've still got it.' He tapped his forehead. 'But maybe they were right after all.'

Bonnie guessed the Twitter comments were hitting Dennis where it hurt.

'It's not real, you know. It doesn't matter.'

'Just a game,' he said, and that weird look made another fleeting appearance.

Bonnie looked at the TV with its split-screen display of social media comments. They weren't scrolling as it was three a.m. Instagram showed some still images of today's challenges, including one of Grant with the red flag between his teeth and an unfortunate one of Maria in front of the fan, her hair rising like a curly turban above her head and her blouse forced back over her body, accentuating the rolls of fat around her neck and middle. Bonnie felt sorry for her. She was the most impressive of them all and yet she was an easy target. Bonnie turned her attention to the tweets.

P Foulds @PFoulds345
What is Dennis's problem? If you don't want to play, don't go on the show. #Dennistogo

---

LaLa Boyes @Laboy
Like Grant said Dennis is a waste of fresh air. #thefortress #Dennistogo

---

Katy Sky @Katysky
OMG Grant is so muscly. #granttowin #muscleman

Chardonnay @Chardonnay84
What I want to know is when are Grant and Charlie going to get it on?

LaLa Boyes @Laboy
Oh I would scratch her eyes out. #Bimbobrain

Farook @Frookboy99

I can't decide if the fortress is sad or sick? #whychannel5?

ShellBrolin @Brolinblog1

Did you see Maria standing in front of that fan? Hilarious!
Watch the frizz bomb fly. #thefortress

Lee @LeePotts14562

No wind would knock Maria over would it?

Danni @DBiswas23

Why are they playing stupid games when Russ is suffering?

Bonnie looked at Dennis to find him looking at her.

'Weird, isn't it?' he said.

'When Russ is suffering? Why is he suffering – because he went home?'

Dennis nodded slowly and then said, 'Or because he didn't.'

22

'Don't be ridiculous. Of course he went home,' said Jaide.

'It's unthinkable,' said Maria.

'He's been down there all this time?' Charlie looked the sleepiest of the lot of them.

'No. Of course he hasn't, we'd have heard him. He'd have been shouting and banging and God knows what,' said Grant. 'I mean how long has it been?'

'Coming up for two days,' said Dennis.

There was a long silence. 'We wouldn't have heard him. This structure is lead-lined concrete. The doors are metal. The place is built to withstand a mortar attack,' said Maria. 'That makes it pretty much soundproof.'

'I can't believe you got us out of bed to serve up this hysteria,' said Jaide.

'But what if he is down there?' said Bonnie.

'He went home.' Grant looked irritated. 'You said yourself you saw the door open later that day, which means he left.'

'Or someone else opened it,' said Dennis.

'Of course someone else bloody opened it,' said Jaide. 'Whoever escorted Russ out.'

'You can't be sure of that,' said Bonnie, her fists clenched.

'How do you explain the tweets? One says they think the game is sick, the other says Russ is suffering.'

There was an uncomfortable moment of silence.

'We need to get downstairs,' said Dennis.

'Through the locked door with no handles? And exactly how do you plan to do that?' said Jaide.

'I don't want to go down there,' said Charlie.

Grant had paused in the doorway. 'Charl, there's nothing to be scared of. Don't let these freaks freak you out.'

'You're very quiet,' Bonnie said to Jacko, who stood leaning against the kitchen counter.

'I was thinking, *Calling for help is useless, no one is coming.*'

Thank God someone else was hearing her and Dennis.

'It's a game,' said Jaide. 'It's supposed to be stressful. The production company probably planted those tweets.'

'But if Dennis and I hadn't been up in the middle of the night we wouldn't have seen them,' said Bonnie.

Jaide sighed, 'So they'd post them again.'

'Let's say you're right . . .' said Jacko.

'Because I *am* right.'

'What's the point?'

'How do you mean?'

'What's the point of the game? That's what's puzzling me. Usually you enter an escape room and you have a mission to do. We've been asked to do random challenges and we have no specific goal or purpose. Don't you find that odd?'

'They're just messing with us?'

'Or it's crappily designed,' said Jacko.

Bonnie realized Jacko was right. They didn't have a purpose and she hadn't been expecting that. She'd imagined they'd be given some role to play out, like having been stranded here in a storm, or in the midst of battle, and then have to work to plan their escape. She'd done one escape room with Clara and some friends where they were told they'd all recently died and now had sixty minutes to escape the afterlife. It had been exhilarating: that low-level panic of knowing time was running out and if they didn't work together to solve the clues they'd be doomed. It had felt so real.

'There's not much we can do about this now,' said Jacko. 'I suggest we all get some rest and decide tactics in the morning.'

As Bonnie made her way back to her room she felt a headache beginning to form. She also noted that Dennis stayed in the kitchen. Either he knew his insomnia would prevent him from sleeping or he was planning on watching for that camera light to turn green.

23

The green light never did appear on day four. Bonnie, Dennis and Jacko took turns watching for it. It was weird and confirmed to everyone that something odd was going on. Except Jaide and Grant. They insisted it was simply a day of rest. No challenges, no recording. The contract had stated they would be given these. But it was all too much of a coincidence in Bonnie's eyes.

Dennis and Jacko had set about seeing if there was any way to access the basement but all they could find were the two doors on opposite sides of the main floor – both locked and without handles or keyholes. Bonnie remembered how on the day of the duel she'd thought it spooky that the door opened automatically or, to be more accurate, was opened remotely from somewhere else. It made her wonder again if they were really alone or if someone – or even a team of people – might also be here. Maria had told them these places often had multiple spaces, hidey-holes and even secret tunnels, so it was entirely feasible that part of the building was sectioned off. Apart from the rooms they had explored, every door in the place was locked. She had assumed most were storage spaces but now she wondered if they were something else entirely. One thing she felt sure of – their three a.m.

conversation had been overheard and that was why no green light appeared all day.

Calling for help is useless, no one is coming.

When the siren sounded on the morning of day five, Bonnie was dressed and having coffee in the kitchen area with Maria and Charlie. She had chosen to tie her hair back and forget the eyeliner. There were more important things to focus on. Her hands felt clammy and the headache that had begun in the night felt like it had settled in for the day.

'I can't believe you have to duel again,' Charlie said to Maria, who looked like she hadn't slept well.

Given their concerns about Russ, Bonnie could understand Maria's anxiety.

'Really? I can. And Jaide won't make it easy for me.'

The public had given most votes to Jaide and then Maria, the screen announcing that they would face a second duel. Charlie's votes had been close behind and to Bonnie's surprise she had hardly any. Perhaps people admired her ice-smashing rage or maybe keeping her head down as much as possible was working as a strategy.

'Can I ask you something?' Bonnie said to Maria when they were alone. 'The other night you said you couldn't win because it was already decided. What did you mean?'

'Did I?' Maria frowned and then yawned. 'I don't remember.'

'It was after the last duel. What might you have meant?' She wondered if on some level Maria had sensed that something here was off too. If anyone was observant enough to spot such a thing it would be her.

Maria gazed past Bonnie for a long moment before saying, 'Do you ever worry that at some point people will spot you're a fraud?'

'What are you talking about? You're the most talented here.'

'Hmmm,' said Maria, still staring ahead. 'I think it's pretty obvious the public don't like me much, though.'

The group began to gather so Bonnie decided to drop the subject. It wouldn't help Maria to be thinking like this. She needed to stay positive.

Finally the screens displayed an instruction to meet outside Basement Door One at nine a.m. Simultaneously the lights on all the cameras flickered to green. Dennis immediately took up position in front of the nearest one and demanded to know whether Russ had safely left the fort.

There was no response.

'Only half an hour to go and then we can see for ourselves,' said Jacko.

At eight fifty-seven they were all outside Basement Door One and, when it opened, Dennis was first through. Bonnie noted how much her impression of him had shifted in the past twenty-four hours – from a mood hoover to a compassionate man of principle. She could absolutely believe he had been a dedicated and effective prosecutor. Look at how focused he was on ensuring Russ's well-being.

The first thing that hit Bonnie was the heat. She recalled walking down here before and feeling a damp chill in the air. It had been the same later that day when she'd stood at the top, willing herself to walk down the steps but finding she couldn't make her feet move. But now the air was dry and hot; like walking into your grandpa's lounge when he had the heating and the gas fire on.

The group all swapped looks but no one commented.

Ignoring the fact that lights illuminated the corridor to their right when they reached the bottom, the group turned left and walked the same way they had before, into the darkness towards the room where they had last seen Russ. This time the lights above did not come on but Dennis and Jaide lit the way with the torches on their phones. It was deathly quiet apart from the rustle of their footsteps. The air in Bonnie's mouth felt warm and dry and she could already feel sweat forming on her forehead and under her arms.

It was not far to the room but this time no light spilled out of open doorways. As Bonnie reached the room Maria had been in, she could see the door was ajar and just make out a scrap of white paper on the floor. Further ahead Dennis and Jacko stood outside the room Russ had been in.

'The door's shut,' said Dennis, and Bonnie's heart sank.

'Please, please, please, please let it be empty.'

Bonnie heard Charlie's whispered words and reached forward to take her hand.

The group stood silent and still as Dennis lifted the flap in the door and shone his phone light in.

'Can you see? Is he there?' Bonnie said.

Jaide shone her light on Dennis so they could all see him.

Dennis moved the phone and tilted his head, and then he stiffened.

Charlie squeezed Bonnie's hand and Maria made a low whimper.

'Good grief,' said Dennis, and the group erupted with overlapping questions.

'Is he there?'

'Is he OK?'

'What can you see?'

'Can you get him out?'

'Russ? Russ? Can you hear me, mate?' Dennis said. 'He's sitting on the floor, leaning on the wall. He's still upright-ish. I'm not sure but I think I saw his fingers move. This heat won't have done him any good. He'll be dehydrated. We need to get him water.'

'We need to get him out,' said Grant.

'Does he look like he's acting?' said Jaide. 'It could be part of the game. Maybe we are going to be tasked with saving him? He could be part of the production crew.'

In the light of Jaide's torch, Dennis looked towards where she stood and then away again. There was a moment of silence.

'Right, we need a plan. Water first then we find out how to—'

Before Dennis could finish, loud heavy metal music blared out around them. Charlie let go of Bonnie to put her hands over her ears. Maria grimaced at the noise as she reached into her bag for a bottle of water. It seemed she had come prepared. Dennis gave her a thumbs up as she passed it to him and Grant held open the flap on Russ's door, but when Dennis checked to see if the bottle would fit through, it wouldn't. Dennis put his mouth to the flap and spoke but there was no way Russ would hear anything above the blaring music.

Everyone had shuffled towards the room, leaving Bonnie alone at the back opposite the small screen on the wall between the two duelling cells.

Hi Clara
Can you do me a favour?

Bonnie stared at the words as they scrolled up the screen.

Tell the others I send my deepest congratulations.
You have successfully unlocked the first secret of the fortress:
NO ONE LEAVES

The text scrolled up and off the screen as the music stopped and the group all began calling out to Russ. Bonnie's heart was beating loudly in her ears.

'Can he move?' said Jacko.

'Even if you get the bottle through, how does he drink it?' said Jaide.

'We need to get in to him,' said Dennis.

'Or he needs to come over to us somehow,' said Jacko.

'Hey?' said Bonnie.

'Can we roll it to him?' said Grant.

'If we get it through the hatch it will be bent out of shape. It won't roll anywhere; it'll stop where it lands,' said Dennis.

'Hey?' said Bonnie a little louder.

'OK, so why don't we see if we can throw it towards him somehow?' said Grant.

'How would—'

'HEY!'

This time the group stopped talking and Jaide shone her light in Bonnie's direction. Bonnie held up a hand to shield her eyes.

'Something's wrong,' she said.

'No shit, Sherlock,' said Grant.

'No, I mean . . . He sent a message. Here on the screen.'

'Who did? Russ?' said Grant.

'What are you talking about?' said Maria.

'Shut up. Shut up, OK?' Bonnie rubbed her eyes with the base of her palms.

'All right, no need to shou—'

'The Director asked me to congratulate you all on unlocking the first secret of the fortress,' Bonnie said, cutting Jaide off. 'No one leaves.'

'What?'

'How did he—?'

'What are you talk—?'

'He said, NO ONE LEAVES in big red letters. Big red capital letters here on the screen. It said, Hi Clara, can you congratulate the others, tell them they've unlocked the first secret of the fortress. No one leaves.'

At that moment a loud metal bang vibrated around them, followed by another and then another. The sound of metal sliding across metal was accompanied by digital beeps then another loud bang could be heard, this one further away and followed by more distant bangs, clicks and beeps.

The lights above them flickered and then illuminated.

Bonnie looked at all the startled faces staring back at her.

24

Three Months Earlier

CONFESSION: **Russ Wheelan**
DATE: **7 June**
TIME: **12.45**
LOCATION: **Best Western Angel Hotel**

Russ Wheelan looked directly into the camera and smiled. Only moments earlier he had been the first to make it out of one of the seven escape rooms set up for the final selection event.

'Well done,' the man from the production company had said. 'But there is one more test you need to pass.'

And so here he was. The final, final hurdle.

He had been taken to a different room where there was a table with a small camera sitting on top and a single chair he had been told to sit in. He had been given a printed copy of his application form and a small instruction card.

'My name is Russ,' he said, feeling self-conscious. The man had left; it was just him and the camera in here. He looked down at the card in his lap.

Nearly there!
A place on The Fortress *is yours*
IF you are willing to confess.
What is your deepest desire?
What are you most ashamed of?
And
What makes you smart enough to win?

The exhilaration Russ had felt on making it out of his room first began to evaporate. He knew what the TV show wanted: sob stories and character flaws that could be used to pit contestants against each other. He had no problem with that in principle. He always enjoyed those talking head segments on reality TV where people either big themselves up or drag others down. The problem with this was he had worked hard to hide the thing he was most ashamed of. Not even his wife knew about it. He shouldn't have put it on the form. They probably wouldn't take him if he didn't repeat it. He looked down at his application form.

In for a penny, in for a pound.

He shuffled in the seat and began again. He wasn't dropping out now, no matter how embarrassing it might be when people saw this. He was one step away from achieving his dream.

'My name is Russ and I have not always been the fine specimen you see before you. I used to be bigger, much bigger. Picture the guy in the supermarket you see buying cake that makes you think, "I reckon you've had enough already, mate." Well, that was me. I'm pretty ashamed, got rid of all the pictures, moved away from where I grew up and the people who knew me then. Thing is . . .'

Russ took a moment. Should he really say this? Would it work for him or against him?

'I went on a diet but I never addressed why I ate so much. Don't worry, I'm not revealing some deep-seated trauma here. The truth is I just flaming love food, you know. I can't give it up. I have to eat it, so I do what I can to keep the weight off. Hours at the gym, internet diet pills, fingers down my throat, you name it I've done it.'

There it is. Out in the open. Do with it what you will.

'So, yeah, that's that.'

He took a moment to collect his thoughts and readjust his seating position. He felt lighter for saying this out loud, as if a weight had been lifted from his shoulders.

'I'd like to say my deepest desire is to make my kids proud, but honestly, I just want to be on the telly. I've been looking at that thing all my life and I want to be part of it. I want it to be *in* it, not just observing it.'

It felt weirder admitting that than the truth about his weight issues. People would see him as shallow, no doubt, as if everyone who goes on a TV show is doing it for some higher purpose.

'And as for my smarts, I'd say I'm street smart. I'm not into books, not academic, but I know when to sit back and when to step up. I'm not going to play the games, I'm going to play the players.'

25

'What happened?' Charlie was the first to speak, her expression a mixture of surprise and confusion.

Jaide pushed past everyone and made her way back towards the staircase up to the main deck. The group followed in silence. Bonnie swapped looks with Maria and Jacko. Their collective concern about Russ had been overshadowed by something far more primal. Jaide started to run, her Doc Martens thumping hard against the stone steps. Grant and Dennis followed but the others remained at the bottom, listening, their eyes white and wide with panic.

'It's locked,' called Grant. 'Someone go and check the other side.'

Jacko and Bonnie continued on down the corridor, along the section they had not walked before. It was a mirror image of the other side with regular closed doors on the outer wall and a handful on the inner wall. They did not pause to look in any. *It's fine, it's just a game*, she told herself, but somehow the sentiment felt feeble.

When they reached the stairway Bonnie followed Jacko up to the closed door at the top. Together they tried pushing it then felt the edges for any sign of a lock or pressure pad to open the thing. The smooth metal made for an effective seal.

Opposite this door another sign read, DEDUCE NOT. Bonnie ran her fingers across it. It looked like moulded metal, like all the other signs above the doors on the main floor, but they were chipped and a little rusty and this one was pristine and plastic. *Placed here for us*, she thought.

'Why would we be told not to deduce?'

Jacko looked at the sign and shook his head.

'They don't want us to get out.'

Jacko's eyes met hers and Bonnie felt a wave of claustrophobia. She quickly retreated back to the corridor and was leaning over with her hands on her knees taking deep breaths of hot, unhelpful air, when Jacko joined her.

'Are you OK?' he asked, his voice barely more than a whisper.

Bonnie nodded and then stood tall again. 'We need to let the others know.'

Side by side they returned the way they had come, in an unspoken agreement that neither of them wanted to pass by Russ.

Jacko shook his head to let the group know there was no exiting through Basement Door Two.

'What now?' said Maria.

'What the hell is going on?' Dennis shouted at the nearest camera. 'We demand to know. Is this part of the show? Is anyone there? Answer me, goddammit!'

The green light shone back, unblinking.

'Maybe we have to save Russ somehow?' said Charlie.

'Russ is out of it, we need to save ourselves,' said Grant.

A flurry of protest rippled around the group.

'Oh come on,' said Grant. 'You're all thinking it. If we find a way out *then* we can worry about Russ.'

'I meant is saving Russ *how* we get out?' said Charlie. 'You said he might be an actor,' she said to Jaide.

'That didn't look like acting,' said Dennis.

'There must be a way out,' said Grant. 'Let's split up and search.'

'This is a fort. A military fort,' said Maria. 'It's designed to have no weaknesses.'

'The perfect prison,' said Jacko.

'It's not a prison, it's a bloody tomb,' Dennis said, walking back towards Russ's cell. 'Grant's right, though, we need to look for something, whether it be a way out or a way to survive this bloody heat.'

Shit Got Real

26

Expect the Unexpected Podcast
Season 2, Episode 1: 'The Fortress'

'That must have been terrifying.'

'I don't think we really believed it.'

'What did you believe?'

'It's hard to describe. I've not talked about this with anyone, not with the police, not even with my family.'

'Of course. Take your time. I imagine you were all panicking to some degree.'

'Yes and no.'

'How do you mean?'

'I mean . . . we . . . or at least I, didn't fully accept the facts.'

'You thought it was part of the game?'

'I remember wanting to laugh and suppressing it. I felt like I was watching myself in the show at times.'

'That makes sense.'

'I've read a lot since about people's experiences with trauma and, like us, they describe this weird denial your brain goes into. It seems kind of counter-productive in the face of danger but it's so common it must serve a purpose. Maybe it keeps you moving or something.'

'Stops you from freezing?'

'Something like that. Fight or flight.'

'How long did you spend trying to get out?'

'I don't think we ever stopped, but if you mean that first morning locked in, I don't know. Maybe two, three hours. It was long enough for the heat exhaustion and dehydration to kick in. All the rooms were locked so we were literally going around in circles, passing each other, peering through access holes into the shadowy corners of dark rooms.'

'And what did you see?'

'Escape rooms. Lots of them. But no doors or windows and no food or water.

'Sorry.

'I don't want to glamorize it.'

'That's not my intention, either. I only want to help you make sense of it.'

'Once the denial began to wear off, the fear was unlike anything I've ever experienced. It felt like my whole body was alive with this desperation to fight my way out, even if it meant digging through the thick walls with my bare hands. I just wanted that fresh air on my skin and the taste of the sea in my mouth. Which is kind of ironic in hindsight.'

'Why did you think this was happening at that stage?'

'To make us comply. To play the games.'

'Yeah, but why you?'

'Me personally?'

'No, the group. Was there a specific reason why this was happening to you? Why you were all selected?'

'We had our theories.'

'Whoever did this went to a great deal of effort and expense. They must have had a reason. A reason they probably wanted everyone to know.

'Listen carefully, listeners. Someone, somewhere must know something. Who has the means, the motive and the opportunity to put this together? Is there anything in what Bonnie is describing that's making your spidey senses tingle? If so, please get in touch at www.expecttheunexpectedpodcast.co.uk.'

27

'I can't stand it any more. I need a drink.' Charlie sat on the floor in the middle of the basement surrounded by the inner and outer circle of rooms. Her cheeks were wet from a combination of sweat and tears. Grant stood on the opposite side of the space scowling at her. Jaide and Jacko stood near him discussing options for trying to break their way out. Maria and Dennis were in the corridor outside Russ's room, still trying to work out how to get some water to him.

Bonnie sat alongside Charlie.

'It'll be OK.'

'It's just a game, I know, but I'm hot and thirsty and I want to go home.' The sobbing started again and Bonnie chose not to raise her growing concern that this was no game. Or at least no game that was going to be fun.

The door behind where Grant stood had a rusted sign attached to it that read, WELL ROOM. Dennis and Grant had tried to prise it open, hoping there really was a well inside filled with fresh water, but logically Bonnie knew that was unlikely. They were in the middle of the sea, so where would the fresh water be coming from, unless it was in a tank and if that was the case how old would that water be? At some point she knew no one would care. Jaide had already pointed out that there were two toilets down here with water in the basin, but as far as she knew no one had stooped to that level of desperation – yet.

The lights flickered and conversation stopped.

'Guys?' called Dennis from the corridor.

Bonnie and Charlie stood and followed the others out.

Maria and Dennis stood opposite the screen on the wall that had shown the message for Clara. Bonnie could see there was more text on it but this time it was not scrolling. She moved behind Maria to look over her shoulder.

NO ONE CAN HEAR YOU

NO ONE CAN HELP YOU

THE ONLY WAY OUT

IS TO WIN

'Absolutely not, abso-bloody-lutely not,' said Dennis, walking to the nearest camera. 'This has gone far enough, do you hear me? People are thirsty and hot and fed up. It's not clever and it's not funny. We demand you let us out right away. We are not playing your stupid game, are we?' He turned back to the group. 'We need to stick together. We don't play this. OK?'

Bonnie scanned the others, who looked exactly how she felt: scared and angry. After a few moments of silence, Jacko went to join Dennis by the camera.

'I agree. I'm not playing.'

'Me neither,' said Jaide. 'Maria?'

'I don't know. They can just keep us locked in?'

'They want to make us compete. You saw all these rooms. More cells like the one poor Russ has been trapped in.' Dennis swallowed. 'This is not entertainment. This is sick, just like that tweet said.'

'No one will watch it, and if they do, they'll send help,' said Charlie.

'Depends how it's edited,' said Jaide. 'They can make it look however they want. Plus people will watch some sick shit.'

'On the internet, maybe, but not on Channel Five,' said Charlie.

'If you saw an episode of *The Hunted* or *Survivor* and it looked like someone had succumbed to starvation or heat stroke, would you believe it or would you think it was fake TV?'

'I'd think it was fake TV,' said Grant.

No one said a word.

'We stand together and we say no. No matter what happens, these sickos are not using me for entertainment.' Dennis stood tall and stared down each of them in turn. After a few moments he faced the camera again. 'We won't play. This ends now.'

The lights immediately went out and heavy metal music blared once more.

Dennis switched his phone torch on and said something into Maria's ear. The two of them came around the group speaking to people one by one.

When Maria reached Bonnie she placed her cupped mouth around Bonnie's ear and shouted, 'Dennis and I think we can squeeze a half-filled water bottle through the gap in Russ's door. We should share the first half between us then find something to push the bottle over to Russ. OK?'

Bonnie nodded and gave her a thumbs up.

After each of them had taken a swig of water, Jaide beckoned them into Maria's escape room cell and used her torch to scan the space. Grant and Jacko immediately moved to the table, turning it upside down to try and break off the

140

thin metal legs. After a good few minutes of kicking, pushing and pulling they had removed two legs.

They carried the poles back to Russ's door, where Maria and Dennis waited with Charlie. They still had the water bottle but it was now flattened a little, ready to pass through the hatch.

'Russ is moving,' Charlie said in Bonnie's ear. 'The music has brought him round a bit.'

'Great,' Bonnie shouted back.

Jaide came their way. 'We need to find a way of attaching the two table legs together to make a longer pole. String, tape, that kind of thing,' she shouted in Bonnie's ear before saying the same to Charlie. Charlie nudged them both and held out the bottom of her blouse before making a tearing motion. Jaide gave her a thumbs up.

Charlie removed her blouse and began to tear strips of material from the bottom using a jagged piece of metal on one of the poles to get her started. Once again she had chosen to wear her bikini top, which proved to be a good decision, dignity-wise. Jaide passed her phone to Maria and laid the poles end to end on the floor, overlapping them by a couple of inches so she and Bonnie could bind them together. They held better than Bonnie would have thought. The group watched as Jaide passed the bottle through the hatch using another strip of blouse to lower it the floor, and then Grant and Dennis fed through the poles to push the bottle towards Russ. After a few moments Grant looked back towards Bonnie and the others and gave a thumbs up.

Had Russ taken a drink? Or was it just that they had successfully passed the water bottle to him? She moved forward to where Maria stood in the hope of taking a look but Dennis stepped in her way to shine his torch in to see. He then turned and held his phone out moving it slowly around the group so they could all see the photographs he had taken. On the screen Russ could be seen with eyes half open and the bottle held firmly in one hand.

The group erupted into jumps, hugs and pats on the back. Bonnie had never felt such relieved hysteria. She hugged Maria and Charlie, and then Jacko, who gave her an unexpected little squeeze. Even Jaide gave her a high five and something close to a smile.

In the light of Jaide's phone, Bonnie watched Grant remove the poles and walk to the nearest ceiling heater. It was a long strip of black metal with a small red light on one end, similar to those Bonnie had seen in her local hot yoga studio. Grant hit it with the end of the pole five or six times in different places until it dislodged from the ceiling and crashed to the floor. This resulted in another whoop of delight from the group.

Grant beckoned for Jaide to follow with her torch as he moved down the hallway scanning the ceiling for other heaters. The group watched them smash another heater and then disappear out of sight. On the screen outside Russ's room a temperature reading of 38 degrees appeared. It flashed for a few seconds and then increased to 40 degrees and then 42.

Bonnie checked her smart watch – 4 per cent charge left. She wished she'd worn her normal watch instead. They'd been down here for four hours now and she felt a touch elated at the thought of Grant managing to destroy all the heaters and the place cooling down. She'd thought it was so dank and cold that first day down here and now she'd do anything for a cool breeze across her skin. Dennis and Maria were taking turns to shout in each other's ears. The two of them had become Russ's unofficial guardians and Bonnie hoped he was doing OK.

When Grant returned he began to high-five the group, that

was until the screen once more displayed the temperature. It flashed a few times on 42 degrees and then began climbing again from 42 to 43 to 44 and finally 45. How was that possible?

And then she felt it swirling around her ankles. Hot air. They were pumping in hot air.

28

The group were all gathered in the central space, sitting on the floor where it was coolest to conserve energy. For a while, Dennis and Jaide took turns shining their torches across the group to check everyone was OK, but at some point they both ran out of battery.

Bonnie swore it was getting warmer. Even the stone under her legs felt hot and she had to keep bending her knees to lift them off the floor. Sweat dripped down her face and stung her eyes. She tried not to think about the amount of fluid her body was using up. Her head ached from the screaming guitars and pounding drums and she had lost track of time after her watch died.

A foul stench came from Russ's room whenever she looked through the hatch at him. It was bad enough sitting out here in the heat and dark without food or water, but he was in there with his own mess for company.

She and Charlie held hands and Bonnie was thankful for the physical contact.

A hand on her head made her jump and then she heard Jacko's voice in her ear.

'If you're doing OK tap my right shoulder, if you're not tap my left.'

She let go of Charlie's hand and reached up to find his face and then moved her hand to his right shoulder and tapped it. She was hot and thirsty and freaking out but otherwise OK. He tapped her right shoulder in response and then moved past her to Charlie.

At least Jacko was letting them all know he cared, even if there was nothing he could do to help. Maybe she should be doing more. But what could she do?

Which is when she realized the mistake she had been making. She had come here to play a role and that role was Clara, her fun-loving, needy little sister, the person who would stand back and wait for someone else to decide what she should do, who would let the likes of Jaide and Grant intimidate her. But that wasn't Bonnie. Bonnie was the capable one, who picked up the slack when Mum was too distracted or poorly to run the house or make decisions, the person whom Mum had described as stubborn and Clara's friends often said could be a bit scary. She was strong. She just needed to be herself.

She reached out for Charlie's hand but it wasn't there. Bonnie shuffled herself in the other woman's direction, expecting to bump into her at any moment, but after half a dozen movements she knew Charlie wasn't there any more. Had she gone with Jacko? What if they'd all moved away and she was now here alone? She knew it was irrational, but the more movements to the right she made without meeting another person, the more desperate she felt. She began shuffling faster, scraping her hand against the rough wall in the process.

Where've you gone? Where've you all gone? she chanted in her head. So much for being strong.

And then she collided with someone. *Thank God.* She felt down the arm for the other person's hand. It was rough and calloused so not Charlie, plus this person wore a long-sleeved shirt and only Dennis had been in one of those. She moved her hand back up his arm to find his shoulder and then his head.

'It's Bonn—' She stopped herself. 'It's Clara,' she said louder into his ear. 'Is it Dennis?'

He felt for her head with his other hand and she turned so he could speak in her ear.

'It's not just Russ bloody suffering now, is it?' he said and she could hear the anger even over the music.

She patted his arm because she couldn't think of anything else to do and then she moved slightly away so their warm bodies weren't touching. But she left her hand resting against his arm and he didn't move away.

What was going on here? That was the question they really needed to answer. Was it really some rogue TV production company that had decided to scare the crap out of people for the sake of the ratings, or had the contestants been sold a dud? What if the show was something else entirely? She thought of the various psychological experiments she had learned about in her degree. Is that what was going on here? Were they glorified lab rats?

Her eyes felt heavy and she leaned her head back against the wall feeling grateful that her little sister wasn't the one going through this.

Bonnie jolted forward realizing she had somehow managed to fall asleep. How was that possible in this environment? And how long had she slept for? She had no idea if it was still daytime. It felt like an age since they'd been locked in here with the warm, acidic smell of everyone's sweat. She felt an urge to stand and pace, to do something active and purposeful. The physical tension in her muscles cried out for movement but she didn't want to leave the comfort of Dennis. Instead, she began shaking her arms and legs, at first gently but then more vigorously and eventually violently as she tried to rid herself of the pent-up frustration, anger and desperation that made her body feel taut and tight and curled up ready to go.

Dennis placed a hand on her arm and she immediately stopped, feeling embarrassed. She gave his hand a small squeeze by way of reassurance that she hadn't lost it or had some kind of seizure.

Thirst burned her throat and her stomach rumbled. She'd eaten nothing but half a banana this morning because she had felt so sick at the thought they might find Russ down here. What she would do for a banana now, or some of those dry cream crackers Jacko had eaten. That's when you knew you were hungry, when you started fantasizing about eating dry crackers.

Her mind set off on fantasies of thickly sliced cheese melted on to toast, chip butties like her mum used to make with lashings of salt and vinegar, and the family-size bags of tortilla chips she and Clara would dunk into tubs of sour cream while watching movies, all washed down by pint after pint of cold squash. She tried to rein in her thoughts but they kept returning.

The music suddenly stopped and the lights came on. Bonnie shielded her eyes. The ringing in her ears sounded almost as loud as the music had been. When she felt able to look she saw the rest of the group all sitting around the room, blinking, more dishevelled and sweaty than before. Charlie sat between Jacko and Maria and there were dark tracks of mascara running down her face. Maria's cheeks were puffy and her eyes red. Jaide on the other hand just scowled at Bonnie before looking away. The boys appeared to have fared better; Grant was yawning and Jacko leaned forward to speak to Charlie, checking she was OK.

'I'll check on Russ,' said Dennis, standing and then bracing himself against the wall as he closed his eyes. He blinked a few times and shook his head before walking across the room and out. Maria rose and followed him. The back of her dress was soaking wet where her sweat had seeped through. Bonnie looked up at the camera above them and knew that image would make it on to the Instagram feed.

Along with the others she stood, stretched her body and then braced herself against the wall just as Dennis had done, when a wave of dizziness hit her.

'How is he?' she asked when she reached Maria outside Russ's room.

'Not so good.'

READY TO PLAY?

Bonnie saw the question appear on the screen seconds before Dennis spoke, but not soon enough to stop him.

'No! Fuck off!' shouted Dennis.

Immediately the lights went out and the music came back on.

29

***Expect the Unexpected* Podcast**
Season 2, Episode 1: 'The Fortress'

'How long this time?

'Bonnie?'

'I haven't cried like that since I was a kid. Sorry, give me a minute.'

'Take your time.'

'I sobbed and then I screamed and banged my hands against the floor. When the lights came on again, I was covered in my own blood. I'd taken all the skin off the side of my left hand. It was awful.'

'Do you want to stop?'

'No, it's OK. I need to do this. I need to get it out of my head, I think, to make some sense of it.'

'What happened next?'

'I started pacing back and forth along the corridor, like those animals you see in captivity. It wasn't safe to move around, I couldn't see my hand in front of my face, but I didn't care. It was all I could do to keep myself sane. And then there were the hallucinations.'

'Really?'

'At first it was flashes of light in my peripheral vision. I kept thinking someone was behind me, but then I saw things running, mice or rats, racing up the walls when I got near. But that was impossible because it was pitch black. I knew it wasn't real, that it was my imagination playing tricks on me. And that was even more terrifying.'

'Mental torture.'

'By the time the lights came back on I would have done anything to prevent them going off again.'

'But he didn't break you, did he? Because you're sitting here talking to me, having the last word.'

'That's kind of you to say.'

'You said right up front that you wished you'd paid more attention because the clues were everywhere. Can you explain to our listeners what you mean by that?'

'Well, for those who've ever done an escape room, you'll know everything in the room serves a purpose as a clue or a red herring. We were told that was true of *The Fortress* and, given everyone was an escape-room fanatic, we took that literally. Maria, Jacko and I in particular scoured the place for things that might be part of the game. Stuff that looked out of place or purposefully put there – riddles, hidden messages, count 'ems and place 'ems.'

'Sorry what are count 'ems and place 'ems?'

'Where you have to count the number of red things, or the number of pictures in a room to give you part of a code, or you're looking to place shapes, cubes, pyramids, et cetera, in a specific place. Things sometimes have pressure pads so when you line objects up in a certain order it unlocks a box or a drawer. That kind of thing.'

'I see.'

'But that's not what I meant about the clues being everywhere and it wasn't what the Director meant either. I meant the fact there was no production crew on site, that all the doors opened, closed, locked and unlocked automatically, and that we were in reality totally vulnerable and completely at his mercy.'

'And what did the Director mean, do you think?'

'His clues were the tasks themselves and the signs he put up. He was tipping us off to what he was up to; everything from the five-pointed star and the Morse code message to Divine Comedy, the name of the band in Maria's duel. These were all hints. Big hints. Even the wooden animals. Especially the animals.'

'Really? That seemed a bit silly to me. Something to distract you from what was happening to Russ. When you said it was a survival-of-the-fittest task, I thought it would be a high-stakes, knock-out kind of thing.'

'I think he wanted it to look frivolous. But you should try typing frog, snake, pig, bear, peacock, snail and cow into Google. Then you'll have some idea of what was coming and why we were there.'

30

'Dennis, keep it shut,' said Bonnie holding a hand up to the older guy. 'Take a minute. We need to discuss this.'

'I can't. Don't let it go dark again. I can't do it.' Charlie was still sobbing despite the lights now being on.

'You can't be serious?' said Dennis.

'I think we should do what he says.' Maria looked Dennis in the eye. 'They won't stop until we do.'

'They'll get bored. It's like any bully: if you react, they keep going. Ignore them and they give up,' Dennis said.

'What if they don't get bored or it takes too long?' said Bonnie. 'What if they're sitting there in an air-conditioned office, drinking, eating and laughing? There may be a whole team of them taking turns to do this.'

'They'll have nothing to bloody broadcast if we don't play.' Dennis was getting angry. 'They have no show if we don't do anything. They can't send out endless shows of us sitting in the dark.'

'We're not just sitting,' said Bonnie, gesturing to Charlie, Maria and her own bloody hands.

She couldn't wash the blood off. There was no water in the

sink taps, they'd checked that early doors. She could dunk her hand in the toilet basin but that risked infection.

'She's right, Dennis,' said Maria.

'Just ask what he wants us to do and then decide,' said Grant.

'Are we agreed?' Bonnie looked around the group in much the same way Dennis had hours before.

Everyone nodded, apart from Dennis, who folded his arms.

'We are ready to play,' said Bonnie, glancing up at the camera.

She noted that the cameras down here were all inside metal cages with glass fronts. She imagined this was re-inforced glass.

On the screen a message appeared.

CAESAR'S REVELATION
WILL MAKE IT CLEAR
WHAT TO DO AND WHO TO FEAR
7 21 12 3 21 - 10 6 21 23 25 - 21 - 22 25 14

'Oh, I can't do any more of this,' Charlie said.

Bonnie stared at the numbers, feeling the same helpless desperation. It was too warm and her head ached. She didn't care enough to force her brain into motion. She wanted out. She wanted to go home. She'd had enough.

Clara should have come clean and dropped out. Bonnie should have forced her to. That's what Mum would have done. The thought of her mum brought tears back to her eyes. How she longed to see her one more time, to be able to ask her what she should do and to be told everything would be OK. Maybe if she came clean about things now, they would throw her off the show and it would all be over. But deep down she knew that things had gone too far now, that none of them would be going home.

She moved to Charlie's side and gave her a hug. If Clara was here, Bonnie would fight with everything she had to keep her safe and get her out.

'It's a code for something,' said Maria, looking around the tired group. 'Sorry, I know that's obvious.'

'Anyone got any actual ideas?' Jaide's tone was impatient.

'Perhaps don't put pressure on us,' said Bonnie.

Jaide frowned. 'I'm just asking.'

Bonnie looked away, her cheeks hot. It was as if Jaide looked down at them and saw lesser beings. She was a female Grant without the humour.

'Caesar's revelation, does that mean a cipher?' said Jacko.

'A Caesar cipher uses letters. These are numbers,' said Dennis.

'Think of all the escape rooms you've done. How are numbers used?' said Maria.

'Is the reference to a revelation religious, do you think?' said Jacko.

'As in Revelation from the Bible?' said Dennis. 'What makes you think that?'

'Are you religious?'

'I went to Catholic school,' said Dennis.

Jacko nodded. 'My mum dragged me to church every week. The Director described my pig as gluttonous and Grant's snake as envious. Do you know what all the sins are by any chance?' said Jacko.

Dennis thought for a moment. 'Gluttony, envy, avarice, pride, wrath, lust and sloth.'

'Yeah, the animals represented the seven deadly sins. I thought that was obvious,' said Grant. 'What's that got to do with this, though?'

Jacko was looking at Grant with exasperation.

'None of us had a lusty animal, I'd have remembered that,' said Jaide.

'I did,' said Maria. 'My cow was described as horny yesterday when I was given my challenge.'

Charlie giggled and the group all looked at her.

'What? That's funny.'

Bonnie gave her a reassuring smile. Any humour they could find in this place was worth clinging to. 'I wouldn't have come on this thing if I'd known it was anything to do with religion. They should have told us that.'

'There's a lot they should have told us,' said Dennis.

'What about this code?' said Maria. She pointed to a small black number at the top left corner of Russ's door. 'Russ is in room five; is that relevant somehow?'

Dennis moved along to Maria's escape room. 'This is room four.' He carried on walking down the corridor away from them. 'Three. Two,' he said as he passed each door. As he reached the curve of the building, he stopped and looked back at them. 'That's one,' he said, nodding at the door he had just passed. 'And this is twenty-six.' He pointed to the door in front of him.

'So it *is* a Caesar cipher,' said Maria.

'What is that?' said Bonnie.

'One of the first ciphers invented. Caesar used it to send secret messages to his generals.'

'But these are numbers, like Dennis said.'

Bonnie caught a flash of judgement in Jaide's eyes.

'Twenty-six numbers,' said Jaide, looking back at the screen. 'So can we match any of these numbers to a letter? There's a twenty-one on its own so that must be an A, yeah?'

'Look up there.' Maria pointed to the wall above the opening to the central area where they'd all spent the initial hours in the dark. Printed over the archway was the letter L. 'He's turned this whole floor into a Caesar cipher. Numbers on the twenty-six doors around the outside, letters on the opposite wall.'

'How appropriate we were stuck in L,' Jacko said, making Bonnie smile for the first time since they'd descended into this place.

'Check if twenty-one is A like I thought,' Jaide said to Dennis, who walked away and out of sight.

'What letter's opposite seven, as that will give us our first letter?' Maria said, moving along past Jaide and a few doors down from where Russ was. She looked up at the wall opposite. 'It's an M.'

'If twenty-one is an A, twenty-two will be a B and twenty-five an E,' said Jaide, looking at the screen again.

'Correct,' said Dennis, walking back from further around the building where he had checked the other doors. 'Twenty-one, twenty-two, twenty-three and twenty-five are A, B, C and E.' He walked to where Maria and Jaide stood in front of the screen.

'I think I know what it says,' said Maria, her voice quiet.

Bonnie looked at the numbers again.

7 21 12 3 21 - 10 6 21 23 25 - 21 - 22 25 14

'Maria place a bet.' Maria's voice had a tremor to it and Bonnie reached out to touch her arm.

'We'll all be with you,' said Jacko.

The group watched the screen expecting further instructions but nothing happened.

'We need the key,' said Jaide. 'The key to the cipher. How many steps to the right did he use? What letter was number one?'

'G,' said Dennis.

'So that means six steps, right?'

'Right.'

'I don't get it. What's going on?' said Charlie.

'Seriously?' Jaide glared at her. 'Sorry, but come on, it's a Caesar cipher. In one step A becomes B and so on. But he used numbers instead of letters. Lined up right A would be number one, but move the numbers one step and B would be one. Get it?'

Charlie nodded.

'So six steps would be?'

'G.'

'Well done,' said Jaide like she was talking to a child.

'Guys?' said Grant. He stood next to room six, one along from Russ's. When he pushed the door with his hand it swung gently inwards.

Maria went to join him and the rest followed. The room was much smaller than Russ's; just a long narrow storage area with a low curved ceiling. The walls were whitewashed bricks like the corridor and a single bulb hung from the ceiling. In each corner there was a metal boxed camera. There were only two other things in the room.

'What is this?' said Grant.

Maria walked in to look more closely as Dennis shouted, 'No!'

But it was too late. Maria was in the room alone. The door swung closed behind her with a bang that made Bonnie jump.

31

Three Months Earlier

CONFESSION: **Maria Bowers**
DATE: **5 June**
TIME: **09.45**
LOCATION: **Best Western Angel Hotel**

'Oh my goodness, this is so exciting. I can't believe it. I'm on the show! Sorry . . . hi, I'm Maria, Maria Bowers. This is the best day. I'm so chuffed. I never thought I'd get this far. I can't believe it. Right, what do you want me to say? Let's see.'

Maria glanced at the card in her hand.

'Oh yes, let me think. So, what am I ashamed of?'

Maria thought of how her mum would try to explain her daughter's lack of a career or lack of a husband to people. How she would make excuses based on Maria having been ill, or being treated unfairly or let down by others. But both Maria and her mum knew none of these things were true. Only Maria was at fault. The truth was after winning the chess competition at age fourteen so many opportunities had come her way but she had refused to take them. Her parents had encouraged her, pressurized her and even at times berated her for wasting her life but she simply couldn't stand the pressure. *I can't do it, I'm not as good as the others, I'm going to make a fool of myself, people will judge me and resent me.* These were the thoughts that ran around her head on a continuous loop.

Maria forced herself to push the memories aside and focus on the task at hand.

'The truth is ... I am ashamed ... I'm ashamed of not doing more with my life. Not doing anything, actually. My parents had such high hopes for me but by the time they passed away they simply had their out-of-shape, unmarried daughter living in the spare room doing temp jobs. It's only since they've gone I've realized I don't really know what was stopping me. Well, I was afraid of letting them down but I did that anyway. And now here I am in my forties and I thought, "What have you got to lose, Maria? Just go out there and do something with your life." So here I am doing something.

'What do I desire? That would be to prove to myself that I can do this. I want to stop hiding from life. I want to know what I can achieve if I'm not scared to try.

'If I'm really honest with you, I don't think for one minute that I can win this. Other people will be more intelligent, more capable and more popular than me. I hope I can maybe get to the final if I keep my wits about me and focus on the challenges. I think I'm at an advantage in that I don't really care what people think of me so much now I'm a bit older, but I do hope that, you know, I can make some friends and have a giggle as we go.

'Like I say, I want to look back and be able to say I did something, something other people haven't done. And what's more unique than this? I simply cannot wait.

'Thank you.'

32

The Fortress @thefortress
The SLOTH or the SNAIL, will she prevail? Watch Maria face her toughest challenge yet on Channel 5 and My5 live NOW. #TheFortress

33

'Maria?' called Jaide. 'Maria, can you hear us?'

Silence.

'So much for we're all in it together. Happy now?' said Dennis, pushing past Jacko.

There was no opening flap in this door. It was solid metal. They couldn't communicate with Maria to help her. All they could do was huddle around the screen attached to the wall and watch.

Maria stood by the side of the waist-high cabinet and stared at the roulette wheel sitting on top. After a few moments she picked up the small card resting in its middle. The camera zoomed in so the others could read what it said.

Faster and faster you must go
Never take a break
A triangle from this circle
You must make

'The running machine,' said Grant.

Maria had no choice but to stand on the narrow, flat oblong in the centre of the floor in order to see the small card.

'That's a treadmill?' said Charlie.

'One of those space-saving ones. They're really cool actually, they work by remote control,' said Grant.

'That doesn't sound cool at all,' said Dennis.

'And what does it mean?' said Bonnie. 'A triangle from this circle you must make?'

Before anyone could answer, they saw Maria stumble a little and grab the roulette wheel before starting to slowly walk on the spot.

'Shit,' said Charlie.

Maria was facing the camera and her fear was clear to see. The group watched as she blinked quickly a number of times before taking a deep breath and slowly blowing the air out through pursed lips. Her eyes had narrowed in concentration and she began chewing her tongue as she studied the roulette wheel.

'A triangle from this circle you must make?' said Grant. 'You can make an equilateral triangle within a circle, can't you? That could give her three numbers from the wheel.'

'Good thinking,' said Jaide. 'How many numbers on a roulette wheel?'

'Thirty-seven,' said Dennis.

'Thirty-eight,' said Grant with a smirk. 'There's a zero and a double zero.'

'In the American version, yes, but traditionally the slots are zero to thirty-six.'

'Can anyone see what version Maria has?'

'It doesn't matter. The numbers aren't consecutive, they're randomly placed to combine odd and even numbers, high and low numbers. Without seeing the wheel we couldn't work out what number was where.' Dennis looked at Grant. 'What matters is whether she can see the wheel clearly enough from where she is.'

'She's pretty close.'

'How would she know where to start? Is the number zero always at the top?' said Jaide.

Grant nodded. 'I think so.'

'So if zero is the top of the triangle could she work out where the other two numbers would need to be from that?'

Bonnie listened to them discussing it as she watched Maria chewing her lip and pressing each of the fingers of her right hand against her thumb, one at a time. If Maria failed to solve the thing she'd be locked in and then what? More darkness? More music? More hours in the heat without water? Bonnie's hand throbbed in pain where she had torn the skin and she couldn't stop thinking about that small amount of water in the bottom of the toilet.

What to do and who to fear, thought Bonnie.

'If she counts twelve places from zero she'd get the first line of a triangle and a number, then another twelve places. It's basic geometry,' said Grant.

'There's one slot too many.' Dennis watched the screen intently. 'It has thirty-seven slots, not thirty-six. It doesn't divide by three.'

'So what then?' said Jacko.

Maria was walking increasingly faster. It was far too warm and they were all horrendously thirsty. How long would Maria be able to last walking faster and faster before she passed out? She was hardly the most physically resilient. Was this so the show could post more cruel images of her and garner ever more abusive tweets? Or was something darker going on? Dennis had been right to try and stop her from going in there.

Maria started to jog as the floor moved faster and faster under her feet, but to Bonnie's surprise the woman looked up at the camera and smiled. Then she started to call out numbers.

'Fifteen,' she said first, then after a few moments of

mouthing words she said, 'fifty-five.' She held her hands up with both sets of fingers splayed.

'What's she doing?' said Bonnie.

'Panicking?' said Grant.

'Sixty-six ... seventy-eight ... ninety-one,' said Maria, blurting the numbers in quick succession before pausing and saying, 'a hundred and five.'

'Is she calculating something? She keeps pausing to think,' said Bonnie.

Charlie spoke under her breath so only Bonnie could hear. 'Sixty-six to seventy-eight is a difference of twelve, seventy-eight to ninety-one is a difference of thirteen, ninety-one to a hundred and five is a difference of fourteen.'

'What's that?' asked Bonnie.

'Nothing, I just . . . I think Maria's solved it.'

The others were all paying attention now.

'What do you mean?' said Jaide.

'She's adding up the consecutive numbers.'

'So?' said Jaide.

'Well, I'm pretty sure, if I remember right, that if you add one plus two plus three plus four and so on it's called a triangular number,' said Charlie. 'So, if she adds up the numbers one to thirty-six consecutively—'

'She turns the circle into a triangle,' said Jaide. 'At last, Charlie has arrived. Welcome to the party. Took you long enough.'

Charlie shrugged and blushed a little. 'I like maths.'

'Can't you just say something nice and leave it there?' Bonnie said to Jaide.

'Not usually.'

Maria's numbers were getting bigger but she was running now and her breath sounded laboured as sweat poured down her face. 'Two hundred and ten,' she said briefly, holding both hands up again.

'That's number twenty; sixteen more to go,' said Charlie.

'She can't take much more of this,' said Jacko. 'And there's no water for her at the end. She'll be in a rough state. What do we do?'

They watched in silence as Maria pumped her arms and called out breathless numbers.

'Four hundred and ninety-six . . . five hundred and twenty-eight . . . five hundred and sixty-two . . . no . . . five hundred and sixty-one . . . erm.' Maria coughed and stumbled.

The group held its collective breath. If she fell, that treadmill would throw her into the harsh stone wall.

'Five hundred and ninety-five,' Maria shouted at the camera defiantly.

'Two more to go,' said Jaide. 'Come on, Maria.'

'Six hundred and thirty,' she said and then something changed in her face. Where she had looked defiant to the point of self-satisfaction, a darkness clouded her expression. Her eyes stared widely at the camera and she gave a small shake of her head. When she spoke again she did so too quietly for Bonnie to hear the number.

Bonnie did the maths in her head and realized what had spooked Maria. They had been right. This was something religious. Something darkly religious.

The final number was 666.

34

Annabelle @Annadom22

Holy crap that freaked me out when I did the maths! Loving the dark twist. Bring on the beast. #TheFortress

---

Adrian @aghopen12

I thought Maria was going to have a heart attack. She is a legend. #TheFortress

Sophie @Sophie_walker

I agree. I take it all back. The Frizzonator has won me over. She's a tough old bird. #TheFortress

Adrian @aghopen12

She's putting the rest of them to shame. I mean has anyone else actually solved anything? #TheFortress

---

Maise Mowlem @maisie_mow3

666! Who should you fear? The devil has you locked in here. #TheFortress

Lola @lolabelle

I'm so glad I'm not on that show. My nerves couldn't stand it. #TheFortress

Maise Mowlem @maisie_mow3

If Maria's challenge is anything to go by this is going to get harder and harder. I reckon a few of them will break. My vote's on Charlie and Grant, he's all talk.

Dave @Davecakes765

Maria rocks. How did she work that out? Whoever goes next has a lot to live up to. #Mariatowin

35

No one said a word as they watched Maria fall to her knees and hang her head low. The treadmill had slowed to a stop after she had spoken the final number and a door on the far side of the cabinet had swung open.

'Poor love,' said Dennis.

'I can't take any more. I can't watch.' Charlie clamped her hands over her nose and mouth as she moved away and Bonnie caught an eye roll from Grant.

For a while Maria did nothing. She remained doubled over, her back rising and falling in a quick rhythm that Bonnie wasn't sure was due to exhaustion or sobbing. The group all watched her in silence. They all knew what Maria's triangular number had revealed. A fleeting question occurred to Bonnie: had whoever designed the roulette wheel known what its numbers added up to? Had it been an intentional message hidden within the game itself because gambling was a sin?

After what seemed like an age, Maria lifted her head and with one shaky hand she pulled the cupboard door a little wider to look inside.

Her sobs grew louder and Bonnie braced herself for what was to come.

'What is it?' said Dennis.

Maria reached inside the cupboard and began to pull something out.

Bonnie thought she might be hallucinating again, like people who see an oasis in the desert simply because they want to. When Maria turned her face to them, she was beaming. In her hands she held a box filled with food and bottles of glorious, glorious water.

The door opened and Maria stepped out. 'You did it! You fricking legend!' said Grant, picking her and the box up. She coughed as he placed her down again and planted a large smacker on her forehead.

'You are amazing, well done,' said Bonnie.

Maria smiled but struggled to speak. Her face was bright red and she smelled sweaty. She placed the box on the floor. It contained twelve small bottles of water, a sandwich each, bags of nuts, a large packet of chocolate digestives and some apples.

'Oh my God,' said Charlie, taking a bottle of water and nearly drinking it in one go.

'Take your time,' Jacko said, handing an open bottle to Maria, who had sunk down to sit on the floor leaning against the wall. 'Small sips at first, OK?'

Maria nodded before taking two large gulps.

Jacko placed a hand on her arm and she paused before starting to sip it.

'We need to keep some aside for Russ, too,' said Dennis.

'Is he still with us?' Grant was already halfway through his ham sandwich. 'These are cold, was that cupboard refrigerated?'

'Grant!' said Bonnie.

'What? Oh, the Russ thing. Look, I like the guy, but has anyone checked on him lately, that's all I'm saying.'

Dennis scowled at Grant as he grabbed a bottle of water and bag of cashew nuts and carried them to Russ's room.

Bonnie watched him lift the hatch and look in, expecting the worst but hoping for the best.

'All right, mate. I've got you more water and some food.'

Bonnie breathed a sigh of relief and allowed herself to enjoy the water filling up the dried-out husk of her body. She had selected a cheese sandwich but knew she needed to take her time to eat it after so many hours without food. One of her closest friends was Muslim and had told her once that in Ramadan when people have fasted all day they would first have small snacks to build up to a meal, otherwise it could make them sick. Bonnie watched the others stuffing food into their mouths.

'Take it easy, guys. Don't eat too fast. You don't want to be ill.'

'Oh, Mum's back,' said Grant but his eyes were full of humour and he winked at her.

Maria's win had done something wonderful. It had given them hope.

Bonnie glanced back to see Dennis passing a packet of something through the hatch. Russ must be doing better if he'd made it to the door.

Charlie took a second bottle of water, opened it and began to pour it over her head.

'Oh no!' said Jaide, grabbing her hand to stop her. 'What are you, an idiot? That water could save our lives. We drink one each and ration the rest. We don't waste it cooling off like we're on some spa break.'

Charlie looked like she might cry again as she fastened the top back on the bottle and returned it to the box.

'Things are looking up, team,' said Grant, selecting three biscuits from the packet. 'Things are looking up!'

'What are you talking about?' said Maria, her voice raspy and low. 'What about six-six-six? Does that not scare you?'

'Ooh, the devil has got us,' he said, grabbing both his cheeks and opening his mouth wide. Then he laughed.

'It's not funny,' said Jacko.

'It's a game, like we said upstairs. Right, Jaide?'

Jaide raised an eyebrow and didn't answer.

'You still think this is a game after what happened to Russ?' said Charlie. 'He almost died.'

'But he didn't. We were sent down here just in time. This is a survival-based escape room, obviously. And the toughest will survive.'

'And that's you, is it?' said Jacko.

'Only the toughest?' said Maria. 'What about the others?'

'Come on, Maz, you of all people know we can beat this. If only one of us was meant to survive they'd have given food and water to you alone, wouldn't they?'

Grant had a point. This was why everyone felt so hopeful. If they won every task, chances were they'd keep getting food and water. And if someone became stuck they could feed them, like with Russ. Bonnie looked along the corridor at room six.

'There was no flap to raise in the door of room six where Maria has just been,' she said. 'What if one of us gets stuck in a room like that? There are plenty of them.'

The group became quiet as they contemplated that. If Maria had become stuck in there they wouldn't even have been able to speak to her. Bonnie couldn't imagine how any of them would cope in that situation.

'Do you still think it's a game?' said Charlie quietly.

'We'll be fine. Don't worry.' Bonnie smiled at her, thinking again of how freaked out Clara would have been in here. 'That was impressive, knowing about triangular numbers.'

'Maria knew it, too.'

'But the rest of us didn't. You shouldn't hide like you do. You don't have to apologize for knowing some of the answers.'

'I'm not like all of you.'

'I'm no genius. Look, we all have our talents. Maria's knowledgeable, Jacko's caring, Dennis is determined, Grant is . . . nice to look at.'

Charlie giggled and took Bonnie's hand. 'I don't think Jaide likes me.'

'Who *does* she like? Ignore her. She's mean. I'm serious, though.' Bonnie gestured to Charlie's bikini top. 'People don't usually wear this under their clothes, you know.'

'Mum always told me my looks were all I had.'

'Well, she was wrong. You won your place on this crazy thing. Don't let the rest of them intimidate you.'

Bonnie watched Dennis walk by and frowned at the packet of nuts in his pocket. Hadn't he passed those to Russ?

'Has he eaten something?' asked Maria.

Dennis swallowed before saying, 'Uh-huh.'

Bonnie caught his eye and frowned a question. Dennis held her gaze for a long moment and then gave an almost imperceptible shake of the head.

Russ. Oh God, Russ. So much for Grant's theory that no one would be allowed to perish.

Bonnie suppressed the scream that threatened to escape her. Dennis was keeping it quiet for a reason, probably to protect the group.

'Are you OK?' Charlie said, seeing the tear roll down Bonnie's cheek.

'I'm just exhausted and it's so hot.' She rubbed her face to try and wipe away the grief and the dread.

If Russ had been allowed to die, what did that mean for the rest of them?

36

The Fortress @thefortress
Who goes next? You decide. Vote now on www.thefortress.
co.uk

Carl @Carlrocks7
Did you see Grant sidling up to Jacko and Dennis? The girls
need to watch their backs. #TheFortress

Adrian @aghopen12
He's a player all right. I reckon he'll stab them all in the back
soon enough. #TheFortress

Sophie @Sophie_walker
I reckon that Jacko's hiding something. He's too nice all the
time. #TheFortress

P Foulds @PFoulds345

Let's see if cracker boy can do a real challenge.
#Jackotoplay

Freya @lolababe

If you have time to comfort others you're not working hard
enough. #thefortress #Jackotoplay

Freddie @FRBrown5

Does anyone else think Jacko is just kinda pathetic? Would
you have him on your team? I'd even prefer Dennis, at least
he has some balls. #Jackotogo

Liz Renton @l_renton

I think he's a sweetheart.

Freddie @FRBrown5

My point exactly. Who wants a 'sweetheart' on a survival
challenge? Man up princess.

37

The Twitter feed appeared on the screen a few hours after Maria had won them food and water. Bonnie had been asleep dreaming of trying to catch a train in the face of endless obstacles. She woke with a start when someone touched her arm. It was Jacko. He was crouched next to her. He had lovely eyes and a kind smile.

'I might need you for this,' he said.

She sat up and rubbed her eyes. The air in her throat was warm and her head still pounded. She'd hoped some sleep might lessen the intensity of it but no such luck. She had been curled on the floor of the central area and her shoulders ached from the pressure of the stone slabs. She began to rub her left shoulder with her right hand.

'What's going on?' She couldn't help the large yawn that followed her question. 'Sorry.'

'Come see.' He held out a hand for her.

When she took it, she felt a ripple of electricity that landed in her gut as if she had ridden a big dip on a roller coaster.

'You OK?' said Jacko.

'Uh-huh.' She forced herself to look him in the eye. He smiled and looked at their hands still clasped together.

'Are you really? You seemed upset . . . more upset, after we got the food.'

He had seen her reaction to Russ's death, of course he had because he watched her as much as she watched him. She thought about telling him but stopped herself. Dennis wanted it kept quiet and she respected his view. Sure, she had disagreed with him refusing to play earlier and dooming them to hours more in the darkness, but in that situation Dennis had acted in anger. In this, he had been calm and composed. He was older and wiser and she needed to pay attention to that. She knew only too well what grief could do to people, how it could engulf you.

'I'm OK. Thank you. What did you need me for?'

Jacko met her eyes again for a long moment and then turned slightly to his left before correcting to his right with what sounded like a half laugh, half cough, after which he walked back out towards the hall.

Bonnie let go of his hand a little reluctantly and followed him to the screen where the group were gathered reading the latest tweets.

'The Director asked the public to vote who goes next,' said Dennis matter-of-factly.

On the right of the screen next to the Twitter feed, where the Instagram posts usually sat, was the vertical bar chart with all their names listed along the bottom. She watched the bars of the chart grow for different members as votes came in. She was mid-table, higher than Grant, Charlie and Maria but lower than Dennis, Jaide and Jacko, who currently topped the charts by a significant amount.

'The public have spoken,' said Jacko and winked at her.

Bonnie wasn't sure what to say. She looked at the Twitter feed for some clues as to why people had voted this way. As she scanned the list she noticed people seemed to think he was finding the whole thing too easy. She wanted to take hold of his hand again but wasn't sure how he'd react. It was one thing to have a moment in private, a whole other to do so in front of the group.

'This time we stick together. No one goes in any room alone and we take supplies of water and food,' said Dennis.

'I'm not sure that's how it works, Den,' said Grant. At least he had refrained from calling Dennis old man all the time.

'You can either roll over and be a victim or stand up to this like a man.'

'Since when did taking your mates in with you make you a man?' Grant raised his eyebrows in Jacko's direction.

'He won't be so cocky when *he's* in the frame,' said Jaide.

'Half an hour ago you were asking me to team up with you against the girls,' said Jacko to Grant. 'Is that what you think makes a man?'

'Team up how?' said Jaide.

'He thinks we stand the best chance of surviving because we're stronger and have more stamina. But I told him you girls are far superior in mental strength and intellect.'

'You are such a suck-up,' said Grant.

'It's the truth.'

'How exactly were you planning to use this man gang to defeat us?' Jaide stared at Grant until he looked away. 'Pathetic.'

The screen turned black for a few seconds before displaying its familiar red typeface.

Jacko,

THE ONE WHO HAS A CROSS TO BEAR
NEEDS TO TAKE A STAND
WHEN THE BEAST HAD BEAUTY IN HIS EYE
WHAT WAS IN HIS HAND?

'There's that religious theme again. A cross to bear – isn't that a reference to Christ carrying his own cross?' Jacko looked at Dennis, who nodded. 'Bear could also mean the animal, though. You had the bear, didn't you, Clara? Do you remember what the Director said about it?'

Bonnie took a moment to collect her thoughts. 'It was something about the fierce bear protects what it loves, then I had to smash through the ice to get to the baby bear toy.'

'The fierce bear, so in terms of the seven sins that's anger, wrath.' Jacko looked back at the screen. 'I expect the need to take a stand references what I have to do, like Maria placing a bet.'

'What was Maria's sin?' said Charlie. 'If this is all about sins, wouldn't her challenge be linked to one?'

'Gambling is all about money so greed, maybe?'

Everyone was quiet for a moment. Bonnie watched Grant, thinking he might be the one to throw gluttony out there but to his credit he didn't. Maybe he thought it was the same as greed or maybe he had finally decided to be kinder.

Jacko said, 'When the beast had beauty in his eye, what was in his hand? Anyone any ideas on that?'

The beast – 666, thought Bonnie, and despite the heat she felt a distinct chill in her veins.

'It's familiar, I think I've heard it before, I think it's a famous riddle but I can't remember the answer,' said Jaide. She glanced at Maria, who looked exhausted. She sat on the floor, her breathing laboured.

Bonnie read the words on the screen and thought of all the religious references: cross to bear. Revelation. 666. Seven deadly sins. Then there was the star as they entered the building. Was that reference to something religious too? The kings and shepherds followed a star to the stable in Bethlehem where Jesus was born. The memory of something had her walking a few feet away to the entrance of Maria's first escape room. She stood in the doorway and looked again at the two old posters on the wall. She had noticed these when Maria was solving the music riddles. A desert island on one wall and bonfire on the opposite. She had thought nothing of them, assuming they were left behind from some earlier inhabitants, but she had been wrong.

'Dennis?' she said, looking in the direction of where everyone gathered. 'The answer to this first duel was the Divine Comedy. That's a religious thing as well as a band, isn't it?'

'Dante's *Divine Comedy*,' he said with a nod.

'Is that about heaven and hell, by any chance?'

'Yes and no. If memory serves me correctly it's about the journey through purgatory.'

Dennis looked at Maria, who was now slumped over with her eyes closed.

'Is she OK?' said Charlie.

'Maria?' said Jaide. 'Hey, you OK?' She walked to kneel by the other woman and placed a hand on her shoulder. 'Maria?' she said a little more urgently and gave the woman a slight shake.

Maria jolted awake with a small yelp and wide eyes.

'You gave us a fright there.'

'We thought you were a goner, Maz,' said Grant, causing Dennis to tut loudly.

Bonnie looked at Russ's door and then at Dennis. *When do we tell them?* her eyes tried to ask, but Dennis looked away. She knew telling Jacko before he went into a challenge would freak him out too much and she'd never forgive herself if he failed because he was panicking. Dennis was right to keep it quiet – but for how long? Surely the group *needed* to know at some point. She wanted to talk it through but how was that possible in this place?

'Is this reference to beauty and the beast, do you think?' Jacko was still focused on solving his riddle. Bonnie could understand it. He wanted the thing over and done with.

Purgatory, thought Bonnie. The place where you pay for your sins. What possible sin could Russ have committed to deserve his fate? And why was Jacko facing wrath? From what she'd seen he was the least likely to get angry. It would make more sense for Dennis or Jaide to have that one; Grant, even. Were the public told which sin they were voting for or was it random?

'If the beast has beauty in his eye, if he *sees* beauty,' said Jacko, 'what does he have in his hand?'

'Got it! GOT IT!' Grant was pointing at the screen. 'Ha! That's good – I like that. I'm going to remember that.'

'Are you going to tell us, then?' said Jaide.

'Hell, no. The winner of this is the one who can solve the riddles and unlock the secrets. If you can't work it out for yourselves don't be looking at me to help y'all.'

38

Once they knew Grant had sussed it out there was a kind of collective acceptance that it couldn't be that hard. Worryingly, Maria didn't participate at all. Bonnie suspected the woman simply wanted them all to leave her alone so she could sleep but they all instinctively knew not to let her do that.

'When the beast sees beauty, what is he holding?' said Jacko.

Grant sniggered then held a hand up. 'No, it's not that. It's clean.'

'Wait, it says the beast has beauty in his eye. How about beauty is in the eye of the beholder?' Jaide said.

'It says it's in the eye of the beast,' said Charlie.

'The *be*holder,' said Dennis, looking around the group and waiting for people to react. When no one did he said, 'When the beast has beauty in his eye what is he holding in his hand? A bee. Beauty is in the eye of the *bee* holder!'

'Oh, that is clever,' said Charlie.

'Holding a bee. What does that mean?' said Jacko.

Grant was looking at the floor. Clearly he hadn't thought to consider how the answer helped them.

Bonnie wondered if it was something to do with honey. The riddle referenced a bear and a bee. Or was it only Pooh

Bear that ate honey? She had no clue. It was ridiculous how they had nothing to help them in this godforsaken place. Where were the clues or the reference documents? All they had were brick walls and locked metal doors.

She pushed away from the wall where she had been leaning and walked along the corridor to the left. The others followed but no one asked where she was going. She passed the exit stairway up to the main deck and almost stopped. Was it worth checking one more time? Instead she continued on until she saw what she was looking for. As she suspected, not all the letters on the inner wall were written on the stone, some were on the doors.

'B,' she said pointing to the black letter on the top left.

'Try it,' said Jaide.

'But don't go in,' said Dennis.

Bonnie stepped forward and pushed the door inwards as Jacko came to her side. As with door six, this one swung easily open. The room was bare apart from a square podium in the centre of the floor with what looked to be another cupboard under it and, in the far corner, a wooden baseball bat. She looked at the door and was relieved to see it had a hatch and a flap to lift. Not that this had saved Russ, but it was something.

On the left-hand wall, written in large black letters, it said,

Mary, Mary quite contrary
How do your bruises grow?
If you can stand and feel my pain
I might just let you go.

'Looks like you're fighting something,' said Grant.

Jacko looked at him and gave a slow nod.

'You're not going in there alone,' said Dennis. 'Come on, I've got two bottles of water and some food.' He held up the items to show Jacko.

'Err, what's with the boys' club again?' said Jaide to Dennis. 'Who voted you the best one to help him?'

'I'm not going in there,' said Charlie.

'Me neither,' said Grant, winking at her.

'Well, I will and Bonnie will. You stay out here, Maria. You've done enough.'

'The room isn't big enough for three of us. Not if I have to swing a bat. I'll hurt someone,' said Jacko.

He was right; this room was small like Maria's treadmill room had been. Bonnie saw that around the walls there were holes that looked to have been purposely drilled, some small and some larger, the size of an orange or, she realized with dismay, a baseball.

'I think I know what you have to do,' she said.

'Hit balls that come from those holes?' said Jacko, scanning the room as she had. 'That is definitely a one-man job . . . sorry, a one-person job.' He flashed a smile at Jaide.

Dennis was also looking in and gave a nod.

With arms outstretched to swing a bat there was no chance of avoiding another person, and if the balls came from different directions you'd be spinning this way and that, making it even more dangerous.

'Plus there's only one bat,' said Bonnie. 'Not that I'm refusing to help, it's just—'

Jacko touched her arm and smiled warmly. 'It's OK. It's my turn.'

'We'll jam open the door,' said Dennis. He took off his shoe and placed it in the doorway.

'Will that be enough to hold it?' said Charlie.

'Give me your shoe too, Grant.' Dennis held his hand out.

'Absolutely not. These are £140 high-tops. That door will destroy them.'

'I'll go back to get the scales,' said Jaide. 'They're heavy and made of metal.'

While they waited, Jacko remained outside the room.

Bonnie stepped to his side.

'Do you have anything to be angry about?' she asked. He looked at her for a second or two longer than was polite and then smiled. 'Why do you ask?'

'Channel the rage.'

When Jaide came back they placed the heavy scales next to the door frame so the door could not fully close and Jacko entered. Nothing happened. He picked up the bat and they waited and waited but the door did not close on its own. Grant and Dennis pulled it closed by hand until it met the scales blocking the way. It stayed where it was but, inside the room, nothing came out of those holes.

Dennis looked up at the nearest camera and then through the gap in the door at Jacko.

'The challenge won't start until the door can close, will it?' Jacko said.

Dennis slowly shook his head. 'Looks that way.'

'OK, we tried. I'll just have to do the damn thing.'

Dennis held out the food and water he'd brought along. Jacko took one bottle of water only. When Dennis suggested he take the other too Jacko flatly refused but he did take the packet of nuts and some biscuits.

Jacko used his foot to push the scales out of the doorway towards Dennis and the door slid into place.

A few seconds later Jacko began to cough. Bonnie lifted the flap in the door and thick black smoke snaked out of the hole into the hallway. She could no longer see him, or the platform or even the walls of the room. She rushed to the nearest screen, where everyone else had already gathered.

'He can't see a thing in there. It's full of smoke.'

'That explains the thermal imaging,' said Dennis.

On the screen the bright white image of Jacko stood out against a grey background.

'What kind of smoke is it?' Dennis looked at Bonnie.

'It's black and thick.'

'Did it smell of anything? Was there a burning smell?'

Bonnie shook her head.

'Dry ice, maybe?' said Jaide.

'That's white,' said Dennis. 'And it would be problematic in a room so small, it's pretty toxic.'

'How do we know that what they're using isn't?' said Bonnie.

Dennis held her gaze for a moment and then looked back at the screen.

'What does he have to do?' said Charlie.

'Take a stand,' said Dennis, as they watched Jacko move carefully across the room until his foot made contact with the podium. He paused for a moment, probably to steel himself, before stepping up on to the small square that was not much larger than his feet.

'And feel the pain,' said Jaide.

Bonnie could just make out the swirling of the smoke around Jacko's bright white image and then a flash of motion caught her eye a second before his upper body jerked backwards.

'Did you hear that?' said Dennis. 'The ball made a noise, a kind of rattle.'

'He'd be best to close his eyes and listen then,' said Grant, who despite his reluctance to help was front and centre to watch the show. The longer Bonnie was in the guy's company the less she liked him.

'If he closes his eyes it'll affect his balance,' said Jaide.

A second ball flashed across the screen, this time from a different direction, and again rocked Jacko off balance. They watched as another ball hit his body and then another. The balls came from four different directions and they came fast. Jacko spun and swung the bat but to no avail; he failed to make contact and the missiles hammered into him over and over.

Come on, Jacko, Bonnie thought, even though in her gut she knew he would never be able to withstand this.

39

Three Months Earlier

CONFESSION: **Jackson Decker**
DATE: **5 June**
TIME: **12.45**
LOCATION: **Best Western Angel Hotel**

'How-do, I'm Jackson Decker, Jacko, and I am here to confess my secrets to you lovely folks. Heads up, this is some saucy stuff.' Jacko winked at the camera.

'What do I desire? Ooh, that's a personal question, isn't it? Do you want to know who I find hot? Men, women, blondes, brunettes? As I'm not applying for *Love Island* or *First Dates* I'm assuming you want something deeper, as in what do I desire most in life? That would be peace. Not world peace, although I wouldn't turn it down; I want peace of mind, peace and quiet. To be at peace.'

You sound like some hippy, New Age ponce. Jacko laughed at himself. This was harder to do than it sounded. He needed less honesty and more humour.

'OK, joking over, what I desire most is to smash it on the newest reality TV show, to beat the competition into the ground, win the cash, get the girl and become one half of the next Ant and Dec.'

Not what he'd written on the form but as he had no intention of revealing what he was most ashamed of on camera he may as well have some fun with it. If it lost him his place, so be it. What will be, will be.

'And so to what I'm most ashamed of. That's pretty obvious, I imagine. I've got the hair, the face, the bod but also the freckles. So many freckles. There should be some kind of law against it. There must be a million cute kids out there desperate for just a few scattered across their noses, and I have all these. I'm in possession of an unfair proportion. It's impossible to be manly and impressive with the things. I'm not claiming it as a disability, obviously, but the afflicted of us do deserve some sympathy. Life is harder when you're covered in so much cuteness.'

That felt good, more comfortable than sharing the sob story he'd written about not standing up for his mum. He wished he could take that back now. If she ever found out he'd written about it, it would crush her. She couldn't bear the thought of anyone knowing what went on behind closed doors. She had never exactly told him to keep it to himself, but he had watched her cover the bruises and mask her pain with a smile too many times to not get the message.

He wasn't lying when he said the thing he most desired was peace. The prize money would enable him to buy a home without drama. He wanted to escape his past and start afresh, somewhere Mum could come and live with him. Not that he suspected she ever would.

What made him think he could win? That was a tough one, as in truth he didn't hold out much hope. *What to say? What to say?* After a few minutes of thought, he decided to drop the façade and tell the truth.

'I don't know if I'm smart enough to solve the secrets of the fortress but I do want to escape. Make of that what you will.'

40

Jacko anticipated the next ball. His arms swung in the direction of the flash and Bonnie heard the satisfying sound of wood against rubber. She watched as he hit another ball and then another. Maybe he would be OK after all. She shuffled forward within the group, willing him on. Of all the people in here Jacko was special. They had a connection and a chemistry. She needed him to keep her sane. But more than that, he represented hope. She could imagine meeting up with him after all of this and having a drink while they debriefed the whole goddam mess. He was the promise of a future.

The balls began firing at an increased frequency. Jacko spun and twisted, swinging the bat in all directions, but the balls came too fast. They hit him in the torso, the legs and the arms.

'How are they doing that?' said Jaide. 'How are they firing the balls?' She looked at Dennis and then Grant.

It was Grant who answered. 'Tennis ball machines or something similar in each of the side rooms behind the holes. The electronic ones are remote controlled.'

'This is unfair. How long is he supposed to put up with this?' said Bonnie.

'It makes it all the more torturous if you don't know when it's going to stop,' said Grant.

'Yeah, but how far can a remote control signal travel?' said Jaide.

'They have to be using radio control as remote control relies on infrared and line of sight. Radio control can travel over distances and through materials such as brick and concrete,' Maria said, coming to Jaide's side.

'How far away could the controller be?' Jaide asked. 'Would it need to be here on site?'

'I'm not sure. It might be possible to have it on land near by or a boat? I'm not an expert.'

Bonnie remembered Jacko saying he might need her help and she made her way back to the door, lifting the flap and shouting in, 'You're doing great. It'll be over soon.'

'Thanks.' Jacko's voice sounded breathless and pained. A second later she heard the flat thudding sound of another ball making contact with his flesh.

Bonnie strode to the nearest camera. 'Are you getting a kick out of this? Well?'

'He's not going to answer you,' said Dennis.

'It's not just one guy. There's a whole production company. We only need one of them to see sense.'

'You're wasting your breath.'

'I have to try.'

'What if it is just one guy?' Dennis was facing her now as the others looked on. 'What if he's the only one who can hear you and he's not listening?'

'You were the one shouting the odds at him before.'

'Like I say, you're wasting your breath. He's not interested.'

'I think he wants us to know how clever he is. He's been showing off about it since we arrived. He's desperate for us to know what he's doing.' She turned back to the camera and said, 'Aren't you?'

The light looked back, unblinking.

Charlie made a sound that took Bonnie rushing to the screen. Jacko's silhouette was rocking precariously on the stand. His arms swung without any real purpose now.

'Don't give up,' said Maria.

'How many did he hit? Is that significant?' said Jaide.

'Not that many. Let's hope the target isn't six hundred and sixty-six,' said Grant.

Bonnie's fury reached breaking point and she strode back to the camera.

'Why are you doing this? WHY?'

'Come away.' Jaide came to her side and took hold of her arm, but Bonnie shrugged her off.

'You can't let people die. You're sick. You're a sick bastard.'

'Calm down, love,' said Dennis. 'It's not doing any good.' He helped Jaide steer Bonnie away.

'Dennis is right. Don't give him the satisfaction.' Jaide's tone was a little softer than usual.

Charlie was staring at Bonnie with wide eyes.

'What do you mean he's letting people die?'

41

The news of Russ's death, followed by Jacko falling off the podium and failing his task, was more than any of them could take.

Once the smoke had cleared from Jacko's room and it was clear it was going to remain locked, Dennis had quietly informed him about Russ before advising him to ration his water and food supplies carefully. The rest of them then shared a few sips of the second bottle of water Dennis had with him.

Bonnie stood opposite Charlie. Her eyes were bloodshot and swollen, her cheeks streaked with dried tears, and she was biting her fingernails to the quick. Next to Charlie, Grant stood with his head back and his eyes closed. Bonnie suspected he was avoiding having to comfort Charlie. She clearly had a soft spot for him despite the fact he was intolerant of her emotional outbursts. Jaide, Maria and Dennis stood a little further away; each lost in their own thoughts.

And then there were six.

Six.

Six.

Six.

When Dennis, Maria and Charlie had walked back to

where they had left the food supplies, and Jaide had gone to the toilet, Bonnie was left outside Jacko's locked room with Grant.

'What made you come on this thing?' she asked, feeling the pressure to make some conversation. It struck her that she'd never spoken one on one to the guy after that moment on the boat.

'I knew I could win it.' Grant's expression was a mixture of boredom and frustration.

'How do you feel about that now?'

'Same.'

'Seriously? You still think this is winnable after Russ?'

'I don't think that was intended. I imagine it was acciden-tal. Bad risk assessment or something. I expect someone's head will roll for it when it comes to light.'

'So why has no one come to get the rest of us out, then?'

'Whoever's in charge is covering it up.'

'Why on earth would they do that?'

'To avoid the sack. I don't know. Maybe they'll turn up any minute but until then we have no choice but to try and win our way out.'

'I can't believe you still think this is a game.'

'It was inevitable that at some point a TV show would kill someone on screen. It's been on the cards for years. It's not like others haven't died because of some reality TV show. It's only the fact that they died afterwards that has saved things so far. This will probably sound the death knell for all of these shows. They're probably trying to figure out what to do about it.'

Bonnie was surprised by this insight and the fact she agreed with it. It made her think of all those shocking psycho-logical experiments again. Could that really be what had happened here? And, if so, who else would they be willing to sacrifice to hide the crime?

'I hope you're right. I hope Russ was a mistake and that someone will stop this soon.'

'I need to believe it. It's not good for me to dwell on the downsides.'

'We've got to be realistic, though, haven't we?'

'Realism's overrated.'

Bonnie wanted to challenge that. Surely to survive they needed to see things clearly for what they were, but something in Grant's eyes told her to drop it; some deep sadness she detected. Russ's death had maybe hit him harder than she'd thought. They had bonded very quickly. On some level perhaps Grant needed to think this way to keep going.

When Jaide returned, Bonnie walked with her and Grant back to the central area and selected an apple from the now small pile of food. Then she walked back to Jacko's locked room and opened the flap. He sat leaning against the opposite wall. The bruising to his face and neck was coming up in red and purple weals.

'I thought you might like some company.' She used the apple to prop open the flap. 'How are you feeling?'

Jacko looked at her but didn't speak or smile. His eyes looked glazed and distant.

'You did really well given there were no bloody instructions and a pretty horrific task to face.'

He looked away and swallowed.

'Hey, you should be proud you lasted as long as you did. No one else would have.'

'Apart from Super Grant.'

Bonnie studied Jacko carefully. She needed to distract him. 'He said something interesting earlier.'

'Yeah?'

She told him what Grant had said about reality TV shows and how Russ's death could have been an accident.

Bonnie watched Jacko adjust his position.

'I'm surprised it came from Grant, if I'm honest.'

'Yeah, more of a Dennis insight.'

'Maybe the guy's maturing.'

'At least something good would come of this, if so.'

Jacko smiled and then winced and touched the side of his face. Bonnie turned away and sat down with her back against the door. She let out a deep breath.

'There are two posters on the walls of the original duel rooms – did you see them? One shows a desert island and the other a bonfire. I think they are supposed to depict paradise and hell. So this is purgatory, the place in between heaven and hell.'

'You're smarter than you look,' said Jacko with a smile in his voice.

'Do you think that's what this is?'

'I think some religious nut is responsible.'

'Do you think Grant could be right that this is all still a game?'

'If so, it's a bloody brutal one.'

'So you agree with Dennis that this Director has gone rogue?'

'Maybe he's trying to teach the world a lesson. Maybe Grant's idea that such shows are increasingly irresponsible is the point.'

'We are being made an example of?'

'Perhaps.'

'We have to get out of here. We have to.'

'I'm getting the feeling that's not up to us.'

Jacko was silent for so long that Bonnie had to stand up and check through the flap that he was OK.

'I think my challenge was designed specifically for me.'

'Being hit by baseballs?'

'Being made to take a stand and fight back.'

'How so?'

'Can you sit down again? I'm not sure I can say this to your face.'

Bonnie did as he asked, her stomach tight with nerves.

'For as long as I can remember, my dad . . .'

Jacko paused and coughed.

Bonnie waited.

'My dad hurt my mum and I . . . well, I did nothing.'

'I'm so sorry,' said Bonnie, not knowing if that was the right thing to say.

'I never fought back, you know. I just watched her take blow after blow. I've been sitting here thinking about that. If this is some kind of judgement, that's what I'd be made to face. That whole "Mary, Mary quite contrary how do your bruises grow?" thing. Well, Mary is the mother of Jesus, isn't she?'

'But that would make this personal and you weren't selected for this, you applied.'

'We were kind of selected, though, weren't we? There were half a dozen people at my selection event; they could have chosen me in particular from that group.'

Everything is a clue.

Bonnie stayed quiet, realizing she had never asked Clara what she had had to do to win her place on this. Clara had been so excited and Bonnie had never even bothered to talk to her about it in any detail. *Whenever I've needed you, you've never been there for me.* Clara's criticism echoed in Bonnie's head with renewed impact.

'I realize I was too open on the questionnaire. You know that bit about secrets? I was . . . well . . .' Jacko became quiet again and it was a good while before he spoke. Bonnie distracted herself by counting the bricks on the wall opposite. When she got to 304, Jacko said, 'I selfishly thought if I had some tragic backstory I'd be more likely to get on the thing. I used it and it was a disgusting, low thing to do.'

What had Clara confessed to, Bonnie wondered? It struck her as particularly awful that the production company would use people that way. But like Grant had said, when it comes to reality TV, anything goes.

The Fortress: are you smart enough to unlock its secrets?

She thought about the tag line. It had been all over social media for months. But what if the secrets belonged to the contestants rather than the show? Was the tag line meant for the viewers rather than the applicants? They had no idea what was really being broadcast to the world and what personal details were being revealed.

'If I'm right, whatever you wrote on that form and said in your video clip will be a clue to what you'll be made to do,' said Jacko.

She stayed quiet, knowing that if she said she couldn't recall that would be suspicious. Fortunately Jacko didn't press her on it. It crossed her mind that she could tell him her own secret now. Surely he wouldn't hold the lie against her, but before she had the chance to think of how to say it, he changed the subject.

'If I don't get out of here . . .' Jacko started to say.

'You will get out of here. I'm going to make sure of it. We all are.'

'But for argument's sake, can you do me a favour?'

'Sure.' Bonnie wanted to protest that no favour would be needed but she knew that was not what he wanted to hear.

'Tell my mum I'm sorry and that she should leave that low-life bastard. Maybe my demise will be the kick up the arse she needs, excuse the pun.'

'I'm sure that won't be necessary but I'll tell her.' Bonnie couldn't imagine how awful it must have been to grow up surrounded by anger and violence. Her home had always been full of love.

Jacko gave her his home address and she tried her best to memorize it.

'I bet you wish you'd not spent all that time worrying about what to wear now,' she said to lighten the mood.

'Oh, I don't know, it had its advantages.'

'Don't tell me you enjoyed being the cowboy.'

'Not so much that, but I liked that it made you smile.'

Bonnie looked up at the open flap. 'You know I was laughing *at* you and not with you?'

Jacko laughed and it turned into a cough.

'I've never been confident enough to go up to a girl and ask her out—'

'But dressed as a cowboy you think you could pull it off?'

'Yeah, I reckon. I could be like, "Are you from Tennessee? Because, babe, you're the only ten I see."'

'Oh, God,' Bonnie said with a giggle.

'Or how about, "Will you be the yee to my ha?"'

'Did you look these up?'

'"Hey, girl, do you raise cattle? Cause those are some nice calves."'

'Promise me you will never use that!'

'What would you like me to say, then?'

Bonnie paused. Was he about to ask her out? She felt the heat race up her cheeks. She hadn't been interested in a relationship for years, first because she wanted to focus on her studies and then because of Mum's illness. But in here everything had been put into perspective. What was important in life really? It was the people you love and the people you could love. She had never before realized the power of feeling supported by others but in here that's all that mattered. None of them would survive this without each other.

'Nothing yet,' she said. 'Wait until you get out.'

'Sure thing, preddy lady,' he said in his best cowboy lilt. 'Bloody hell, it's so fricking hot in here. What's it like out there?'

'If I say I'm trying not to breathe too deeply when I'm around the others that tells you what you need to know.'

'I thought I'd be able to acclimatize to it, but there's no way, is there? It feels thick when you breathe in.'

'Stop talking about it. It makes it worse.'

'I really want to drink but I need to save this. I'd also like a few co-codamols.'

'I'm sorry. We will do our best to win the next one and get more supplies.'

Jacko said nothing.

Bonnie moved on to her knees and raised herself up to look through the gap in the door. Jacko smiled back at her despite it looking like it hurt him to do so.

'Clara, Jacko, have you seen the screen?' Maria rushed towards them from the end of the corridor. Bonnie rose to her feet and moved to the nearest TV.

'What does it say?' called Jacko.

Bonnie read it aloud.

Jacko,
Congratulations.
You have identified the second secret of the fortress.

ALL SINNERS WILL SUFFER THEIR OWN SINS

42

Expect the Unexpected Podcast
Season 2, Episode 1: 'The Fortress'

'Do you want to take a break, Bonnie? I realize this is tough going.'

'No, no, I'm fine. It's just hard to think about that moment when Jacko . . .'

'You and he were becoming close? You light up when you talk about him.'

'Do I? I remember feeling so desperate and angry when he was in there. The situation was out of control. Russ had died in the most horrible way. I didn't want that to happen to Jacko. I didn't want it to happen to any of us.'

'Calling for help is useless, no one is coming.'

'Was this the point at which you realized what was really going on?'

'No way. I don't think my mind would go there even after Russ. People might think we were foolish or naive but we had to believe someone would stop this, or we'd get to the end of the challenges and be released. Grant was pretty convincing on this, actually. He was the one who held fast to the idea that everything was part of the game.'

'Even a fellow contestant dying?'

'Grant could be pretty convincing when he put his mind to it.'

'So this game – if we can call it that – placed you all in purgatory to face the seven sins. Everything that happened in the first few days, on the upper decks, hinted at what was to come. The reality that you were trapped and couldn't call for help, the animals which represented the seven sins being used in a survival-of-the-fittest competition, the reference to Dante's Divine Comedy, in which paradise is called Paradiso, the sign you said was placed above the sun-deck room. Even the five-pointed star you mentioned as the access key to the whole game is filled with symbolism because if you know anything about this stuff the inverted five-pointed star and the pentagon are related to devil worship. I think even at that point you were being told you were entering the beast's lair.'

'It's a relief to hear you say that, if I'm honest. I'm not sure the police see the relevance of all this.'

'Well, speaking from experience, the police are primarily focused on proving who did what. There's not much room for why, which I often think is where you really get a handle on things. If you get why someone did something, kind of get in their head, it can lead you to uncovering who is likely to have done it.'

'Which is why you're good at solving mysteries.'

'Well, I don't know if I can take the credit for that. It's mainly the listeners who make the breakthroughs. But I hope it helps.'

'Can I tell you a little more of what we found?'

'Yes, please.'

'There were some fairly sophisticated elements going on in the challenges you've described. I wanted to see if there were any clues to who was responsible for this whole thing in the *choice of tasks you were given, so my team and I did a bit of digging. I know the use of Caesar ciphers are pretty standard in escape rooms. In* The Fortress, *once you were locked in the basement you also had the reference to Caesar in your first set of instructions. You said, if I check my notes here, "Caesar's revelation will make it clear, what to do and who to fear." You most likely know that six-six-six comes from the book of Revelation in the Bible, but what does Caesar have to do with it? Well it turns out six-six-six itself is thought to be a secret code used within the Bible that tells you who the beast is. This is based on the fact that in Hebrew, the original language of the Bible, letters were used to indicate numbers, a bit like roman numerals. It's thought that the followers of Jesus were sending a coded message about who they viewed as the source of all evil at that point in time. Logically, this would be their greatest persecutor: the Roman Empire and its leader. So, if you add up all the numbers associated with the name Nero Caesar you get . . . guess what?'*

'Six hundred and sixty-six?'

'Exactly. This is just one example of how seriously the designer of this game was taking things.'

'Is that important?'

'Well, I'm no profiler but as an ex-copper I'd say this thing mattered to someone. They cared.'

'About what? Scaring people? Hurting people?'

'Well, that's the million-dollar question. What did they have to gain or what were they trying to prove?'

'Jacko had a bit of a theory on that.'

'Have you read Dante's Divine Comedy? *Do you know what punishments he describes for each of the sins?'*

'No. I've avoided anything like that. I couldn't, you know.'

'I'm sure, but this is pretty critical. You see, the punishment for wrath in purgatory is to constantly battle within clouds of

black; the punishment for sloth is to run without rest; and the punishment for gluttony is to experience excruciating hunger and thirst. Sound familiar?'

'Oh my God, Jacko, Maria and Russ's challenges.'

'And I'll tell you another thing. To survive the game, and win your food and water, you had to defeat the seven sins and, in essence, escape purgatory. But here's the thing, in the Divine Comedy, the people Dante meets, the people battling the seven sins, they're souls. They're already dead.'

43

The Fortress @thefortress
Seven deadly sins for seven deserving sinners. Watch
Jacko's fall on Channel 5 and My5 live NOW. #TheFortress

Annabelle @Annadom22
Talk about taking a beating. That was brutal. This show is
out there! #TheFortress

Fido @Feedthedog3
No way those balls were hard. It's all fake. #TheFortress

Adrian @aghopen12
He watched his mother take a beating and did nothing. He
deserves every ball he gets. #TheFortress

Sophie @Sophie_walker
You can't say that. You have no idea what it was like for him.
He obviously feels awful about it. #TheFortress

Adrian @aghopen12
So call the police or tell a relative, a teacher, anyone. Don't just sit there and say nothing. #TheFortress

---

Maise Mowlem @maisie_mow3
Why was Charlie crying AGAIN?! She's such a sap. It's supposed to be fun. Anyone else sick of watching her weep? #TheFortress

Lola @lolabelle
She's after the sympathy vote. Has she done anything worthwhile yet other than take her kit off and cry? #TheFortress

Maise Mowlem @maisie_mow3
OMG you are so right. Charlie to play next.

The Fortress @thefortress
See the sinners face their sins. Watch this space for when to vote for who plays next. #TheFortress

---

Carl @Carlrocks7
I vote for Dennis the drain. Talk about sucking the fun out of a place. What's his sin I wonder? My guess is Sloth or Pride. #TheFortress

Roger @rodgerdoger_

Errr Grant is clearly pride. Let the peacock FLY! #TheFortress

Aslan @A_hT56

Maria was the SLOTH. She had to work her brain and her body. #TheFortress

---

Adrian @aghopen12

My vote is for Jaide because she rocks and I want to see her smash it! #TheFortress

44

'I'm so sorry,' Bonnie said to Jacko, who sat with his arms wrapped around his legs and his head buried. 'I never thought they'd hear our conversation. I thought the camera was too far away.' She looked at the metal cage attached to the wall a few yards away with the camera and mic inside.

'There's one in here. I should have smashed it with the bat. It's not your fault. I said it.'

Of course there was a camera and mic in Jacko's room.

'I can't believe it. Your poor mum.' The screen had displayed the latest Twitter feed after the Director's message. Bonnie read it with growing dismay and then had to tell Jacko what it said.

Jacko lifted his head enough for her to see his eyes were red and wet. 'He'll have gone nuts. No one ever knew. He's a copper. This will wreck his career.'

'He's a policeman?'

'He likes the power.'

'I'm so sorry.'

Jacko stared into the distance and blinked a few times.

'Maybe it will force her hand,' Bonnie said quietly, aware she was clueless about situations like this. 'We all need to be careful what we say. Everyone feels bad for you.'

Jacko dropped his head back on to his knees. His bruises looked larger and more painful as the hours ticked by. Maria had offered to change places and sit with him for a while but Bonnie said she was OK. The others were all gathered in the central area. Maria said the mood was sombre as everyone reflected on the latest secret to be revealed.

When she had not heard anything from Jacko for a while, she checked through the door to see he had curled up on the floor and fallen asleep.

She had no idea what time it was or how many days they had been in here now. Not knowing if it was day or night was one of the most disorientating things. The heat was exhausting. Her head constantly pounded with dehydration and now her limbs ached and her chest felt tight and restricted like she couldn't suck in enough oxygen.

'How are you?' she asked Dennis as she sat on the floor near to him. Maria and Grant were both curled up and sleeping. Jaide was sitting cross-legged and drawing patterns on the floor with a small stone and Charlie sat staring into space without blinking. Her mouth was open a touch and her lips looked dry and sore.

'Peachy,' he said.

'What's everyone been saying about the new message?'

'The general consensus is we've somehow been specially chosen for this hellhole. Which is a depressing thought because it implies we have done this to ourselves. I may have said I thought the challenges he set would come easy to me so I'm expecting to face the punishment for pride.'

'Ha, I figured that would be Grant's sin.'

Dennis smiled a little. 'No one is admitting to anything so we may all be facing pride.'

Bonnie felt uncomfortable. Ordinarily she would match his confession as not only was it the polite thing to do, it was an opportunity to strengthen their friendship, but she had no idea what Clara had written on her form.

'Maria did confess to being a sloth,' said Dennis.

'She shouldn't put herself down like that.'

'Well, apparently she had many opportunities come her way from her chess success in her teens but she decided to hide in her house, as she put it. It's probably a confidence thing because that woman could have been anything she wanted to be. She'd have wiped the floor with most of the lawyers I worked with.'

'Maybe this will make her grasp some opportunities . . . afterwards . . . hopefully.'

Dennis frowned deeply and chewed his lip before shuffling closer to her and dropping his voice to a whisper. 'We need to find a way out. We can't keep going along with this.'

'But how?' she said in the same whispered tone.

'We need to get in there.' Dennis nodded towards the well-room door near where Jaide sat. 'It might be a way out.'

'Down the well? Are you crazy?' Bonnie couldn't think of anything more terrifying. It brought to mind the movies she had watched with Clara where people climb through tunnels or shin along air vents to escape prisons. Whenever she watched such things she always thought, who would ever really do that without knowing what was at the other end? But now here she was.

Dennis whispered, 'What if it's a play on words? The well room as in doing well or feeling well? It could be a clue. There has to be a reason it's the only wooden door in this place.'

45

Three Months Earlier

CONFESSION: **Dennis Allen**
DATE: **8 June**
TIME: **09.45**
LOCATION: **Best Western Angel Hotel**

Dennis Allen straightened his tie and coughed. He expected some of his ex-colleagues would think he was selling out by doing this, some might even believe he was bringing more unwanted media attention to his profession. The Crown Prosecution Service had a history of being tabloid fodder, something that was fairly infuriating when you saw how hard people worked within it. There was a time when he would have cared, when he would have done anything to defend and protect the people he worked with, but those days were long gone. The way they had treated him had lost all of them the right to have an opinion.

He looked into the lens. His ex-wife always said he was worth more. She thought he should have become a barrister or a judge and she was right.

And this was his chance to prove it.

'Why do I think I'm smart enough to beat the fortress? If I'm brutally honest, there are not many people who have a mind as sharp and well honed as mine when it comes to seeing the truth of things. I have spent my life sifting through clues and evidence to gain clarity. This will be no different. If the challenges you have put in front of me so far are anything to go by, it will be child's play.'

Dennis put his reading glasses on and checked the card to see what else he was required to talk about: his deepest desire and the thing he was most ashamed of.

'I'm not ashamed of anything. I don't see the point in regrets. What is done is done.'

He tried to recall what he had written on the application form about his deepest desire. He knew it wouldn't have been the truth, the whole truth and nothing but the truth because that was something he'd never told anyone, not even his ex-wife. She had been so devastated when they failed to get pregnant that he'd had to take on the role of optimist; they needed a new purpose and a new route towards some quality of life. But in truth he had wanted to be a father so badly it had eaten him up inside to have the chance denied.

He must have said something about his career, but that was over now. He was retired and redundant in all senses of the word.

He checked the copy of his application form, ignoring the lens that stared at him expectantly. It was critical he got this right. Not only did he need to accurately represent what he had written, because that is what was required, he was also conscious this would probably go out to the world, to his ex-employers and colleagues.

He pictured himself completing the form on his laptop in the too quiet kitchen at home. Removing his glasses, he looked into the camera and repeated it word for word.

'My deepest desire is to get the respect I deserve.'

He nearly left it at that, but realized it might come over as a bit arrogant.

'What I mean is I want to feel valued for the things I achieve. I want people to see what I can do and appreciate my skills and efforts.' Dennis looked squarely into the lens. 'Isn't that what we all want?'

46

'Anyone who sees someone else being bullied or beaten should step up.' Jaide was biting her thumbnail as she spoke.

'I agree,' said Grant. 'I knew there was something off about him right from the start. It's his shifty eyes.'

'He doesn't have shifty eyes,' said Bonnie. 'Plus he clearly feels guilty about the whole thing.'

'I don't think so. I think he feels embarrassed and ashamed,' said Jaide.

'What's the difference?' Bonnie said.

'Guilt is what you feel about yourself and your actions; shame is how you feel when others find out.'

'Well, I expect he feels both,' said Bonnie. 'How can you know, anyway?'

'He had multiple chances to say something. If it was me, I'd feel so guilty that I would have to speak up.'

'Sometimes it's not as simple as that,' said Dennis. 'He may have been a little kid when it started. He may have thought it was normal for years. You don't know. Plus in my experience kids in situations like this are often too terrified of the abuser to stand up for themselves.'

'Thank you, Dennis. How do we know he's not a victim

too? Is it not victim-shaming to think people in those situations should do something?'

'Have you ever been bullied or attacked?' Jaide said to Bonnie.

'That's not the point.'

'No, I bet you haven't.'

'What do you mean by that?' Bonnie felt her hackles rise.

'I bet you were the one doing the bullying in the school playground, you and your princess mates laughing and pointing at the girls who didn't fit in.'

'You don't know anything about me.' Bonnie clenched her fists. She had never been the popular girl. She had been the quiet kid at the front of the class doing all her work on time and behaving like a good student.

'I know your type.'

Before Bonnie could react, Grant spoke up. 'Do you know what's really disappointing? He couldn't even take his beating like a man, couldn't stand up to the pain.'

Grant sounded like he was enjoying himself. Bonnie suspected they were seeing something of the real Grant; the truth hiding behind all that poncing and preening for the cameras.

'We can't turn on each other like this. The public are listening and they're too gullible to know you're only stirring,' said Maria.

Bonnie looked up at the cameras, triangulated to see and hear every angle in the small room. What had Jacko said about smashing them down with his bat? Would that be possible? The metal cages around them were sturdy and bolted to the wall.

'Is he stirring?' said Jaide. 'Or is he simply speaking the truth?'

'Oh come on, you were all friendly with Jacko before this. I think we should admire his honesty,' said Dennis.

'My mum used to hurt me.' Charlie's words stopped the discussion in its tracks. All eyes turned her way. 'Not so anyone would know, just slaps and hair pulls and occasionally dragging me across the floor.' She looked at Dennis. 'I thought it was normal, like you said, until someone told me it wasn't.'

'What happened?' Dennis's words were warm and sympathetic.

Charlie shrugged. 'After I told on her, she never did it again.'

'So what do you think of Jacko's confession, then?' asked Bonnie.

'I think if he wasn't going to help his mum, he shouldn't have said anything at all. Ever. I wouldn't have.'

Bonnie knew Charlie was right. Sharing what had happened to get on a TV show was not a good move. There really was no defence she could think of for that.

47

Bonnie had been snoozing outside Jacko's room after finding him still sleeping. It had crossed her mind that he might have passed out from internal bleeding or concussion, but she pushed her concerns to one side. She didn't want to wake him to face the wrath of the group.

She awoke to the sound of chatter and sensed something had happened. She checked Jacko. He was still sleeping and she watched to make sure she could see his chest rise and fall before looking at the nearest screen.

Grant and Jaide
I have a test for you

I'M AT THE OPENING OF YOUR VISION
AND AT THE HEART OF BEING CLEVER,
AND FINDING ME TAKES YOU
TO THE MIDDLE OF NEVER

'Jacko?' she said quietly at first and then a little louder. 'Jacko?'

He stirred and opened his eyes briefly.

'The next challenge,' she said. 'It's for Grant and Jaide to do together.'

Jacko sat up a little straighter, winced and wiped the sweat from his forehead. Bonnie could feel the heat from inside his small cell. It felt much warmer than out in the hallway and that scared her. He had hardly any water left and some of the group might not feel so inclined to give him more after their recent rant.

'I'm going to check it out,' she said, starting to leave and then coming back. 'How are you feeling?'

'Never better.' He rubbed his eyes and met her gaze. 'I'm fine, really. Thank you.'

She smiled at his lie and nodded. 'I'll be back soon.'

The others had already begun to gather around a doorway to her right.

'V?' she said on joining them.

Maria nodded and glanced up at the small V on the top of the door. When Grant pushed it open Bonnie could see this room was a little bigger than Maria and Jacko's had been. There was a white cabinet in the middle of the room and a table above it with two white moulded plastic chairs tucked underneath. Other than that and the camera cages, the room was completely bare. No holes in the walls, no treadmills in the floor, nothing.

Grant looked at Jaide. 'Shall we?' He had a full bottle of water and she had the last apple and a few biscuits in her hands.

Jaide hesitated and looked at Dennis.

'It makes no sense for more of us to go in with the two of you,' he said.

She frowned and nodded. It was safer for some to remain outside, plus Bonnie knew Dennis had plans to try to escape so there was no way he was volunteering to get locked in.

'You could refuse to go in,' said Charlie.

Grant winked at her. 'You won't find me shirking my responsibilities. Watch and learn, people.' He walked in and pulled out the nearest chair. Jaide followed, looking less enthusiastic about what was to come.

The rest of them watched the door swing back into place before turning their attention to the screen opposite. There was no hatch in the door again like with Maria's room. On the screen, they could see the back of Jaide and Grant. Grant sat back in his chair like he hadn't a care in the world but Jaide's foot was shaking under hers.

All of a sudden an image appeared on the facing wall of the room. It was nothing more than a black silhouette but it moved as the Director's voice broke the silence.

'You two are fast becoming my faves.' His laugh raised the hairs on Bonnie's neck. 'Before we start I should make it clear this is a little bonus I dreamed up as a bit of fun.'

'Is that really him?' Charlie said, leaning into the screen.

'If it is there are no clues in it.' Dennis stood with folded arms and a concerned expression.

The black figure on the screen tilted his head as he spoke, but not enough to reveal any features.

'I thought the tinny sound of his voice was down to something technical but it's also a disguise, isn't it?' said Bonnie.

'That's good news, really. If he's not showing us his real self, it's because he's planning to let us out,' said Maria.

'I hope that's true,' said Bonnie.

'Your friends out in the hallway can't hear you so don't worry about them,' the Director said.

Bonnie and Maria exchanged glances. Did he not realize they could hear?

'Your friend Jacko is not faring well so I'm going to give you one chance, and one chance only, to release him from room B.'

'Oh my God,' said Bonnie, touching Maria's arm.

'But if you choose to do so you forfeit the food and drink in this room.'

Bonnie felt a little sick as her hope disappeared quicker than it had arrived.

'On the desk in front of you there is a touch screen. I'm going to ask each of you in turn to select food or freedom. If you both select the same, I will grant your wish. If you do not, I will not. If you confer, you invalidate the game. Have I made myself clear?'

'Can I clarify?' said Jaide.

'Go ahead.'

'If we both vote food do we get supplies straight away for the whole group?'

'You may share what is in the cupboard below you.'

'And if we select freedom for Jacko, when do we next get the chance to win supplies?'

Bonnie was impressed that Jaide had the wherewithal to make sure there were no tricks.

'Soon enough,' said the Director. 'Jaide, you will go first. Grant, if you could walk to the door and face it, please. No peeking, now.' The humour in the Director's tone turned Bonnie's stomach.

'Come on, please vote freedom,' Bonnie said.

'Those two were selected for a reason,' said Dennis. 'They've already written the lad off.'

'Even if they do hate what Jacko did, they should still let him out.'

'But we might starve if we don't get more food soon.'

'Maria!' said Bonnie.

'Sorry, I'm just saying. What if all of us end up without food because they made the wrong call? It won't matter that they let Jacko out. It won't help him. We can pass him food.'

If we're here to, thought Bonnie, looking at Dennis. If they were going to make an escape attempt, they couldn't leave someone behind. It was unthinkable. 'That didn't work out so well for poor Russ, did it?'

'Maria's hungry, obviously.' At Charlie's comment, Maria turned to stare at the younger woman. 'Tell me I'm wrong?'

'Thank you, Jaide,' said the Director. 'Kindly swap places with Grant.'

Bonnie watched as Jaide moved to face the door and Grant walked to the table and pressed his option without any hesitation.

Bonnie held her breath. She imagined rushing into Jacko's room and taking his hand. Dennis would help her lift him and bring him out. At least out here she could take care of him. But then the cupboard door underneath Grant and Jaide's table swung open and the Director began to laugh.

Bonnie stepped away from the screen. They had chosen to leave Jacko to suffer. Both of them.

Before Grant and Jaide emerged from the room, Dennis held a finger to his lips as he looked around the group outside.

'You're welcome,' said Jaide, emerging with a box of supplies and a large grin.

'What did you have to do?' said Dennis, his voice full of innocent enquiry.

'You didn't see?' said Grant, glancing at the screen on the wall.

'We could see you but not hear.'

Grant and Jaide swapped a look.

'He made us do a quiz,' said Grant.

'What kind of quiz?'

'The kind where you answer questions. What other kind of quiz is there?' said Jaide.

'He made you answer separately, we saw that. How come?'

'Who knows?' said Grant.

'He wanted us to agree,' said Jaide at the same time.

Dennis stepped towards Jaide. The prosecutor in full flow. 'Agree on what?'

'The answers. What else?' said Grant.

Dennis looked at them both with a smile. 'What are you not telling us?'

'I don't know what you're talking about.' Grant's laugh sounded a little fake.

'I'm talking about the fact you both look guilty.'

'We look relieved,' said Jaide. 'I did not want to get trapped in there with him, no offence.' She looked at Grant.

But it's fine to leave Jacko trapped, thought Bonnie.

Dennis looked from Jaide to Grant and then back again with a small nod. 'Was he speaking to you live or was it a recording?'

'Live,' said Grant.

'So you asked him why he had locked us in? What he was up to? How and when we can get out?'

The smug looks on Grant and Jaide's faces dropped a little.

Dennis continued. 'You demanded that he tell you how the hell he let Russ die and if he intended that fate for all of us?'

'What is wrong with you all?' said Grant. 'We won food. You should be thanking us.'

'What's wrong with us?' said Bonnie, unable to hold her rage in any longer. 'I'm beginning to think this guy is right about you people. You might well deserve every shitty thing he throws at you.' She walked away towards where Jacko sat, unaware how close he had come to standing a fighting chance of surviving.

48

The Fortress @thefortress
Puzzle me this: The world's most popular game totals
nothing. What does that tell you about humanity?

Philleus @PFogg80
That people are obsessed with the wrong things. Who cares
if one football team beats another? #realitycheck
#TheFortress

Jamtart @jamesTK55
Football is a sport. This says game. The biggest game in the
world is Minecraft or Fortnite. #TheFortress

Wayne @Waynesmith303
That tells you people have their heads stuck in a fantasy.
I agree with @PFogg80. We need a reality check.
#TheFortress

Scott @ScottHYFC

Is it the world's most popular game or history's most popular game they're looking for? Because that would surely be chess. A game of war. #Checkmate #TheFortress

49

'I can't believe they did that,' said Charlie, following Bonnie to the door of Jacko's room.

'They're a couple of selfish, judgemental pricks.'

'Would they have done the same if me or you were in there?'

'They'll do whatever they can to serve themselves. I don't think they give a shit about any of the rest of us.' Bonnie knew this was an exaggeration but she was so incensed she didn't care about accuracy. 'I thought you were Grant's biggest fan, anyway,' she said, turning her rage to Charlie.

The younger woman shrugged and glanced down the hallway to where Grant and Jaide still stood outside room V. The two of them were deep in a conversation and it looked to be getting heated. Jaide was gesturing with both arms and Grant's face was contorted into a sneer.

'What have they got to be so angry about?' said Bonnie.

'What's happening?' Jacko had lifted the flap in his door to look out at them.

'Grant and Jaide just gave up the chance of setting you free.'

'Charlie!' Bonnie said. She'd not intended to tell him this because in his shoes it would drive her crazy to think she'd come so close to freedom.

'What? He has every right to know.'

'Why would they do that?' said Jacko.

'They had the chance to win more food,' said Dennis as he arrived to join them.

'OK, well, I suppose that's a fair choice.'

'Don't be so gracious,' said Bonnie, moving to look Jacko in the eye.

'We know you're talking about us,' called Jaide. 'If you've got something to say, say it to our faces.'

Bonnie looked at Jaide and then at Grant as she slowly shook her head. They were pathetic.

Grant strode her way. 'What is your problem?'

'My problem?'

'We just did you all a favour. How long do you think we'd have survived on the last few nuts?'

'Did you do us all a favour? Or did you look after number one as usual?'

'You need to wind your neck in, sweetheart. I don't know who you think you're talking to.'

'Oh, I know exactly who I'm talking to, Mr I Won *University Challenge*. Well, newsflash, brain box, this isn't a game show. Haven't you worked it out yet? This is life and death. Russ died. He's never going home. He's never getting famous. He's dead. Dead!'

Grant stared at her. His jaw tensed and his dark eyes were filled with rage. Bonnie guessed he was rarely challenged by a woman.

'You know, don't you?' said Jaide as she arrived at Grant's side. She looked from Bonnie to Charlie and then towards where Dennis stood with Maria. 'You heard everything?'

Grant looked at her wide-eyed as if to say, *What the hell are you doing?*

'We won more water. We were down to the last two bottles. We *had* to pick supplies.'

Dennis watched Bonnie and Grant for a moment as if trying to assess what was coming, then he turned his attention to Jaide.

'I'm not sure that's justification for dooming someone to God knows how long locked in there.' Dennis pointed at Jacko's door.

'That's not fair. We didn't do this to Jacko. We didn't do this to any of us. This is them out there. Why are you blaming us?'

'Because you could have helped someone and you chose not to,' said Charlie.

'Or you could have got us some bloody answers,' said Dennis.

'What difference does it make if he's in there or out here if we have no water?' shouted Jaide. 'You're being ridiculous.'

'Let's see how happy they are without any supplies, then.' Grant led Jaide away, taking the box of food and water with them.

50

Bonnie heard footsteps. She was sitting on the floor with her head buried in her bent knees and her arms hugging her legs. She wanted to cocoon herself from this whole place and disappear. Grant and Jaide had stalked away with no apology for Jacko. Not that Bonnie was surprised. It was quite clear the two of them thought they'd done nothing wrong and little would change their minds at this point.

'I came to check you were OK.' Charlie sat beside her and touched her arm.

Bonnie shook her head from side to side without looking up. She didn't want to see anything or do anything. She wanted to hide.

'Maria is trying to solve the latest puzzle *The Fortress* has tweeted. There are a few public tweets about it.'

'Who cares?'

'She thinks it could be a clue.'

To what? How we get out of this place? How we avoid Russ's fate? How we get home? This was nothing more than the latest sick bit of entertainment at their expense.

'Maybe it will tell us who has to go next.'

Bonnie hugged her legs a little tighter.

'I don't want to go next. I don't want to get locked in,' said Charlie.

Bonnie reached out and took Charlie's hand.

'But I'm not going to cry. I'm not giving them all the satisfaction.' There was a new steeliness to Charlie's tone that had Bonnie finally looking up.

'Good for you.'

She and Charlie sat for a while in companionable silence. Bonnie couldn't face going back to Jacko just yet, knowing he had been so close to coming out. She felt the tears sting her eyes but forced them back. She needed to be strong. If taking her sister's place was the last thing she ever did for her sister it was a good thing.

'It's irresponsible. There are consequences,' Dennis shouted from down the hall.

'You're not the boss here,' Grant shouted back.

Bonnie looked at Charlie.

What now?

They rose to their feet and walked quickly towards the argument. As they rounded the corner, they saw Grant and Jaide sitting behind the now empty food crate.

'What have you done with it?' Dennis was almost purple in the face and his hands were balled into tight fists.

'Please, Jaide. This isn't fair.' Maria stood to Dennis's left by the well-room door.

Open it and all may be well, Bonnie thought.

'What's happening?' said Charlie.

'They hid the bloody food and water, that's what's happening.'

'If you behave, I may let you have some,' said Grant. He smirked at Jaide.

Bonnie stepped in between him and Dennis, guessing the

older guy might be tempted to take a swing and Bonnie didn't fancy his chances against muscle man Grant, ex-boxer or not.

'Right, well, it can't have gone far. There are very few places to hide things in here. You've made your point, Grant.' Bonnie felt weary of it all, of the drama, the heat, these people.

'From now on,' said Grant, 'I control the supplies, get it? You need food, you ask, you need water, same. This is not a democracy any more. We won those supplies and they're ours to use or share as we see fit. Right, Jaide?'

'Right.' Jaide met everyone's eyes with defiance. They were serious.

'What about Jacko?' Bonnie said.

'What about him?'

'You can't leave him without food.'

'I think you'll find we can do whatever we want.' Jaide held Bonnie's gaze with defiance.

Bonnie stared back at Jaide, willing her to give Bonnie a reason to really lose it.

Jaide moved to get up and Grant put a hand on her arm.

He let out a long sigh. 'I'm so done with your constant bleating about how we all have to take care of Jacko. This is dog eat dog now. We are on our own.'

'Well, that's an amazing strategy, very intelligent, very mature,' Dennis said.

Bonnie stalked out of the room. She would find those supplies and play them at their own game. If they wanted war, they could have it. She would not let Jacko die. No way. Never. If it was the last thing she did.

On her second circle around the corridor Bonnie heard Grant laugh at her as she passed. He and Jaide still sat together on the floor. They didn't seem at all concerned that she might find their hidden stash.

She met Maria coming the other way.

'Any luck?' she said.

'Nothing. You?'

Bonnie shook her head. 'What could they have done with it? I've checked the toilets, all the open rooms and every inch of this corridor.'

'What exactly was in the box? Did you see?'

A loud bang had them investigating. They found Dennis in room six kneeling next to the cupboard under the roulette wheel and bashing on its base. He had dragged the running machine into the doorway to avoid the door closing on him, meaning Bonnie had to clamber across it.

'Have you found something?'

'Uh-huh,' he said, sounding out of breath. 'There's a space under this shelf. The cupboard base sits higher than the floor so I . . .' He paused as he pressed his weight into each corner then sat back with a sigh. 'There's no give in it. They can't have used it.' Beads of sweat glistened on his forehead and Bonnie worried at the toll this heat was taking on him.

'Let's think about this. After they took the supplies, they left you two with Charlie by Jacko's room and I moved past the toilet to get some peace and quiet near room twenty-four. So they had to have brought it over to this side of the basement somewhere. Has anyone checked the stairway up to door two?'

'Yep, no joy,' said Dennis.

Realizing something, Bonnie looked around and said, 'Wait, where's Charlie?'

Maria looked down the hallway on either side of them and shook her head. 'Maybe she went to search elsewhere?'

Dennis stood and climbed over the treadmill to pass Bonnie and Maria. He strode the few yards it took to reach the central area where Grant and Jaide remained, then stopped in the opening, bowing his head before looking Bonnie's way. 'She picked a side.'

No. Why would Charlie side with them? She knew Charlie had the hots for Grant and probably vice versa but she'd been equally appalled about them leaving Jacko locked in. *Do you think they'd have done that to one of us?*, she had said to Bonnie. Was that what this was about? Saving her own skin?

'What if they won't give us anything to eat and drink?' said Maria.

Bonnie pushed her thoughts of Charlie aside and focused on the current problem because Maria raised a valid point: *What if?*

51

'The whole thing ripped a hole in the group. Until that point we'd been really together, at least since getting locked in the basement, but now we had two factions forming. Jaide, Grant and Charlie versus Dennis and me. Jacko kind of divided us with his confession about his mum and once Grant and Jaide had selected to leave him to suffer and keep the supplies, Dennis and I couldn't get past that.'

'*How long did they keep the supplies for?*'

'Until they were gone.'

'*Wow.*'

'Grant really did seem to think it was all a game. I don't know if he simply couldn't let himself believe the alternative, but if I'm being kind I expect it affected his judgement. He maybe didn't see the consequences as clearly as we did.'

'*And Jaide?*'

'I don't think she liked that Dennis and I disagreed so strongly with them about not releasing Jacko. She absolutely thought they were right to choose the food.'

'So they kept it all for themselves? They didn't share it at all?'

'Well, it wasn't as simple as that, and to be fair, Charlie did try to do the right thing.'

'You really liked her, didn't you?'

'Don't get me wrong, I was so disappointed with her when she joined Grant and Jaide, but I do think she did it in part to make sure they shared things with us. I felt very protective of her, not only because she reminded me of Clara, but because she seemed more vulnerable than the rest of us. She wasn't that much younger but she had an innocence. She went there to have fun and get noticed, simple as that. That's what makes it so sad.'

'And what about Maria? You said this formed two factions – Grant, Jaide and Charlie versus you and Dennis, so where did Maria sit in all this?'

'Well, Maria became obsessed with the latest puzzle posted by *The Fortress* – "the world's most popular game totals nothing". She was convinced it was a clue but we were all too busy fighting with each other to pay her much attention. I still feel bad about that. She had been so insightful and we should have listened to her. Because she was right and if we'd known what that clue revealed earlier it might have bonded us again. It might have prevented me from saying and doing the things I did, things I now feel awful about.'

'You couldn't have done anything that bad, I'm sure.'

'You weren't there.'

'*This is* Expect the Unexpected, *the podcast that blows your mind with crimes that beggar belief. I'd like to thank our show sponsor this month on* Expect the Unexpected. *As regular listeners will know, I'm a huge advocate of effective home security and the importance of keeping yourselves and your families safe. SecureIT is a digital home security system that gives you peace of mind at the touch of your fingertips. Through their app you can secure your home from wherever you are and even see who's calling. I have it at my house and I have to say it was so easy to install and very easy to use. Check out SecureIT today so you can feel safe at home, every day.*

'And now back to our conversation with Bonnie Drake.'

52

'What are you doing?'

Bonnie rounded the corner to find Jaide with her hands on her hips challenging Charlie, who was moving quickly away from Jacko's door.

'I'm worried about him.'

'So you thought you'd give away our food?'

'I didn't think I needed to ask.' Charlie sounded childlike in the face of Jaide's challenge.

There was no way of knowing how long it had been since Grant and Jaide had taken possession of the new supplies, but it was long enough for Bonnie to feel faint from hunger. It turned out they'd never really hidden the food: it had been a trick, an illusion. They had used the original box from Maria's first win to make everyone think they had ferreted everything away, but in reality the new box was nowhere more concealed than behind Grant and Jaide's backs where they had been sitting on the floor. It showed how exhausted and dehydrated they all were that they were so easily fooled. And what did that mean for how they would cope with the rest of the challenges?

Grant had still kept possession of the crate, only sharing one bottle of water with Bonnie and Dennis on Charlie's insistence. Dennis had suggested they could try to overpower him but they didn't fancy their chances and agreed he would tire of his power play soon enough if they ignored him.

Jaide stared Bonnie's way. 'I'm so sick of how you look at me. You're such a judgemental little shit.'

'I have good reason to be judgemental.' Bonnie took her usual seat on the floor outside Jacko's room.

Jaide towered over her. Her Doc Martens looked even more intimidating from this angle and Bonnie noted that the other woman had a tattoo of a finger gesture on her ankle that read, *Up Yours*.

'Get up and face me. I want to have this out.'

'I'm comfy here, thanks.'

'I said GET UP!' Jaide reached down and grabbed Bonnie's upper arm tightly, yanking it upwards.

'GET OFF ME!'

'Stand up and look me in the eye.'

'Leave me alone.'

Jaide still gripped her arm and the woman's nails dug painfully into Bonnie's skin.

'You're hurting me.'

'Get up or I'll hurt you more.'

Bonnie stared at Jaide without blinking. For all her hot air about bullies and abusers, here she was lashing out in anger.

'What's going on?' Dennis walked towards them holding the bottle of water he, Maria and Bonnie were sharing.

'I'm done with you two treating me like I'm the bad guy here. The sneering little looks and smirks.'

'Why don't you try being nice, then?' said Bonnie.

'Care to explain this?' Dennis held up the bottle. 'This was our only bottle and I was saving the last of it for Jacko but someone drank it.'

'Good God,' said Bonnie, yanking her arm free of Jaide

and rising to her feet. 'Is it not enough that you're rationing the water, you have to steal what we have too? Do you want us all to die in here?'

'This is what I'm talking about. Why would you think I would do something like that?'

'Because you're determined to win at whatever cost,' said Dennis.

'That is not true. I wouldn't drink the last of your water.'

'Well, somebody did and given that Charlie is the only one of your gang with a shred of decency, it must have been you or Grant. You're as bad as the sicko who has us locked in here,' said Bonnie.

Jaide pushed Bonnie hard and she hit the wall with enough force to make her bite her tongue. Instinctively Bonnie pushed Jaide back with all her strength. Jaide stumbled, her arms flailing. Charlie tried to move out of the way but it all happened too fast. Jaide slammed into her, sending Charlie crashing to the floor.

'I'm sorry, Charlie,' said Bonnie, 'but she deserved that. You can't throw your weight around in here, Jaide. You're not the tough girl now who gets to scare people with your piercings and tattoos and big boots. If you're mean to people, people will be mean to you.'

'You're a horrible person, you know that?'

'OK, ladies,' said Dennis. 'Perhaps we should calm this down. Are you saying this wasn't you, Jaide?'

'Absolutely.'

'We need to speak to your partner in crime, then.'

'How do we know it wasn't you?'

Jaide's words brought a look of stunned surprise to Dennis's face.

'How do we know this isn't you demonizing us because

you disagree with our choices? You probably enjoyed the last of the water while Bonnie and Maria were out of sight.'

'Dennis wouldn't do that,' said Bonnie. 'You really do have a twisted mind. Why don't you try to see the good in people for once instead of lashing out with your spiteful bile?'

Jaide laughed as she looked at Bonnie with disgust.

Bonnie's anger erupted. 'I hope *you* get locked in and learn what it feels like to be scared for your life, knowing no one is coming to help you.'

For the briefest moment Bonnie saw tears well in Jaide's eyes and the mask of rage slip from her face. She looked younger, paler and vulnerable as she brushed her hand across her eyes and Bonnie saw the faded signs of self-harm running all the way up her arm.

53

Three Months Earlier

CONFESSION: **Jaide Walsh**
DATE: **6 June**
TIME: **12.45**
LOCATION: **Best Western Angel Hotel**

'I'm Jaide Walsh. I'm not sure what to say. I'm not the best with communication, I'm better at tasks. Apparently I have the kind of brain that struggles with emotions, my own and other people's. That's not an excuse, only an explanation. People often take me the wrong way.

'I'm not ashamed of that, though. I'm not ashamed of anything, really. Everything I've done has been to survive. Even the situation I got myself into a few years back when I was used by men. I think that's a polite way of saying it. I'm not sure you can broadcast stuff about the world's oldest profession on this kind of show. I'm not ashamed of it because I wouldn't have survived without it. It was a stepping stone. It just happens to be one others judge you harshly for. But that's their problem, not mine.

'What do I desire? To do more for the world and for people

in need. When you've survived a tough upbringing you spot it in others. I see the vulnerability and I want to do something about it. People like me who have survived, or who are different, have a tough time. I want to win this show for all the misunderstood and mistreated people, the outcasts who rarely get a chance to change their lives. I want people to see we are just as smart as anyone else. I hope that by going on the show I can demonstrate that.

'And I think I can win because I'm a survivor. I've escaped much worse than anything you can throw at me on a TV show.'

54

Kimberley Hayes @HayesKim123

Oh that Clara is such a bitch! Did you see her attack Jaide and knock poor Charlie over? #TheFortress

Captain_dude @DudeCaptain_

At least Charlie didn't cry for a change. #crybabybimbo #TheFortress

Sophie @Sophie_walker

Are they really wanting us to believe Jaide couldn't take Clara in a fight? There's no competition. That was totally edited. I bet there was a proper catfight off screen.

Kaoru @Riverslad

I'm loving this! They've turned on each other. It was only a matter of time. Bring it on #Lordoftheflies

55

'Don't read that nonsense,' Dennis said as he left Bonnie staring at the screen.

Bonnie nodded but couldn't help wondering what Clara thought of all of this. How would she feel about Bonnie arguing and showing a not so flattering side to herself in her sister's name? She wondered if Clara had already disowned her on social media and come clean about this not being her. But if she had, the show would have ousted Bonnie, surely. The thought simultaneously gave her hope and brought despair. Again, she considered coming clean, but something told her it wouldn't make a damn bit of difference. There was no way he would let her simply go home.

NO ONE LEAVES.

She had used the empty bottle Dennis had left with her to wedge open the flap in Jacko's door. He wasn't doing great, his breathing sounded raspy and laboured, so she wanted to be able to hear him all the time.

'Howdy, partner,' she said, forcing the best smile she could as she looked in at him. He was sitting in a new spot on the floor with his head back and eyes closed. She wondered what he spent all his time in there thinking about. *His mum? His life outside of this place? Her?*

'Howdy,' he said, opening his eyes with what looked like some effort. His bruises were darker now; blacks and purples covering his arms and legs and one particularly angry one on his right cheek.

'Charlie brought you something to eat?'

'Yeah, half a ham sandwich. She's an angel.'

'You don't get many of them in hell.'

'Oh, I don't know. I think there are a couple.' When he smiled at her the look in his eyes brought a lump to her throat. She wanted nothing more than to give him a hug. He looked so alone. 'Even the devil was an angel at one time.'

'Really? I never heard that before.'

'Because *you* weren't dragged to Sunday school every weekend. Lucifer was a fallen angel, cast out by God and doomed to rule hell.'

'Do you believe in any of that? God, the devil, hell?'

'I'm beginning to in this place,' he said before adjusting his position, carefully. 'But no, I don't buy it. I think we're here and then we're gone. Nothing before and nothing after.'

'You should be an inspirational speaker.'

Jacko's chuckle was brief but lovely to hear. 'I think people want to believe in an afterlife and that there's a reason for everything because they're scared of the chaos. Anything bad can happen to any one of us at any time. That's the reality but we don't like it. We want to control it by following the rules of a religion.'

'They call it the "just-world hypothesis" in psychology. The belief that if we do good things, good things will happen.'

'Look at you. Trying to take Maria's crown by any chance?'

Bonnie admired how well he was coping. She was not sure she'd be up for any banter in his position.

'Speaking of Maria, has she asked you about the puzzle on

Twitter? Something about the world's most popular game being nothing?' she said.

'Totals nothing, I think she said.'

'Oh yeah, totals nothing. That probably matters.'

'I think the bit it says afterwards is the important section.' Jacko paused for a moment and closed his eyes. 'What does that say about humanity.' He opened his eyes and looked at Bonnie again. 'I think that's a clue to why he's making an example of us.'

56

'What's going on?'

Bonnie arrived at the central room, having heard loud banging, to find Dennis trying to smash his way through the well-room door with one of the metal legs they had used to push water to Russ, what seemed like an age ago. Dennis had said they needed to be smart and subtle about an escape attempt. Clearly he'd changed his mind.

'Honestly, Dennis, you're never going to break through that. It's solid oak,' said Maria, looking concerned.

Grant smirked from what had become his favourite spot, sitting on a small stone step to the left of the door guarding his box of food and water. *Little king on his throne guarding the spoils of war.*

Charlie and Jaide stood close together talking quietly. When Charlie saw Bonnie, she stopped talking and moved a fraction away. 'If Dennis is right and this could be a way out, it's worth a try,' she said, picking up the other table leg from the floor and proceeding to help Dennis bash into the centre of the door.

'You do know you've yet to make a significant dent,' said Jaide, who had also avoided looking directly at Bonnie. 'And you have no idea what's on the other side of it.'

'Exactly,' said Dennis, giving the door another pointless

whack. 'Maria says these places have secret passageways. "Well room" could be a clue to all being well behind here.'

'It's worth a look,' said Charlie. 'There were steps down to this level outside in the courtyard, weren't there? This could take us out there.' She gave the door another couple of hard whacks.

Bonnie had to admit this was a good point. None of them had explored those stone steps in the centre of the fort. They had been too busy enjoying the upper decks. Perhaps that's why Dennis had thought there might be some way out through here, too. Bonnie looked at the sign above the door again: WELL ROOM. Would it really say *room* if it was a door to the outside? But like Charlie said, what did they have to lose?

'You think they're going to sit up there and watch you get out?' said Grant, pointing at the camera.

Dennis stopped battering the door and waved the leg at Grant. 'If they're on the mainland, they have to get here to stop us and then they have to get past me.' Dennis lunged the metal leg towards Grant. 'And I'm ready to take on anyone stupid enough to try and stop me. You included. I'm getting out of here today. We're not standing for it. Stay here with your precious stash if you don't like it.'

Grant sniggered.

'Is there anything I can do to help?' said Bonnie. 'Shall I see if there's anything we can use as a crowbar to prise it open?'

'I already looked,' said Dennis as he and Charlie continued making no significant dent in the wood. 'This is our only option.'

'Could we use the legs to knock down the cameras?' Bonnie said.

'Oh, that really would bring the Director running,' said Grant. 'You think the fella who locked us in and turned up the heat will let you take his fun away?'

'Scared?' said Bonnie.

'I'm afraid Grant's right, Clara,' said Maria. 'I'm not sure we can take the punishment.' When Bonnie started to protest, Maria said, 'I know Jacko definitely couldn't.'

Charlie cried out in pain. Somehow she had slipped and hit her wrist with the metal table leg. She dropped the leg and placed her wounded hand under her armpit.

Maria rushed to her side. 'Let me see.'

'Give me a minute.' Charlie was blowing out slow breaths through pursed lips.

Bonnie picked up the table leg and began helping Dennis. She heard Maria check Charlie's wrist to make sure nothing was broken. She could still bend it so Maria told her to sit for a minute and rest.

Bonnie had to admit taking all her inner rage out on the door was pretty therapeutic. Dennis must have felt the same because he relentlessly powered his table leg into the wood over and over without slowing. They would be even more in need of food after this. Would Grant bestow any on them? She expected if they didn't have any success breaking through the door the answer would be no.

After a while, Charlie said she would check on Jacko. Bonnie knew he would ask what all the noise was and she also knew Charlie would probably tell him they were trying to break out. The girl could be far too honest. Bonnie should have told her to make something up.

She stopped for a breather, wondering how Dennis managed to keep going without a rest. Maria was talking quietly to Jaide and Grant. Were they trying to recruit her to their gang too? It wouldn't surprise Bonnie. What did surprise her was that Maria was giving them the time of day.

'Jacko? Jacko!' Charlie shouted in the distance. 'Help, everyone. I need help!'

Gangs or no gangs, the group responded as one.

57

'I came to check on him and the room is full of smoke again. I can't see him and he's not answering.'

Bonnie pushed her way through the group to see for herself. As before, thick black smoke snaked out of the hole in the door when she raised the flap.

'Jacko? Are you OK? How long has it been like this? When did someone last check on him?'

'He's your bestie,' said Jaide. 'When did you last bother to check?'

Bonnie felt the panic rising. How long had the smoke been pumping into his room? Had he called for her? Could she have helped him?

'You should have let him out. I told you.' The tears stung Bonnie's eyes.

'He's going to be OK, isn't he?' Charlie looked from person to person. 'What do we do? What do we do?'

'Chill out. Panicking won't help.' Grant sounded almost bored.

'Chill out?' said Charlie. 'Would you want us to chill out if you were in there?'

Bonnie was pleased the younger woman was finally getting a backbone.

'He's not choking to death,' said Grant but he didn't sound entirely sure.

'Where's the bottle gone? The one holding the flap open?' The group looked at her blankly. 'Was it not in here when you arrived, Charlie?' Charlie shook her head. Had Jacko removed it? Had he been annoyed by all the banging and taken it out to dampen the noise? 'We need something to prop the flap open,' said Bonnie, removing a Converse from her foot and wedging it into the space.

'Why is this happening?' said Charlie. 'Jacko did his challenge.'

'Maybe something malfunctioned,' said Grant.

'Or the sicko running this game is getting bored,' said Dennis.

The group stood in silence, none of them knowing what to do next.

And then the lights went out and the music began to blare.

58

They're stopping us from helping Jacko, Bonnie thought. *Why?*

She could not think of a legitimate reason. But what she did know was that this completely blew Grant's theory out of the water that Russ's death had been an accident. How could you argue that this was a malfunction now?

Were people at home entertained by this? Were the ratings high? She tried to think of anything she had ever enjoyed watching where people were suffering. She knew there had been reports of people having breakdowns on shows like *Big Brother* and *Love Island* but that was nothing close to what was being done to Jacko; the pain and discomfort he was experiencing. Not even *Survivor* came close to this.

In that moment Bonnie felt sure of one thing. Dennis was bang on. There couldn't be a full production team behind this show. This had to be the work of one twisted mind who had no one with him to put on the brakes.

The first thing Bonnie saw when the lights came on was that her shoe no longer propped open the flap on Jacko's door. She searched for it on the floor. Had it fallen out? She had wedged it pretty tight. It was too big for the hole so she'd had to squeeze it in place.

'Is everyone OK?' said Maria.

'Where's the shoe?' Bonnie walked closer to Jacko's door.

'At least that didn't go on too long this time,' said Dennis.

Long enough to achieve what? thought Bonnie with dread.

'I hate that music. What is it, anyway?' said Charlie.

'Metallica,' said Jaide.

'It's awful.'

'And yet they're one of the biggest metal bands ever. Go figure.'

Where is that bloody shoe?

And then Bonnie saw it, resting against the wall at Grant's feet.

The rage erupted within her in a flash. Before she knew it, she was throwing her whole weight into Grant so that he fell backwards on to the floor with her on top of him. Scrambling on to her knees she began thumping him in the chest. She heard him swearing as he attempted to grab her arms while other people's hands tried to pull her off him, but she wriggled and twisted and landed as many blows as possible. And all the time she wailed like an animal, such was the rage and frustration pouring out of her.

'STOP. STOP!' Grant tightly grabbed both her wrists.

Bonnie heaved in a heavy breath as the sweat dripped into her eyes.

'Someone get her off me. She's lost it.'

'Are you OK?' Charlie said as she gently took hold of Bonnie's left arm.

Jaide was not so careful in grabbing her right arm.

'He took the shoe.' Her voice sounded hoarse and her throat felt sore. She pointed to where her shoe sat by the wall.

All eyes were on Grant.

'I did not touch it.'

'How did it get to you, then? You were nowhere near the door. It can't have fallen there?'

252

Grant stared at Bonnie. 'How should I know?'

'Liar,' said Bonnie, walking to Russ's door. Grant was single-minded in this thing. Always looking to win at any cost. It would not have passed him by that the fewer people there were to compete with, the better his chances. It made her feel sick that he could still be so bothered about winning when their lives were in danger.

'Jacko? Hey, Jacko? The smoke has gone.' Bonnie glanced back at the others in time to catch an exchange of looks between Grant and Dennis.

Maria and Charlie came to see.

Jacko sat slumped on the floor, his arms spread wide and his clothes soaked with sweat. His eyes were closed but his chest rose and fell in shallow breaths.

Bonnie turned towards the nearest camera and stared into the lens. *You want us to see this,* she thought. Was this because she had suggested destroying the cameras? She turned her attention back to Jacko. He gazed into space.

'Are you OK?' she asked. 'We're all still here, just outside.'

He looked down at his hands, which still rested on the floor, then closed his eyes.

'No. Don't go to sleep, Jacko. Hey, Jacko?'

His eyes opened again and he frowned.

'You're going to be OK. Just try not to sleep for a bit. Do you have any water or food left? Jacko, don't close your eyes. Talk to me. Please?'

59

Three Months Earlier

CONFESSION: **Grant Withenshaw**
DATE: **6 June**
TIME: **09.45**
LOCATION: **Best Western Angel Hotel**

'I'm Grant Withenshaw and I came here to win. People might think they're clever. That they are strong. Attractive, popular. But let me tell you, line 'em all up in a room and it's clear to see, I'm just better.'

Grant smiled into the camera lens.

'I'm not sure that's what you want; maybe it's a bit too arrogant. Let's try that again.'

He took a moment.

'I'm Grant Withenshaw. I'm a competitor, someone who likes to win, and I'm here to play the game. I'm sure the other contestants are great people, some of whom might make good friends, but I'm not here to make friends. I am here for the glory and the cash. I know how these things work. If it takes acting the fool, then I'll do it. If it takes being the villain, then I'll be the villain. My plan is to take every opportunity to influence the group. Competition in my experience is not just about your physical strength or your IQ, it's about the mental game. If I can make them all believe I'm stronger, faster, smarter then I'm already winning.

'Is that OK? Is that what you want? It's hard to know in here on my own. This would be easier as an interview.'

Grant read the card again and collected his thoughts.

What did I say I desired and what did I say I was ashamed of?

He flicked to the relevant section on his application form, thinking it was nothing to do with Sofia because that had all happened after he applied. She was his boss and had said their relationship was a conflict of interest, but he knew that was her trying to let him down gently. When he'd asked her to move in, he could see the panic in her eyes. She didn't want to live with him, in his house. She wanted the detached five-bed in the suburbs and the Range Rover. He really was the bit of fun she'd always said he was.

The last thing he wanted to do following all of that was to be on a TV show. What he really wanted to do was sit and drink in the dark, but his dad always said if you start something you have to see it through. So here he was, and he was close to winning a place. The competitor in him felt a thrill and for the first time in weeks his depression lifted.

'What am I ashamed of? That's an easy one. It's pretty tough to grow up with swimming pools and holiday homes, and attending the best university in the country, and then to have nothing. Dad is a wealthy man but he believes my brother and I have to make our own way in life. No more handouts after the age of twenty-one and no chance of an inheritance. He's a fan of the tough love approach. I get it, he's trying to make us like him. He came from nothing and is very proud of that. Difference is we didn't come from nothing. We had everything and lost it. Now I live in a modest two up, two

255

down on an average estate because that's the best I can afford working as an accountant. Needless to say, I don't invite the ladies home.

'And as for what I desire? That would be my lifestyle back as quickly as possible. I want the stable of cars, the designer threads. I want the five-star holidays and I don't want to wait for all of that until I'm in my fifties. I don't want to just make my way slowly towards success. I want to have it all now. It's not a huge amount, it won't make me rich, but I can invest it, build on it, so yeah, I desire the money.

'But I expect that's what all the contestants are going to say.'

60

Bonnie was in the toilet when she heard Grant's shouts. She had been standing looking at that yellowish pool of water. She was so damn thirsty. The hot air felt drier with every breath, like it was sucking all the moisture out of her. As she walked back down the hall she saw Jaide, Maria and Grant striding towards Jacko's room where Charlie and Dennis had stayed to keep an eye on him after encouraging Bonnie to take a few minutes to calm down. Grant and Jaide had gone back to the central area to guard their spoils and Maria had accompanied them to fetch water for Jacko.

'Where are the supplies?' Grant shouted again.

'What?' said Dennis.

'Everything's gone. The food, the water, even the box. So I'll ask you again, where are they?' He was looking at Bonnie, Dennis and Charlie. 'Someone has taken them.'

'When? How? We were all here,' said Charlie.

'Yes, but it went dark for a while,' said Dennis.

'And music was blaring,' said Bonnie.

'Exactly. So which one of you jokers took it?'

'Well, it wasn't me,' said Dennis.

'Nor me. There were more important things going on than

your stolen goods, in case you hadn't noticed.' Bonnie held Grant's gaze.

'They were not stolen goods because they were mine and Jaide's. We won them fair and square so it is up to us what is done with them. So give them back.'

'Fair and square? You keep telling yourself that. They weren't yours and yours alone. The Director himself said they were to be shared with the group,' said Bonnie.

'He said we *could* share them with the group,' said Jaide. 'As in if we chose to.'

'We don't have your precious supplies. So it must be one of your lot that's hidden them again.' Dennis looked from Grant and Jaide to Charlie.

'Why would I take them? I already had access to them,' said Charlie.

Dennis's attention moved to Maria.

'Hey, Maz, they're accusing you now, too,' said Grant.

'I wouldn't—'

'We know.' Grant put an arm over Maria's shoulder. 'But these idiots are stuck so far up their own arses they can't talk anything but shit.'

Maria smiled and Bonnie was disappointed in the woman. She was brighter than that. She didn't need a Neanderthal like Grant. But as he planted a kiss on Maria's head and said, 'I'll look after you, Mazza,' Bonnie saw the thrill in Maria's eyes and knew this was a woman who would always be a sucker for a good-looking guy making her feel important.

Dennis sucked air in through pursed lips. 'Look,' he said, making his tone calmer, 'whoever took the supplies needs to put them back. I'm not being dramatic when I say our lives depend on it. We don't need to know who did it and why.' He scanned the group, meeting every person's eyes. 'Put them back and that'll be the end of it.'

61

'Sorry to interrupt again. Did anyone put the supplies back?'
'No.'
'Who would steal the remaining food and water?'
'I don't know but it was getting very competitive. People were becoming irrational.'
'But surely taking the water was dangerous. No one was that desperate, were they?'
'It was a way of weakening the rest of us.'
'You never considered that something else was going on?'
'Such as?'
'Well, you've told us about the dummy in the hot tub going missing on your first day and about finding the basement door open and then closed when all of your fellow contestants were on the top deck. Now your supplies go missing while you are all distracted by the smoke in Jacko's room. Are you sure someone wasn't there messing with you all along?'
'Yeah, we did discuss that. Jaide wondered if it was really possible to control all the doors and heaters and cameras remotely or if someone had to be there with us. But in the

259

end I think we figured, what did it matter? They weren't in the basement with us and unless we could get out of there they might as well be on the mainland.'

'*I think Jaide had a point. I've seen the police report on what they found on site after this was all over, and it's not such amazing tech that you could trust it would work without glitches. Someone had to be on hand in case of any malfunctions.*'

'Maybe we should have tried harder to find out what was behind the locked doors when we were on the main deck.'

'*Did you ever manage to break through the well-room door?*'

'No. It turned out to be solid wood as Maria said and no amount of smashing against it with table legs achieved much more than scuffing the surface. Don't get me wrong, Dennis and I gave it a good go but it was clear early on that this wasn't going to be our great escape.'

'*We looked at the plans. There was nothing behind that door other than a very deep well. The secret passage actually runs around the perimeter of the basement and is accessed through one of the rooms behind the central area.*'

'There really was a secret passageway?'

'*It wouldn't have been much use if you'd found it; it simply travels around a section of the basement perimeter. It has a sign above the opening that says BOLT HOLE. You can see it on historical pictures of the place.*'

'So what was it for?'

'*To bolt into, or hide in. Like an old-fashioned panic room.*'

'So someone could have used that to hide in the space?'

'*I think it's an angle worth investigating. Are you OK?*'

'He could have been there the whole time, only inches away from us?'

'*It's possible.*'

'Thinking of him skulking in the background, listening to us suffer. It makes my skin crawl.'

'*There is another possibility.*'

'Which is?'

'*One of your fellow contestants could have been using the space to store their own supplies.*'

'No, I can't believe . . .'

'*Bonnie?*'

'I'm just thinking . . . that final secret we uncovered.'

'*What about it?*'

'No, it can't be.'

'*Can't be what?*'

'Saying that one of us was in on it.'

62

'How's Jacko?' Maria said as Bonnie sat down next to her on the floor. Since the argument about the missing food, Maria had taken up position alone opposite the screen showing the social media live feed.

'What are you doing?'

'I'm trying to figure out this riddle, "The world's most popular game totals nothing." Maybe it will tell us why there was a second attack on Jacko.'

'No, I mean what are you doing teaming up with Jaide and Grant? They're only being nice so they can gang up against Dennis and me.'

'Jaide's not. She's been nice to me since we got here.' Maria remained staring at the screen as the posts scrolled.

'I find that hard to believe.'

'You see what you expect to see and not what's really there.'

'What does that mean?' Bonnie heard the indignation in her own tone. She was not a judgemental person, never had been, and she didn't like being labelled as one. 'She's the one being rude to everyone all the time.'

'Jaide and I understand each other. We've both been picked on most of our lives for being different. To her you represent the people who have it easy, you know, because you're pretty, thin and clever.'

'That's no defence.'

'Have you ever considered she might need to be that way just to get through the day?' Maria looked at Bonnie and her eyes were kind. 'Not everyone finds it easy to laugh along with the jokes.'

Bonnie felt uncomfortable under Maria's gaze, as if the woman had uncovered some fundamental truth about Bonnie's character.

Bonnie knew that psychologically everyone tends to think of themselves as normal and so are prone to viewing those who differ significantly as being odd or wrong. It was the basis of most prejudice and discrimination to make judgements on limited insight and understanding. Wasn't that why viewers loved reality TV so much? It allowed them to judge others openly, laugh at their differences and subsequently validate how normal they are in comparison? But she wasn't doing that, was she?

'What about Grant, then? Why befriend him? He's just out for himself.'

'Grant is what Grant is. At least he's honest about it. So, how is Jacko?'

'He's awake but doesn't remember much. He's getting more disorientated in there. It's so much hotter than out here and he's down to his last drops of water.'

'We'll keep an eye on him. We're not having another Russ on our hands.'

Bonnie watched the text scroll up the screen without reading it. She hoped Maria was right but she was unsure what power they really had to help Jacko now.

'I'm thinking the phrase "totals nothing" is a code of some kind. I don't think it's an anagram but maybe it has another meaning, like "equals zero". It could be a mathematical clue as there's been a good amount of maths in things so far. There's no room zero here but maybe we should check out if there's a room with the letter O. What do you think?'

Maybe it's saying we are all worth nothing, thought Bonnie, but said instead, 'Let's take a look.'

There was no room O. The letter was displayed on a plain patch of wall. The two of them carried on walking, checking if any other doors were unlocked as they went. Eventually they came across Jaide, Grant and Charlie, who were gathered together near the stairs up to the main floor. Charlie was giggling at something Grant had said but stopped abruptly on seeing Bonnie.

'We need to put our heads together on this world's most popular game question,' said Maria.

'We haven't been asked to solve this, have we?' said Jaide.

'No, it was on the Twitter feed for viewers,' said Charlie.

'OK, well, why are we paying it any attention?'

Bonnie chipped in to help Maria, who looked crestfallen. It was clearly bugging her that she couldn't solve it. 'Jacko thought the fact it says, "The world's most popular game totals nothing" and then "What does that tell you about humanity?" might be a clue as to what the point of all this is. He thought maybe we are being used to make a point about reality TV or the media or something.'

'I said that,' Grant said to Jaide and Charlie.

Bonnie forced herself to look at Grant and nod. He was right, he had started that whole line of thinking. 'Jacko thought you had a point,' she said, trying to act on Maria's feedback not to be so judgemental and write people off.

None of them looked her way. They continued to talk to Maria as if Bonnie wasn't there.

'"The world's most popular game totals nothing." What

does that mean? That there is no single game that's the most popular?' said Jaide.

'That's stupid. There must be. Some games are famous for a reason,' said Grant.

'But averaged out across the world, maybe no single game comes top.'

Grant shook his head. 'I don't think that's it. It would be a pointless riddle if so. Why bother saying anything about the world's most popular game if there is no such thing?'

'I agree,' said Maria. 'I think this is telling us something else. I'm wondering if it's a maths thing again, like my triangular number.'

'Has anyone solved it on social media yet?' Charlie said.

'There are lots of suggestions for what the game might be, like Minecraft or chess.'

'Dennis might be able to help. Where is he?' said Bonnie.

No one answered.

Bonnie was about to go and look for him when Charlie exclaimed.

'Wait. Could it be a zero sum game? I remember that from my maths lessons.'

'Totals nothing and zero sum could be the same, yes. What is it?' said Maria.

'Argh, I'm not sure. It was something about winning and losing. A game with a winner and a loser.'

'All games have a winner and a loser,' said Grant with a smirk. He clearly thought Charlie was a bit of an airhead.

'I think gambling is an example and also chess from memory,' said Charlie, ignoring his jibe.

'Gambling is a game of chance and chess a game of skill so that makes no sense,' said Grant.

'So are we looking for a specific game or a type of game?' asked Bonnie.

Jaide and Grant stared ahead as if she hadn't spoken.

Charlie said under her breath, 'Come on, come on.' She crouched down to the floor and put her head in her hands. 'Zero sum, zero sum.'

'What other games were examples, can you remember?' said Maria. 'If we could find the similarities we could work it out.'

'Tennis, maybe?' said Charlie.

'What do gambling, chess and tennis have in common?' said Grant. 'They are all totally different kinds of games.'

'Dennis, do you know?' said Bonnie, seeing him approach from behind Jaide. 'Any idea what a zero sum game is?'

'Why do you want to know?'

'Maria thinks it might be the answer to the riddle about the world's most popular game.'

'I'm beyond working out these riddles,' said Dennis. 'Our biggest puzzle is how to survive without water. The last drink I had was hours ago. How about everyone else?'

'Same,' said Grant.

'I just spoke to Jacko, he's not really with it but I wanted him to know we weren't withholding water from him on purpose. I'm hoping we get our next challenge soon as that's our best chance.' He didn't say *of surviving*, but they all knew that was what he meant.

Bonnie saw Maria wipe a small tear from the corner of her eye and Jaide briefly placed a hand on Maria's back. They really were friends; Bonnie had totally missed that.

'Unless whichever one of you has taken the supplies gives them back now,' said Grant. 'We'll know who you are soon enough, anyway, when you're the only one who's not dehydrated and starving.'

Would he say that if he had been the one to take them? Bonnie thought of Jaide hiding the small black Morse code card from Dennis and Jacko that first day and figured, yes. It's exactly what a player would do, mask their advantages. Blimey, she really was judgemental. Maria might have a point.

'Poker, not gambling!' said Charlie. 'The example was poker. I remember now because that was the game that helped me to understand the theory. It's any competition where the amount the winner gains is equal to the losses of all the losers. So in poker everyone puts money in and the winner takes all.' Charlie looked so pleased with herself that she didn't sense the mood shift in the group.

The winner gains at the expense of the losers, thought Bonnie with a new wave of dread. She left the group and quickly walked back towards Jacko's room and the screen near by. There was a closer one to where they had all been standing but that meant passing Russ's door and she avoided that whenever she could. The smell was getting bad.

As she approached the screen she thought it was blank and felt a flash of relief. Maybe Charlie's theory had been wrong. Maybe the answer had nothing to do with zero sum games. But then she saw that the red block text she had come to dread was there waiting, like the next chapter of a horror novel that you're scared to read but can't stop yourself from doing.

Did you unlock the final secret?
Were you smart enough to do it?
Did you really want to know?
Because this one is a blow

SURPRISE, SURPRISE
ONLY ONE OF YOU SURVIVES

63

Jonny @JT45

Who knew Charlie had a brain in there? Identifying poker as the world's most popular game. #Gothebimbo

PeterP @P_banner_1

Clearly she's brighter than you. She didn't say poker was the most popular game she said zero sum games were. Any game where the winner gains at the expense of the loser. #Useyourbrain

Ayo Aminade @Goshblog

Is that really necessary? Do you get a kick out of picking on @JT45? What does that say about your intelligence?

PeterP @P_banner_1

Err, I'm just pointing out that if you're going to judge you should get your facts right.

Julie Hathersage @HathersageJulie
What does it say about humanity that the world's most
popular kind of game is to win at the expense of others? It
says we are an awful, awful species. #TheFortressisdeep

Lulu @Lukehere3
Only one survives! My vote is on Grant as he's the only one
ruthless enough to do whatever it takes. #Granttowin

64

'Hey?' Bonnie said quietly.

Jacko lay on the floor curled loosely into the foetal position.

'No, it's OK, don't move. I'm just saying hi.' She knelt by the door like she had outside Maria's duel room and held the flap open with her thumbs. 'Dennis said he's explained about the water. We're hoping for another challenge soon so we can win some more.'

Jacko blinked at her a few times. She wasn't sure if he was trying to communicate or if it was a purely reflexive thing. His skin glistened with sweat and his T-shirt was damp around the neck and armpits.

She had intended to tell him about the latest secret to be revealed before someone else did, but couldn't bring herself to do it. What could be gained? Jacko was already fading fast; she needed to give him reasons to fight, not to give up.

'So I've been thinking . . . about this date, where would we go? Because if you were thinking of an escape room you know the answer is no, right?'

She saw the faintest sign of a smile touch Jacko's lips.

'Then again, if we're talking a nice meal where I get to wear a new dress and sip some fine wine, then I could go for that.'

'OK.'

The word was raspy and whispered but it still made her smile.

'There are some nice restaurants near where I live if you don't mind travelling, or I can come to your neck of the woods.'

The mention of restaurants had her mind spiralling off on fantasies of food again. No doubt it would do the same for Jacko. She needed a change of subject.

'I totally lost it with Grant, did you hear? He's so bloody competitive, he'll do anything to win, even sabotage other people's chances. It's disgusting. I imagine I'll get roasted on Twitter for it. I must have looked pretty crazy. I didn't know I would knock him off his feet and I hurt my hands hitting him. He's made out of granite or something. Probably spends too much time in the gym.'

She caught another flicker of a smile.

'Maria gave me a talking to, though. She said I was being too judgemental. Do you think that? She was talking more about Jaide than Grant. She said they were good friends, which I have to admit I can see now. I think this place is bringing out the worst in me. I feel angry all the time and it's getting harder to hold it back. Sorry.' She realized she had started to cry. 'I didn't come here to bring you down, but you're my best friend in here.'

She moved away from the flap for a moment to compose herself. *You came here to cheer him up.* But the tears kept coming and she couldn't stop them. The chances of her surviving this were extremely slim. She wasn't as clever as Maria and Dennis or as competitive as Jaide and Grant. She might fare better than Charlie but that only made her feel bad because that would doom the young woman to some awful fate like Jacko was facing.

Even if she did stand a chance of surviving, did she really want that? Zero sum games may be the world's most popular, but what nightmares await a winner who only survives because everyone else does not?

65

The Director

The problem was never going to be who to save – that would be easy. The problem was not dishing out the punishment too early to those who deserved it most.

As he edited the latest footage, he watched them all complaining, arguing and playing up to the cameras. Every one of them, without exception, kept doing it. He doubted the others saw it, doubted some even knew they were doing it themselves, but if he counted those little eye flicks upwards he reckoned they'd tally out equally.

They wanted him to see them. To like them enough to choose them. They were desperate and tragic. What they had all failed to see was that their destiny was already set. It had been so from the moment they signed up to do the show. Anything and everything they said or did from that point on was irrelevant. He held the strings, all of them, and his puppets would do exactly as he intended.

It didn't matter to him that the world would brand him the bad guy, in fact he was banking on it. He would become more famous than any one of them, but he didn't need his name in lights or his face on everyone's screen. He was happy just to be known for having done something breathtakingly real in a world of frivolous fakery.

This was his favourite part. The basement section. The opening parts, upstairs, had been necessary to set the scene but this was the meat in the sandwich. He had enjoyed designing the games. He had relished every thrilling detail of Dante's purgatory in his late teens. The dreadfulness of how souls were made to suffer for their sins was darker and more delicious than anything to come from Stephen King or James Herbert. The gluttonous being starved of food and water, the sloth being made to run without rest, the angry shrouded in black smoke as they faced battle. What was not to love? And all relatively easy to recreate. Sure, he'd had to get a bit more creative with envy as he couldn't very well sew people's eyes shut with wire. It had taken him a while to think of an alternative. Blindfolds were too naff, darkness too similar to what he'd done already, but eventually inspiration had struck. At this stage, what would this sinner be most envious of? Other people's freedom – so why not give them a taste of that?

66

The Fortress @thefortress

Green-eyed girl beware. The next SIN is to be served. Watch it on Channel 5 and My5 live NOW. #TheFortress

67

Charlie

SLITHER AND SLIDE
YOU WHO'S GREEN-EYED
TAKE MY FIRST
MAKE IT MY LAST
NOW I HAPPENED IN THE PAST

'I don't want to do it. I don't want to.'

Charlie was on the verge of hyperventilating and Maria was telling her to breathe.

'Why me? Why have they picked me? I solved the riddle.'

'And that makes you a competitor,' said Grant. 'You'll smash it,' he said, but his expression looked a little too concerned to convey any genuine confidence.

Bonnie watched the interaction with intrigue. Maybe he really did care for Charlie. Like Maria said, she needed to open her eyes to what was really going on rather than jumping to conclusions.

'Let's find out what it is. It might not be so bad,' Maria said, rubbing Charlie's hand. 'Anyone any ideas?'

'I say we try every door and see which one is open, save messing about,' said Grant.

'They don't get unlocked until we solve the clue,' said Jaide. 'How do you know?'

'Because I have a brain and so does the Director. We tried every door when we first got trapped in here. They were all locked. They only open when he unlocks them.'

Grant bristled a bit at his new bestie's put down but did not argue back. Again, not what she would have predicted.

'This must be envy as it says green-eyed,' said Dennis.

'And has references to a snake with the slither and slide,' said Jaide.

'So those last three lines are the puzzle. "Take my first, make it my last, now I happened in the past." Anyone know that?'

The group looked at each other, hoping one of their number would come up trumps, but no one did.

It kind of made sense that Charlie was envy. Bonnie imagined that the younger woman constantly judged herself against others. Why else would she walk around in bikini tops and tight jeans? What other people thought of how she looked was important. Bonnie also imagined that out of all of them here, Charlie was the one who most aspired to fame and a job in TV.

'It has to be wordplay,' said Maria. 'Swapping the first letter of a word for the last letter, which then turns it from present to past tense.'

'Agreed,' said Dennis. 'Aren't S, E and T the most common letters to end a word?'

'I think R and D would be pretty common too,' said Jaide.

'OK, let's take a letter each and see what words fit the bill. I'll do S words, Maria you do E, Grant take T, Jaide, R and Clara, D,' said Dennis.

'What about Charlie?' said Grant.

'She'll have her own work to do in good time.'

Bonnie began thinking of D words, taking the first letter and making it the last. *Do would become Od, Don't would become a nonsense word, Did would be Idd, Dive would be Ived, Drink would be Rinkd. They were all nonsense.* She needed words with a vowel at the end or it wouldn't work. *Die would be Ied, Dye would be Yed, Dupe would be Uped.* Her brain seemed stuck.

Jaide was pacing, her lips mouthing various words. Dennis stood still, his back against the wall, his head up to the ceiling and his eyes closed. Grant was crouched down on his haunches and tracing shapes on the floor. Maria sat by Charlie stroking her hand and staring into the distance. Every one of them was focused on solving the puzzle. Why? Why were they continuing to play his games? She knew it was nothing more than a survival instinct now. He controlled the food and water supplies. He didn't need darkness and deafening music any more, he had two far more powerful motivators on his team: thirst and hunger.

'Got it!' said Maria. 'It's *eat*. If you move the E to the end it becomes *ate*. Past tense.'

'Typical that Maria would find *eat*. What? It's a joke. You people have totally lost your sense of humour.' Grant began walking. 'Come on, then. To room eight it is.'

'It might be a good omen,' said Dennis. 'We could really do with you winning us something to eat, Charlie, not to mention something to drink.'

Bonnie watched Grant and Dennis walking side by side ahead of them. Their heads were tilted a little towards each other. It had felt good to have the group working together as a team again, even if she didn't quite feel part of it the way she had before. Grant patted Dennis on the back and Bonnie tried to tell herself this was a good thing.

The smell as they approached Russ's room had her holding

her breath. Part of her brain wanted to take a look. Just a sneaky peek to see what he looked like now. It was the same compulsion most people felt on passing a road accident. On some level you really, really want to look at what you should not.

Dennis abruptly stopped outside of Russ's room and Bonnie thought he was actually going to do it, but then he turned slowly to look back at the room next to it. The room Maria had done her Divine Comedy challenge in. The room whose door was now shut.

'Maria, just push against that door,' Dennis said.

Maria stood next to it and did as he asked.

'What's going on?' said Grant, walking back to them.

'It's locked,' said Maria.

'What? Maybe it just closed by itself,' said Grant.

'None of the other open doors have done that.'

'Stop it, you're freaking me out and I'm already freaked out,' said Charlie.

'There's nothing to worry about. We are all here. No one is locked in so what does it matter?' said Jaide.

'It matters,' said Dennis, 'because nothing in this place happens by accident.' He moved back and opened the flap to look inside. It put Bonnie in mind of the moment he had done the same to Russ's door, just before she'd had the message telling them that no one leaves. 'I hope you're happy with yourself,' said Dennis in anger as he stood up straight, 'because your little stunt has shafted you as much as the rest of us.'

'Who are you talking to? What have you seen?' said Bonnie. When Dennis didn't answer, she moved to take a look for herself. 'Oh my God,' she said on seeing the full box of supplies sitting on the top of the keyboard.

Dennis said, 'Whichever joker tried to hide the supplies in here got shafted, because in case you hadn't noticed he can remotely close the doors!'

The rest of the group all took turns looking in the room and Bonnie watched them, trying to see who looked guilty.

'I think we need a strategy based on need. So think about the last drink you had and when that was. We can make a list of who might suffer the effects of dehydration first.' Dennis wrung his hands as he spoke.

'And do what with it?' said Jaide.

'Take care of one another. We're counting on you, Charlie, love.'

The group moved silently to room eight.

'I can't do it, I'm not going in. It's not fair. I'm not doing it.'

Grant put a hand on her shoulder. 'Charlie, calm down. It's OK, you don't have to go in on your own.'

'You're going in with her?' said Bonnie to Grant, thinking that if he did her opinion of him might shift significantly.

The guy took a small step away from room eight as Jaide pushed the door wide. The interior was brightly lit. There was no opening in the door but to Bonnie's surprise there was a window in the outer wall. A porthole with a view to the outside. It was dark out but a few stars sparkled in the night sky. She felt a small thrill at the prospect of seeing the world again.

Something was bugging her and she knew she had to say it, even though Charlie would hate her for it.

'I'm not sure having someone go in with you is allowed. It might forfeit the task and do nothing more than result in two people getting locked in there.'

She expected some agreement from the others but their silence was the first hint at what was to come.

'I don't think Charlie should go in alone,' said Maria.

'I don't want to be locked in,' said Charlie.

'Who would you like with you?' Grant said and his tone was softer and more concerned than Bonnie had ever heard it.

Charlie reached out for Bonnie's hand.

Despite the heat and the hunger and the exhaustion, Bonnie's brain joined the dots amazingly quickly.

'Oh, I see,' Bonnie said to Grant, realizing she'd had him right all along. 'You think two for the price of one. The more of us out of the game, the more chance you have of winning. Jog on, dirtbag.'

'Please, Clara.' Charlie squeezed Bonnie's hand.

'I don't think it's a bad idea.'

Bonnie turned to look at Dennis. 'You're not serious?'

'Charlie stands a much better chance of success with someone to support her and we really need this win.'

'She's not a child. She's a grown woman, and if you're that bothered, you go in with her.'

'You have a better relationship.'

'I don't think the quality of our friendship is any predictor of success in there.'

'What makes you so precious? You'd let one of us go in, I bet,' said Jaide.

'No. That's not what I'm saying.'

'I don't mind going with her,' said Maria.

'No, Maria. You've done more than enough, hasn't she, Clara?' Jaide stared at Bonnie.

In that moment, with the whole group gathered around her, Bonnie realized what she had missed over the last few hours: that look between Grant and Dennis after she'd lost her temper, Charlie and Jaide whispering then stopping as soon as she entered the room. Maria telling her off for being unreasonable. Grant patting Dennis on the back. The group had found a common enemy. They had decided she was trouble. They already thought Charlie was overly emotional, and since Bonnie had attacked Grant they no doubt thought the same of her. She was a liability. Becoming hysterical. Weaker than the rest.

'This isn't fair. You can't force me in there just because you're annoyed with me.'

'We're not annoyed,' said Maria.

'What, then? Why me?'

No one said a word. No disputes. No apologies.

'Think about it. What if someone going with Charlie means we lose our chance to get supplies? Are we willing to risk that?'

'We said after Russ that no one would go in alone,' said Dennis. 'We need to look out for each other.'

And this is you looking out for me, is it? Or are you just looking out for yourselves? 'But we let Maria and Jacko go alone.'

'We were too slow to go with Maria and Jacko's room was too small. He agreed to that.'

Of course, Mr Prosecutor would have an answer for everything.

'Does everyone agree? Can no one else see the risk? Maria, you're our smartest member. What do you think?' said Bonnie, hoping for a voice of reason to help her out.

Maria looked at Charlie for a long moment. The young woman silently sobbed. Her head hung low as she hugged her bare left arm with her right hand. Maria's gaze moved to Bonnie.

'Fine. If that's how you all feel.'

Jaide held Bonnie's gaze for a moment and Bonnie imagined the other woman was telepathically trying to communicate Bonnie's words back to her: *I hope you get trapped in here knowing no one is coming to help.*

'Good luck,' said Dennis.

Bonnie held the middle finger of her right hand up to him. She had thought he was her friend.

68

The door shutting behind them made Bonnie jump. Bonnie looked back at it. No hatch. No chance of survival if they failed.

Charlie tried to prise it open again then banged against the metal with the sides of her fists. Bonnie gently pulled her away. The door was locked now. No point fighting it.

The room was square and wider than the others they'd been sent into so far. Around the bottom of the walls there were scuffs and empty drill holes where fixtures had been removed. She imagined this was once an operations room filled with military equipment. Had the men working in here felt safe or scared?

Her eyes rested on the text printed on the wall to the left of the window.

More and more is never enough
To save your sorry soul
Jacob's climb is the only salvation
The key is through that hole

What was it with this guy and rhymes? She recalled attending a talk by the Poet Laureate when he had visited her university. He had said that making up rhymes was easy, child's play even, that true poetry was so much more. So this Director was not as smart as he thought. The idea made her feel a little better. *Bring it on, douche-bag*, she thought.

Below the rhyme a crude arrow had been drawn on the wall towards the porthole window that sat two-thirds of the way up the side of the room. Bonnie walked to it. It was dark outside so there was nothing to see. The window was larger than she'd first thought and she was surprised to find it wasn't a sealed unit. It had a small metal latch on one side and a hinge on the other. Reaching up she uncoupled the latch and pushed against the glass. It wasn't going to open, but still she had to try. She imagined the group outside watching her on the monitor and laughing at her naivety. The sicko was not leaving an accessible window open.

And then she felt the thing shift a tiny amount.

'Oh my God.' She looked back at Charlie then pushed the window with both hands. 'Come and help me.'

Charlie came and placed her hands around Bonnie's and together they pushed. The window creaked and budged before sticking and then budging a little more. Bonnie banged her fist around the frame. It could have been years since this thing had been open; decades, maybe. It would be rusted and swollen. She and Charlie continued to push and bang, feeling little movements every now and again that spurred them on until, eventually, finally, it sprung free of its frame and swung wide.

Cold sea air gushed in, and Bonnie began to laugh.

It felt beautiful and clean and she took large gulps of it.

She and Charlie hugged before Bonnie leaned her head out of the window. She could hear the sea pounding against the sides of the fort below them. Its spray hit her face and she breathed in the saltiness with renewed admiration. With her eyes closed she enjoyed the feeling of being alive and just a tiny step closer to freedom.

'What can you see?' said Charlie.

Bonnie reluctantly opened her eyes, breaking the spell.

No one leaves.

Only one of you survives.

She looked down and around the porthole, seeing nothing. As her eyes adjusted to the darkness she began to make out the smooth concrete stretching down to the waves below, and when she looked up she saw the first few rungs of a metal ladder.

Jacob's ladder. Where had she heard of that before? She expected Dennis and Maria would know. How on earth those two crammed all that general knowledge into their heads was beyond her. The fondness she felt towards them drained away as she remembered how they had turned on her. Not so long ago, Dennis had been whispering to her about his plans to try and escape. She had been his confidante. And how often had she stuck up for Maria since they'd been in this place? Almost daily. All Bonnie was guilty of was calling out the bullshit and selfishness. And this was her punishment – being ostracized from the group. At least she had felt fresh air on her face once more. She hoped every one of them was jealous of that.

Envy, that's why there was a window. So everyone would be envious of whoever was in here. Or was it to ramp up that feeling in the room's inhabitants? After all, there was nothing more envy-breeding than seeing something you want but can't have.

The cruelness of it all brought a fresh rush of bile into her mouth.

Bonnie moved back into the room. The supplies cupboard was standing against the wall and, unlike those in Maria and Jacko's rooms, this one had a keyhole.

'What?' said Charlie, her eyes wide and fearful. 'What do I have to do?'

'The rhyme says the key is through that hole and this cupboard has a lock on it.'

'Can you see the key? Can I reach it?'

Bonnie slowly shook her head. 'I think the reference to a climb is literal. There's a metal ladder fixed to the wall above this window. I'm thinking you need to climb that to retrieve the key.'

'Out there? In the dark?'

'Unless we wait until morning, yes.'

Charlie was shaking her head. 'I can't fit through there. It's too small.'

Bonnie looked at the window and then back at Charlie. 'It'll be tight but manageable.'

Charlie backed away towards the door, shaking her head. 'I can't, I won't. I'm not climbing through that, I'll fall.'

'Calm down. Let's think about it.'

'I said I can't. I can't!'

Bonnie went back to the window. The bottom of it was level with her chest. She turned her back to it and then reached out above her head until she found the bottom rung of the ladder. If she stood on tiptoes she could reach the second rung. She let her arms take her weight and tried to pull herself up.

'If I push your legs up you can sit on the windowsill and then pull yourself out.'

'No. No. I can't. I can't. He can't make me do it.'

'Charlie, it's OK.' Bonnie could see the younger woman was close to a panic attack. Her breathing was erratic, and her eyes flicked from place to place. 'There's no rush. Sit here, take a minute.'

'I can't do it. I can't,' she said as she slid down the wall to sit on the floor.

Bonnie sat beside her and took her hand. It felt clammy and every now and then a small tremor passed through it.

'Breathe for me.' Bonnie took a few deep breaths in and out in slow succession to demonstrate. When she heard Charlie's breathing settle a little she leaned in to whisper in Charlie's ear. 'You'll be outside and free. That ladder must go somewhere. You could get us all out of this place.'

'How?'

'Sshhh. If you climb out and find where it goes maybe there's a way to the main deck.'

'What if there isn't?'

'Then . . . stay there on the ladder.'

'What do you mean?'

'When the sun comes up there are bound to be boats. This is our chance to get help.'

'What if I fall?'

'You won't, and anyway, we're not so high above the water here and you are dressed for a swim,' Bonnie said, trying to lighten the mood.

'Is this supposed to make me feel better?'

'Charlie, come on, you'll be our saviour. You can do this.'

'If you're so keen, why don't you do it?'

'It's not my challenge.'

'So? I don't care.'

'He'll know we're up to something if I go.'

Charlie looked up at the camera. 'I don't want to do it. Any of it,' she said at full volume. 'YOU CAN'T MAKE ME!'

Bonnie sat quietly. Charlie was right, no one could make her climb out of that window and up the ladder. Bonnie could see her point. Although she was desperate to get out of this building, the idea of hanging on to the sheer face of this concrete cylinder above the sea was the stuff of nightmares.

'Who do you want to hug first when you get out of here?'

Charlie shrugged.

'For me it'll be my sister. I miss her a lot, which I never thought I'd say.' Bonnie smiled at Charlie but the younger woman didn't smile back. 'We lost our mum a few months ago and since then we've not been getting on too well.'

'Were you and your mum close?'

'Very. She was fab. Totally bonkers at times but fab, you know.'

'Not really.'

Bonnie remembered Charlie's confession from earlier. 'Sorry, that was insensitive.'

'It's OK. I like hearing about nice mums. I always wished I'd had one. I was adopted and I don't think Mum ever really warmed to me. I was just an irritation to her. I always seemed to be getting in her way, or stopping her from having the life she should have had if she hadn't had to look after me.'

And so she took out her bitterness on you, thought Bonnie, but chose not to point this out.

'I don't think anyone will miss me if we don't get out.'

'Don't say that.'

'It's true. I'll be easily forgotten because I never made the kind of friends that stick around.'

Bonnie wondered if this was due to Charlie's mother never teaching her what a positive relationship looked like.

'What about boyfriends? You must have some admirers out there. Look at you. And if you don't already, you will now. I think you'll be the one who could get some kind of career out of this if you're smart about it.'

'If I just keep crying and taking my kit off, you mean.'

'Ignore the trolls. They're people who spend too much time on their phones and not enough time living their own lives. Anyone worth their salt wouldn't have time to be passing petty judgements.'

Charlie smiled for the first time since they'd entered the room.

'That breeze is lovely.' Bonnie closed her eyes and enjoyed the cool wafts of air crossing her face. When she opened them, Charlie was at the window looking up at the ladder.

'What do you think?' Bonnie said.

Charlie reached up to grab the rung. 'Errgh, it's slimy and wet.'

'Can you pull yourself up?' Bonnie rose to her feet.

Charlie twisted her body to look out and down towards the sea and then faced Bonnie again with a kind of steely look in her eyes. She slowly lifted her feet off the floor. She was a slight girl with little body mass, so lifting her own body weight wouldn't be easy. But to her credit she gave it a good go before her hands slipped off the ladder and her bare back scraped down the wall. Charlie cried out in pain and slumped to the floor. Bonnie rushed to her side. There were two red tracks across her shoulder blades where Charlie's skin had grazed against the rough wall.

'It's not bleeding.' Bonnie checked for any grit in the wound and was relieved to see it looked pretty clean. God knows how they'd cope with an infected wound in this place.

Any bravado Charlie had briefly possessed was gone. The panic was back in the young woman's eyes. And yet she made one more attempt to lift herself up and with Bonnie's help almost managed to get her bum on to the bottom of the window.

'I can't do it,' she said when her head and shoulders were outside the building. Her voice sounded high pitched and panicked and her long hair whipped around her face. 'No! No! I can't.' Charlie began sliding back into the room.

Bonnie helped her inside. She knew it was pointless trying to force Charlie. She was too scared. Even if she did get out there she probably wouldn't have the steel to climb very far, or to find an exit strategy.

'Could we hang something out of there to attract attention?' said Bonnie, thinking out loud.

'Like what?'

Bonnie looked at Charlie's denim shorts and bikini top. *Not those.* They'd need something bright and attention grabbing, so her own jeans and dark T-shirt wouldn't make much of an impact. She scanned the room. There was nothing to use, nothing that would attract enough attention. She knew there was no other choice than to do what he wanted. He had set everything up that way.

'It's fine, I'll do it,' said Bonnie, knowing it was the best chance they had of escaping this hell.

'You can't, it's not your challenge.'

'What's the worst that can happen? If I get the key, at least we'll have supplies.' She said this for the camera, knowing she had no intention of coming back into this room.

Charlie hugged Bonnie tightly around the waist and sobbed into her shoulder as she apologized.

'I'll be OK,' Bonnie whispered in Charlie's ear, squeezing her back. 'Don't worry.'

Bonnie hated to admit it, but the group had been right to send someone in with Charlie. She would never have made her way out of this room alone.

Reluctantly breaking free, Bonnie took Charlie's place by the window. She breathed deeply a few times to calm the nerves before reaching up to the ladder as she had before. 'Can you help push me up?'

Charlie took hold of her legs and lifted her as Bonnie slowly pulled herself up and out through the window. Her shoulders only just squeezed through the gap and she had to scrunch her arms in close to her head to get them through.

289

She shook her hair from her eyes as best she could as she reached with one hand for the third rung. When she had a firm grip, she moved her other hand up and then managed to lift herself so that she sat in the window. Her upper body was now outside in the cold, her legs still encased in warmth.

'It's OK,' she said, looking back in at Charlie.

'I think you should come back in. What if you fall? If you fall, you'll drown. This is stupid. It's not worth it.'

Bonnie was looking up at the ladder. She counted ten rungs until she could see no more. Was that the top or simply where the darkness cloaked the rest of it? If it was the top it stopped in a random place. There were no windows as far as she could see. Maybe there would be a ledge or something. Someone had put this ladder here for a reason. It must have been an escape route of some kind.

'Clara? Clara?'

'I'm fine,' she said, steeling herself. She needed to lean back with her arms and slide her bottom out over the sea until she could get a foot on the window and stand up. Charlie was right about the ladder feeling slimy and wet. She tested her grip a few times, tightening her hands as much as she could around the thin metal. Then she took a few more deep breaths.

This is how we escape, she told herself.

69

The manoeuvre went better than she expected. She moved quickly without thinking about the danger or the cold water below her. Before she knew it, she had one foot firmly in place on the window frame, at which point she pulled her body close to the building again, moving one hand up to the fourth rung and checking her grip before following with the other hand and then slowing rising to a stand. Her right hand slipped and she nearly lost her grip but managed to hang on.

The cold wind whipped around her head. It felt so good, despite the goosebumps. She took a moment to appreciate how she had feared she might never experience the outside world again. All her senses were filled with the sea; the sound of it crashing against the fort, its salty smell in her nostrils, the feel of it clinging to her pores. Despite the darkness shrouding her vision, she knew she was surrounded by beauty.

She briefly wondered what the rest of the group watching outside the room might be thinking. They would see nothing but her feet now. Were there cameras out here? She couldn't see any. Would they think she was reckless or brave? Grant would no doubt have a small smile on his face as he willed her to fail. She imagined Jaide with her arms folded and a scowl on her face and she hoped Dennis and Maria were feeling guilty. Really fricking guilty.

Here we go.

Bonnie reached for the next rung. The ladder felt even slipperier under her feet. Maybe if she'd removed her shoes, she might have had more grip. The soles of her pumps were worn flat and smooth, which was probably the worst thing for this activity.

Five rungs to go and then what? It looked like the ladder just stopped. She risked a glance down. Perhaps it had been used to climb aboard boats. Her eyes had now fully adjusted to the darkness and the drop below her was clear to see. The surf rose and tumbled. She pulled herself closer to the ladder, closing her eyes and trying to think of anything other than that cold, black sea.

An image of her mum at a swimming gala came to mind. She had a scarf tied in her hair, which had been a favourite style of hers when they were younger. She was standing in the midst of all the other parents, shouting Bonnie's name with a wide-eyed Clara by her side. Clara never missed the chance to cheer her big sister on. Bonnie recalled feeling mortified at the time. How embarrassing that your mum was the only one jumping up and down and screaming. She had worried that her friends would make fun of her or, worse still, make fun of her mum. Bonnie swallowed back the tears. Mum had always been their biggest fan and if she was here now, she'd be saying, don't panic, take your time, you can do it. Just find the key, that's all you have to do.

Find the key.

The thought had her opening her eyes. Maybe she should go back in once she had retrieved it. She could get food and water then come back out to find help later, even jump in the water and swim for help. The idea of staying outside until sunrise had seemed so logical before she had been here in the slimy, cold reality of it.

She couldn't see a key or any box that might house one. She looked at the rungs above and beneath her, seeing nothing other than dark slimy metal and smooth concrete behind. She strained her eyes against the darkness to see if there was a hook attached to the wall. But every time she thought she saw something promising it turned out to be nothing more than a shadow or a stain.

She was about to give up and climb down to consult with Charlie when something caught her eye, something above, where the ladder was fixed to the wall. Hope lifted her spirits and made her feel brave. She moved up another rung to look more closely and then she froze. Was it her imagination or had the ladder just shifted under her? She stayed there, her body tense and still. She hadn't imagined it, she felt sure. The ladder had definitely moved. There was a container of some kind attached to the top rung, if only she could reach it.

A weird buzzing noise caught her attention. She could just hear it above the sound of the waves. Something man-made. She turned her head one way and then the other while keeping the rest of her body as still as possible. When she looked to the right she knew her hope of staying hidden out here until help came was foiled. The drone hovered a few feet away, watching her.

Bonnie stared into its camera wondering what to do. Retrieve the key and go back in to give everyone the chance of food and water, or wait here and hope this drone had no capacity to prevent her from calling for help.

She thought of Clara watching her at home, no doubt chewing her nails as she willed Bonnie to go on. It was all she needed to get her moving again. Only four more rungs to go.

As soon as Bonnie placed her foot on the next rung and

shifted her weight upwards she knew she'd made a mistake. There was no imagining the shift in the ladder this time. It jerked backwards away from the wall with a horrible scraping sound. Bonnie tried to stay as still as she could but the ladder jerked backwards again, and then again. She had time to look up and see that the top was no longer attached to the wall. There was no time to climb back down. The ladder fell hard and fast, throwing her feet free as it jarred to a stop when the bottom fixings held. Her hands still gripped on to the rung but there was no time for her to feel any relief or hope. She was already slipping and no amount of physical or mental effort was going to be any match for gravity in that moment.

No. No. Please.

Time seemed to slow down as her fingers slipped bit by bit. When she finally fell the wind whipped at her hair and clothes. She thought about the scene in *Die Hard* where Alan Rickman's character falls from the top of the building. She had always wondered how they had done that.

Nothing Is What It Seems

70

'I said to Phil you can't keep doing this. It's unfair. What kind of life is it for me never knowing if you're going to be around or not?'

'I don't know how you cope, Luce. I'd have kicked him into touch years ago.'

'You can't when you've got kids, can you?'

'He's not their real dad, though, is he?'

'As close as anyone could be. He's been in Dougie's life since he was two. He doesn't know any other dad.'

Bonnie heard the conversation in the distance as if the women stood at the other end of a tunnel.

'Hey, Luce, I think she's waking up.'

'Well, hello there. It's about time you showed up.'

Bonnie's eyes flickered open and she caught glimpses of two smiling faces hovering above her. She felt someone messing with her arm and tried to move it away but couldn't. Her body wouldn't respond.

'Go and get Aksha,' someone said.

'What?' Bonnie's mouth felt sawdust dry and her throat was on fire. She became aware of a tube in her nose.

'Let me get you some water.'

The woman lifted Bonnie's head very gently and put a

straw to her lips. Bonnie took a small sip. As soon as the room-temperature water hit her mouth, her body took over, sucking large gulps through the straw until the woman pulled it away.

'Take it easy. There's plenty here.'

Bonnie stared at the woman. She had kind eyes and a large smile. Her badge read LUCY BRIDGES and Bonnie had no doubt she was good at her job. But she knew nothing. Water was precious and necessary and should never, *ever* be taken for granted. Lucy Bridges should be grateful she'd never had to survive for days on end in a hothouse with only the smallest drops to go around.

The fortress.

Bonnie moved herself to sit up as an older woman in a white blouse and smart blue trousers entered the room.

'You have to get them out. Has anyone got them out?'

The new woman swapped a look with Lucy Bridges.

'Hello, my name is Dr Aksha Syed. How are you feeling?'

'Did everyone get out?'

'Were there others with you?'

'Yes, a group of us. Are they OK? What about Jacko?'

'What were you travelling in? Who was bringing you?'

Bonnie frowned at the doctor. 'We weren't travelling anywhere.'

'She sounds English,' said Lucy.

'Where are you from, what country?'

'I *am* English. Why? Where am I?'

The doctor looked at Lucy again. 'You're on the Isle of Wight. We assumed you'd been crossing the Channel.'

They thought she was a migrant.

'No, I swam as far as I could towards the lights. I just kept swimming until . . . I don't know; I can't remember.'

'Swam from where?'

'The fortress. The sea fort. The escape room show on Channel Five. It isn't real. I mean it isn't what it looks like. Someone died, another was dying. Please tell me they all got out.'

Bonnie looked from the doctor to the nurse; their blank expressions bringing a churn of dread to her stomach.

71

The young police officer looked sceptical. It irritated Bonnie that he was here alone. Weren't they supposed to go every-where in pairs? Had she been fobbed off with some rookie trainee? He didn't look much older than Clara.

'A TV show, you say.'

'Yes. Channel Five. It's on now. You should be able to find it on-demand.'

The officer wrote something in his notebook.

'Look, do you have a phone? You can check it now and see who's still OK.'

'You told the doctor that you had been thrown into the sea from a ladder that was attached to the exterior wall?'

'Yes. I climbed about halfway up but then the thing gave way.'

The officer raised an eyebrow. 'And why were you climbing this ladder?'

'It was part of the game. It was a challenge we had to do to fetch a key.' She had been through this twice already, once with the doctor and once with this very officer when he first arrived. 'I don't want to tell you how to do your job, but this is an emergency. Russ already died and Jacko was in a really bad way. I can only assume Charlie is trapped now, too.

You have to get someone there quickly. The coastguard or something.'

'The coastguard only responds to an immediate threat to life.'

'This *is* an immediate threat to life! Didn't you hear me?'

'But you can't give me the full name of the man who died, or the other one?'

'Is there someone more senior I can talk to?'

The officer glared at his notebook. When he left, she assumed he'd gone to call or radio for someone else to come, but a little while later he returned with the doctor.

'Is there a more senior officer coming?' she said, not bothering to rein in her irritation.

'Bonnie, I am still struggling to reach your sister, Clara, but I have left messages for her to call me back,' Dr Aksha said as she entered the room again. As Bonnie had been found with no identification on her there had been no opportunity for the hospital to contact her sister before now.

'The officer here asked me to come and speak to you because he was concerned by something you said.' Dr Aksha sat in the chair by the bed while the officer remained standing with his hands on his belt. 'You mentioned to him that you originally left Portsmouth Harbour on Tuesday fifth September and that by the time you fell into the sea one of the gentlemen on the sea fort with you had already passed away and another was in a disorientated state. Is that correct?'

'Yes. And Charlie, the girl I entered the escape room with, will be trapped too now.'

'And the people left on there have no access to food or water?' Dr Aksha had previously told Bonnie they'd assumed she was a migrant not only due to where she was found but also because of how she looked. She was emaciated and clearly suffering the physical effects of hunger and dehydration.

Bonnie had explained as best she could the conditions they'd all been kept in.

'I needed to find a key to open the next cupboard of supplies, so they'll have nothing left apart from . . .'

'Apart from what?'

'The water in the toilet.'

The door opened and Lucy the nurse came in. 'The sister called us back. She's on her way here.' She looked at the officer. 'She confirmed Bonnie had been away recording a reality TV show.'

The officer blinked and turned away. He paused for a long moment, then let out a sigh and withdrew his radio. 'Officer four-two-six-three requesting an urgent check on the nearest two sea forts by the coastguard, please.'

72

'What are we looking for, again?' Danny Grieves had been with HM Coastguard for over twenty-five years. He was fit for his age and proud of his job. He had personally saved more lives than he could remember and facilitated the arrest of many a trafficker. He was a man who did not suffer fools.

'Some woman in the hospital reckons they're recording a reality show on one of these and someone died.' Danny's colleague Steph Barnett was the kind of woman that even he wouldn't mess with, despite the fact she was half his age. She was a cross between his mother and his primary-school headmistress.

'Bloody kids. Like we've got time to race around after their idiot ideas. Some TikTok prank gone wrong. These places are dangerous. They've been deserted for years.'

The first of the four sea forts in the Solent rose high above them; a huge grey and black cylinder rising out of the waves like something from *Godzilla*. Danny loved them. They were an awesome illustration of the power of British engineering and he always felt awed by their presence whenever he came up close to them.

The boat pulled up by the docking area. Danny zipped up his coat against the cold – the temperature had really dropped this week – then he jumped off the boat and secured it with one of the thick ropes. Steph followed him with a quick wave to their driver.

They both climbed the ladder up to the main deck.

'Looks deserted,' said Steph.

Danny stood still outside the open door into what had once been a pretty cool hotel. 'Yeah, but what's that smell?'

Steph came a bit closer to where he stood and inhaled deeply. She didn't say a word but when she looked at him her eyes said, *Oh shit.*

73

'There's something I need to tell you, Bonnie, and it might be upsetting.' Dr Aksha shifted in her chair. Lucy and the police officer had left the room again. 'You were found washed on to a small shale beach here on the island on September sixteenth, ten days or so after you went to the sea fort.'

Ten days? It had felt like a lifetime.

'The thing is—'

'Sorry, Dr Syed, we need you in room three.' A male nurse stood in the doorway.

'I'll be back as soon as I can.' She stood and left the room.

Sitting alone in the safety of the hospital, waiting for her sister to arrive, it took her a few moments to realize that this feeling was happiness. Relief at being away from that place, of not having the threat of heatstroke or dehydration hanging over her, felt like a freedom she had never experienced. And although she'd never admit this to anyone, she also felt proud. Really fricking proud that she had put a stop to the whole sick process. Now the police would catch the bastard and throw him in jail, see how he liked it.

When she had landed in the freezing seawater, she had sunk so deep she thought she'd never make it back to the surface before running out of breath, but she had. As she'd emerged from the surf and taken her first few gasps of air, she'd heard Charlie screaming Clara's name. She'd almost called back, almost reassured the group that she was OK, but then she heard the buzz of the drone. It was close to the wall of the fort, searching the water. Bonnie took a long, deep breath and slowly sank under the surface again. She needed to stay quiet and play dead. It was her only chance of saving everyone. She swam underwater and away from the fort, towards the lights she had briefly seen in the distance. When she ran out of breath, she resurfaced slowly, only raising her head high enough to take another deep breath. Portsmouth harbour was ahead of her, closer than she remembered, the lights bright as if to guide her back. She had always been a strong swimmer, even competing for the county as a school-girl. It had to be at least a mile but that wasn't beyond her, especially if the currents were on her side. She simply needed to pace herself. There was a long way to go and she was weak and tired.

She sank under the surface again and began her long, lonely swim.

74

Danny led the way into the building with Steph close behind.

The hotel looked much the same as it had when this place was open. The large Union Flag still hung in the entrance hall and inside the room to the right large brown leather chairs surrounded low tables and shipping memorabilia filled the shelves. The curved brick ceiling hinted at the skill and patience of the men who had built the place. Everything was intact and in its place and yet drenched in a smell that made no sense.

The door leading straight ahead and out to the inner courtyard was wide open.

'Right, let's move at pace and make an initial sweep, top to bottom. We'll go out here first then do inside. Agreed?'

'Yup.' Steph followed him out into the fresh air.

'Someone was paranoid about security,' said Steph, pointing to the number of cameras attached to the walls. 'I wouldn't stay in a hotel that had that many eyes on, would you?'

The blustery wind whipped up the seawater, creating the sensation of rain and causing Danny to raise his voice to be heard.

'I don't think they're CCTV. They have microphones attached.' Danny moved around closer and looked up at the camera. It looked like some fancy kit. Not something a group of kids would have used to record a TikTok video. Danny continued on to a set of steps up to the lighthouse deck while Steph went to explore the other raised areas.

After a few minutes they met again back at the door to the inside.

'Anything?'

'There's a full hot tub up there. Water looks fresh, too.'

Danny nodded. 'Evidence of people eating and drinking up here. There were glasses and plates washed by the sink and crumbs on the tables, plus some dry foods in the cupboards and bottles of beer, wine and champagne in the bin.'

'So someone has been here recently.'

'It's like they just up and left.'

They walked quickly back into the main building and that smell hit Danny again. It was acrid and strong.

'You go right, I'll go left.'

Danny walked through to the Victory Bar area. A few yards in he noted a small black card stuck to the wall with the letter H printed on it and what looked to be its Morse code counterpart. A similar card for the letter V was stuck to the window and a third was on the opposite wall for the letter J. On a chair in front of the bar a wooden polar bear toy had been left with its head down and its bum in the air. Danny felt his senses sharpen. Were there kids here? He'd been on shift the day they'd found a whole family deceased in a sister hotel to this one. Carbon monoxide poisoning, apparently. He felt the same dread in the pit of his stomach as he had that day and he did not like it one bit.

Further on, he came to the first of the bedrooms. There were clothes discarded on the bed and a pair of men's trainers by the door. The bed hadn't been made.

'Danny!' Steph rushed up from behind him. 'You need to see this.'

He followed her back to the entrance and then into the other side of the building, past dining tables and chairs, obviously used, and on to the hallway beyond.

'Basement Door One,' she said, reading the sign. 'This is where the woman in hospital said we'd find everyone.'

Danny pushed against the door but it didn't budge. There were no locks or handles.

'I think it's electronically controlled.' Steph pointed at a small square object attached to the wall. 'Like office doors.'

'I don't like the look of this.' The smell was strongest here. 'Fetch us the crowbar and call it in. We might need the brigade for this.'

'Got it,' called Steph.

While she was gone, Danny checked the areas near by.

He came to a small room with a fireplace and a small writing desk. As he entered he saw a large red armchair with a shape slumped in it. He stepped closer, feeling a familiar heat in his chest and ears. He had seen many an emergency in his days but he never stopped reacting in the same way.

'Hello?'

There was no answer. The woman was naked. Her body was slumped to the left and her head hung low over her chest.

Danny moved closer still, hoping she was sleeping but knowing that was unlikely. He knew the drill – check for a response, open airway, check breathing and circulation. But she wasn't unconscious, either. She wasn't alive. In fact she never had been.

Steph returned, crowbar in hand.

'Oh crap.'

'It's OK, it's a dummy,' Danny said. 'One of them Resusci Annes – the dolls used to train people how to administer CPR.'

'Who would leave that there?'

Danny shook his head in answer as he leaned closer and read the small text written on the plastic woman's stomach.

Smile, you're on camera.

Danny looked up at the ceiling to find a camera pointing right at him, its small green light shining.

'Give me that bar, we need to get down there. Now.'

75

'The thing is, we think you hit your head either as you climbed on to the shore or just before. It was a bad injury which caused your brain to swell.' Dr Aksha Syed was back, sitting in the chair again with the concerned look on her face. 'So we had to make sure the swelling reduced and the best way to do that was to put you into a medically induced coma. It's quite normal. It allows the brain to recover more quickly. Do you understand?'

Bonnie understood only too well. This was why the police officer was reacting so slowly to her pleas.

'How long was I asleep?'

'Eight days.'

'Eight . . .?'

Bonnie felt tears rolling down her cheeks.

76

'No, you don't understand. It was broadcasting while we were in there.' Bonnie was desperately scrolling through the search results on Clara's phone. All she had found so far were the same promotional pitches that had caused Clara to apply in the first place. *The Fortress: are you smart enough to unlock its secrets?*

She had searched My5, the Channel 5 on-demand website, numerous times and each visit brought no results and a fresh determination to find the episodes. 'People were commenting on what we were doing, talking about us on social media, mentioning us by name. It has to be here.' She looked under the Popular, Entertainment and Real Lives categories. Then she searched for 'The Fortress', 'Fortress' and 'Escape Room' but found nothing: no episodes, no trailers, not even the smallest hint of a show coming soon.

Clara's worried expression had deepened. She was no longer concerned for her sister's physical health; she was scared for her sanity.

'I swear to God,' Bonnie said as she opened Clara's Twitter app and once more searched for 'The Fortress', 'Channel 5' and reality TV hashtags. The results were many but none of them about the show. She next searched for a combination of their names but again could find nothing. *What was happening?*

There was no reference to *The Fortress* on any other social media platform beyond the promo messages.

'They said it was a five-week filming process.' It was not the first time Clara had said this and her voice was less insistent now. She was simply stating a fact with a degree of impatience.

Bonnie looked up from the phone for the first time in hours. Her eyes struggled to adjust and her sister looked blurry and distant.

'People were voting on who should play next. Who should be punished next. Who should die.'

'No one died, Bonnie.' Clara took her hand and smiled in an infuriatingly patronizing way. 'You've had a head injury. You've been in a coma. None of this is real. It's your imagination.'

Bonnie rested her head back on the pillow and stared at the ceiling. *Could that be right?* Pain pulsated behind her temples and she remembered the feeling of sitting in the heat with music screaming into her ears. She remembered the hunger gnawing at her insides and that primal need for water that had her standing over the toilet basin on more than one occasion, willing herself to walk away but being unable to move her feet. The memories were vivid and sensory. She had not imagined this. It wasn't like a dream which fades when you try to focus on it. It was seared into her brain.

But what if it was closer to a hallucination or a delusion? She knew from her studies that some people report such things as multi-sensory. Was she losing her mind?

77

'Shouldn't we wait for the fire brigade?' said Steph.

Danny placed the back of his hand against the door as they were trained to do if they suspected a fire. 'That's stone cold. Feel it. And I saw a toy out here so there may be kids down there.'

Steph placed the back of her hand against the metal and nodded.

Danny used the crowbar to prise open the metal door as quickly as he could. The smell of smoke hit him when he broke through but the fire was long since out, because there was no heat, only the scent of its aftermath.

'Take care,' he said to Steph as he moved slowly down the stairs.

'Shouldn't we wait?'

'I've put my gloves on. I won't touch anything. I just need to see.' It was a sentiment he would reflect on many times in the weeks that followed. Why on earth he'd been so keen to see. It was clear nothing could be done. The walls were scorched black and the metal handrail on the stairs had buckled like it was made of rubber.

At the bottom of the steps his torch illuminated a small passage that curved away from the bottom of the stairs in

314

both directions. At regular intervals he spotted the mangled remnants of cameras. Had this really been some sort of TV show? If so, someone had messed up big time. He came to a locked door on the inner wall, but there was a thin opening where a metal cover had melted and broken away. Danny shone his torch inside and slowly moved the beam around the space.

'Jesus.'

He had seen something similar once before on a trip to Pompeii, where the reconstructed bodies of those who had died in the volcanic eruption were on show, many of them curled into a foetal position, just like the poor soul who had been trapped in here.

78

The young police officer entered as Clara reached for the remote and turned up the TV volume.

'Ah, maybe I should speak to you first,' he said, but both Clara and Bonnie were focused on the image of the sea fort on the BBC news.

'Police uncovered the tragic scene earlier today after receiving a tip that a group of youngsters had been attempting to film an amateur reality TV show on the deserted fort. A fire appears to have broken out, trapping the group in the basement. Police have yet to confirm the number of deceased, but they have said there is only one survivor.'

'Oh shit,' said Clara.

'We weren't youngsters. Everyone was above twenty-one.'

'Everyone died.' Clara's eyes were wide and scared.

'Who is the survivor?' Bonnie asked the officer, desperate for the answer to be Jacko, or Maria or Dennis or Charlie. Any of them, in fact.

'That would be you, Bonnie.'

Bonnie stared at him in disbelief. Someone else had to have survived because that's what he'd said. *Only one survives.*

The truth of things dawned on her slowly as she watched the aerial footage of the sea fort. Her escape hadn't saved them. It had doomed them to their fate.

79

Expect the Unexpected Podcast
Season 2, Episode 1: 'The Fortress'

'To summarize, listeners, we know what ultimately happened to Bonnie's fellow contestants on The Fortress. *What we don't know is who set the whole thing up and why he thought the contestants deserved to suffer for their sins.'*

'No one deserves that. What happened to them was disgusting. There's no point trying to rationalize a sick person's mind.'

'But can someone be sick and get away with it? I'd expect clues and evidence to have been left everywhere if this was an irrational, disorganized person.'

'You don't have to worry too much about evidence when you torch the place, do you?'

'But he didn't torch the whole place. He left the two upper decks intact. I agree it would have been easier to destroy them too and I'm wondering why he left them. It was a big risk. So I'm thinking, is it a clue? Is this guy still playing? Did the police tell you anything about what they found there?'

'Not much. It's all part of an active investigation so they can't share many details. They did tell me there was evidence the other members of the group had completed more challenges. More of them were locked in rooms when the fire started.'

'Did you look into what they might have had to do?'

'No, like I said, I couldn't bring myself to. It was too painful.'

'Do you mind my summarizing the punishments for the remaining sins in Dante's description now? It might help our listeners understand who might have had the capacity to do this.'

'Sure. If it helps.'

'Well, the first thing to say is Charlie and yourself were very lucky because Dante's envy requires having your eyes sewn shut with wire and all you had to do was climb in the dark. Perhaps because it's hard to wire people's eyes shut remotely.'

'I'm not sure anyone would say Charlie and I were lucky.'

'You survived. That strikes me as pretty lucky.

'So the sins we have left after that are avarice, lust and pride. The punishment for avarice requires lying on the floor, face down with your hands and feet tied, and pride requires carrying large weights.'

'And lust? Dare I ask what that requires?'

'Running through flames.'

'Really? So . . . might something have gone wrong with that one hence the fire?'

'I don't think so. I spoke to an old contact in the force who confirmed the fire was started with accelerant pumped in via the sprinkler system. I think it was always intended to be the finale. Remember that sign you said was inside both doors to the basement, DEDUCE NOT?'

'Of course. They were plastic signs, unlike the metal ones.'

'So he put them there on purpose as a clue. We think it's a play on words because another way of saying deduce not would be infer not, or, more specifically—'

'Inferno.'

'As in the name Dante gave to hell. I think he always intended for the sinners to burn in the fires of hell.'

'Like I said, this is the work of a sick person.'

'And like I said, you were very lucky. I don't think you were supposed to escape with your life.'

'It should have been Charlie. If she'd climbed the ladder, she'd be the one sitting here now.'

'Have you had any contact with her family – or any of the families for that matter?'

'A little. I reached out to Jacko's mum because he'd asked me to give her a message. That was hard because I'd told him there would never be any need for me to do it, and yet there I was sitting in her kitchen relaying the words of her dead son. It was pretty horrific. And then there was Grant's dad, who was pretty furious when we had a Zoom call.'

'Furious with you?'

'Uh-huh. Nothing direct, you know, but a lot of statements along the lines of "Why didn't you check where you were swimming to?" I think he thought if I'd not got confused and swum to the Isle of Wight, I might have been successful in raising the alarm or getting spotted by a boat. He also asked why I didn't insist Grant went into that room with Charlie, because he was an excellent swimmer. That kind of thing. He was just upset. He feels like all of us do: we want to turn back the clock.'

'Do you wish you hadn't spoken to the families, then?'

'No, not at all. It was only right that I did it. They all wanted to know as much as possible about the last days of their loved ones. And, actually, Maria's brother was lovely. He thanked me for trying to raise the alarm and said it wasn't my fault, that Maria would have been proud of me for trying. That was nice to hear.'

'I'm interested to know if you reached out to Jaide's family, given your relationship with her.'

'I asked the police to pass on my contact details to all the families but I've received no response from Jaide's. It might come later, though. Everyone grieves differently, don't they?'

'It does strike me that whoever did this had a real anger towards you all. Do you think that was because of something specific you had done?'

'I can't speak for the others, but I know for a fact that my sister Clara never did anything to inspire that kind of cruelty.'

'What sin did she have?'

'I . . . I don't know, actually.'

'You said Jacko thought he'd been assigned wrath because of what he'd admitted about not standing up for his mum, so what did Clara write on her application?'

'I don't know. We've not discussed it.'

'Really? Why not?'

'I didn't want her to know what could have happened to her, or have her feel guilty about what happened to me.'

'Yeah, I can understand that. It would be helpful for us to know what she wrote, though, don't you think? It might give us a clue to why Clara was selected.'

80

'Hey, how goes the podcast?' Clara said on answering the phone. 'What's Shane Fletcher like in person?'

'He's nice. It's really helping to talk it all through, actually. To get a bit of perspective on it. I think that's what I needed. Shane's team has been doing some research and have some extra insights, which are also useful. I don't think they'll crack the case, but it's good to have some more people working on it.' Bonnie sat in a small room down the hall from where they had been recording, with a tragic-looking cheese salad sandwich someone had bought for her, made by a brand she'd never heard of. It was nice to have a break. Her head had started to ache and she felt exhausted.

'Definitely. I love his podcasts. Do you remember that jewellery thief who broke into that singer's house? I don't remember her name. She was one of the ones Mum liked. Not Madonna, but that kind of era. Do you remember?'

'Vaguely, yeah.'

'Anyway, his podcast led to new witnesses coming forward and the guy being convicted.'

'Are you sure people won't judge me for talking about it?'

'Sis, how many times have we been over this? You're doing the right thing and it's really brave. Sure, some people will get off on the juicy details but most will want to help if they can. Most real-crime listeners would love to solve a case.'

'OK, well, I need a favour, then.'

'Anything.'

'Do you remember what you wrote on the application form? We think maybe people were assigned their sin because of their answers. Any chance you can tell me what you might have said?'

'I can do better than that. I saved a copy. I'll send it to you now.'

Bonnie ate the horrible sandwich while she waited for Clara's email. One of the consequences of the fortress experience was that she couldn't leave food uneaten. It was like her brain was on a mission to ensure starvation was never again a possibility. She needed to up her exercise regime as her calorie intake was off the scale.

Of all the memories stirred up by the podcast, sitting in Jacko's mum's kitchen was the most emotional. It was the moment when the whole thing had become real. She had stared at the picture of Jacko stuck to his mum's fridge. It was a close-up of him with his head flung back in laughter and his freckles out in force. It must have been taken in the summer, maybe even his last summer before he entered the fortress. Had it been on her fridge for a while or had his mum put it there after her son's death?

His mum was petite and nice-looking for a mum-aged woman. Her blonde hair had hints of Jacko's mousy brown when she ran her fingers through it, which was frequently. Bonnie figured it was an anxiety habit.

They had talked for a few hours, laughed even at points, and Bonnie couldn't help but wonder if things had ended differently would she have been introduced to this woman as Jacko's friend, or even his girlfriend? There had been a spark between them and some fun banter right to the end. He was just the sort of guy she would have loved to have had as a partner.

She had passed on Jacko's message as sensitively as she could. Obviously no one had seen the footage of his admission about his mum taking regular beatings from his dad, so the impetus for his mum to get out was not what Jacko had imagined. Bonnie didn't want to reveal what Jacko had endured, so she simply said he'd confided in her that he felt guilty for not standing up to his dad more. Jacko's mum had changed the subject, moved from the table, offered more coffee – anything to avoid the conversation – but Bonnie had promised, so she'd had to say the next bit. And so with his mum standing at the kettle avoiding eye contact, she had told her that when they realized they might not ever get out of that place, he'd said he wished he could speak to his mum one last time to tell her to leave and be safe. Bonnie had watched the tears fall down Jacko's mum's cheeks and be quickly wiped away as the front door unlocked and her husband entered.

Bonnie had not stayed long after that. She had no interest in spending any time in the company of a wife beater, even if he did come over as friendly and considerate; the practised façade of a police officer no doubt.

Shaking the memories away, Bonnie opened Clara's email and the attachment.

The first few questions asked for biographical details such as age, education and jobs, followed by the request for five strengths and five flaws, and then the critical section. *What dark secrets have you kept locked away from the world?* It asked specifically for what people were most ashamed of and what they secretly desired above all else. Underneath, in italics, it read: *Answers will be treated in confidence so please be honest*

324

and truthful. The show relies on contestants knowing the value of keeping secrets.

Bonnie read it again. It was basically saying, *If you want to get on this show, tell me something embarrassing or damning. Something I can use against you.*

81

***Expect the Unexpected* Podcast**
Season 2, Episode 1: 'The Fortress'

'Over the past few weeks we've been asking our listeners to send in questions for you. Would it be OK to go through a few of them now?'

'Sure.'

'People are fascinated. Are you all right?'

'Fine.'

'We can take a longer break if you need to? I can edit out anything we say here. You look upset.'

'No, it's OK. I've just been reading through my sister's application form and it's a bit . . . confusing, but we can discuss that later. Let's do the questions.'

'Are you sure?'

'Yes.'

'Great. The first question from Gracie in Swindon follows on from our last discussion. She asks: do you regret taking your sister's place on The Fortress?'

'Not at all. I'd hate for Clara to have suffered any of that. I think any sibling would.'

'*Do you think you fared better than Clara would have? That's my question.*'

'I've no idea. Maybe. But people would have liked her more.'

'*Harry in Dundee asks: when were you first suspicious that this was not a real show?*'

'I was never suspicious that the TV show wasn't real. It was a shock when I came out. I spent hours searching for it on Channel Five and on social media. I was absolutely convinced it was being broadcast because of the public comments that we were reading every day.'

'*But these were fake.*'

'It must have taken hours to produce them all. None of us thought to question them. In fact, people like Charlie were really hurt by what was being said. It's awful to think she never knew that it was just one nasty person and not the views of the general public. I think she was scared to leave that place on some level, expecting she'd be hated by everyone. It was another kind of mental torture that was going on.'

'*Were you being tested, do you think?*'

'No, I don't think it was that clever. It was divisive and cruel because whoever did this gets a kick out of watching people suffer.'

'*From what you said, it also fired up arguments over Jacko's admission about not protecting his mum.*'

'Absolutely. There were some awful things tweeted, which allowed Grant and Jaide to air their own prejudice. And the treatment of Maria was horrid. The pictures making fun of her weight and her hair. It was childish and designed to cause pain. If it was the general public I could kind of excuse it as people being ill-informed or lashing out because of some personal unhappiness, but this was one person making all of them feel self-conscious and anxious. It was an attempt to weaken our spirits and make us all more vulnerable.'

'*You were largely spared, though, weren't you?*'

'Not entirely, but I didn't get attacked like some of the others.'

'*Why is that?*'

'I'm not sure. Maybe because I kept my head down a bit, especially in the first few days, because I was worried about pretending to be Clara. Maybe I simply didn't come over as very interesting.'

'*Until you argued with Jaide?*'

'I suppose.'

'*There's been a lot of speculation online that you were a group of people creating your own TikTok show because of some of the earlier media messaging. We know that wasn't the case, but you said earlier that the final secret suggested one of you might be in on it. Saffy from Grange-over-Sands asks: do you think the person or persons responsible for this were on the fort with you?*'

'When we were discussing the *Only one of you survives* message, I thought perhaps it was hinting that one of us was complicit and would therefore be the sole survivor. But now I've thought about it, it doesn't make sense. I'm the only survivor, after all.'

'*Are you sure?*'

'How do you mean?'

'*The police haven't revealed how many bodies they found, only that you're the sole survivor. This is why I asked you about contacting the families. You said you gave your details to the police to pass on, but not everyone's family got back to you.*'

'Well, yes, but not everyone wants all the details, do they?'

'So you don't think one of you could have been involved?'

'Bonnie?'

'Do you know how many bodies they found?'

'I don't think the police will release that information until they're ready.'

'That's not what I asked. Do *you* know? Has one of your contacts told you? Is that why they're not confirming who died? You have to tell me. You can stop recording or edit it out, like you said, but you have to tell me. I need to know.'

'I think we should take another break. You're getting upset. I'll get you some water.'

'You do know, don't you? What are you not telling me? Who else survived?'

82

Shane left the room to fetch water without answering her question. She knew he wouldn't want to reveal anything that might jeopardize the investigation, but she didn't care. She needed to know. He had police contacts and he knew something.

She checked her phone and saw she'd had six missed calls from Clara and a text which read: CALL ME. NOW!

'I think someone else survived,' Bonnie said as soon as Clara answered. 'And I think Shane knows who but won't tell me. What do I do? Should I call the police and ask them? Why has no one said anything to me about this? They put everyone's picture in the papers so it implied everyone died, but they never said that. They only said these are the people who went *into* the fortress.'

'Bonnie?'

'This is crazy, Clara. If someone else survived, that means they must have been in on it with the Director. Shit, they might even *be* the Director. Do you know there was a secret passage that went around part of the basement? Shane told me. What if they used that to move around or hide supplies for themselves? They could have been controlling the whole thing and we would never have known.'

'BONNIE!'

'What?'

'The show is out.'

'What show?'

'*The Fortress*. It was released on the internet this morning. The first episode.'

'How? Who by? Channel Five?'

'No. Of course not. Channel Five had nothing to do with it. They've been quite clear about that since this all hit the media.'

'So who?'

'The monster who made it, I expect.'

'Have you seen it? What's in it?'

'I watched a bit, yes, but then I've been trying to get in touch with you.'

'He's not planning to release it all, is he?' It made her feel sick to think people might watch Russ and Jacko suffering, and surely he wouldn't broadcast the fire? She had a memory of standing with Russ as the group read their first social media comments. She had found him irritating at that point, judged him for being lazy and fake. She wished she could go back and say something nice to him, ask about his family or his life. It transpired he was married with twin boys. A picture of his wife being consoled on a visit to Portsmouth Harbour had been in the news a few weeks ago. 'Someone will shut it down, won't they?'

'I don't know. It's all over the internet.'

Oh God. People would see her losing it and arguing with Grant and Jaide. Grant's father really would hate her then. She hadn't realized how relieved she'd been that no one had seen what had happened in that place. She'd been able to frame it her own way, leave out any bits that she felt really uncomfortable about. Even in this podcast she knew she had made herself sound better than she really had been, more balanced

331

and fair, when in reality there were times when she'd been irrational and unreasonable.

'Did I come over OK?'

'You weren't in the bits I watched. Do you want me to watch it all for you and see?'

Bonnie wanted to say yes because she couldn't bear to watch it herself, and Clara was the person she trusted most in the world, but then she remembered what she'd told Shane only minutes ago, that she wanted to shield Clara from what had happened in there.

'No, it won't be nice. Promise me.'

'I'm not sure I can. I think I need to know. I did this to you, after all.'

'No, you did not. This is not on you. It's on him. You entered it in good faith and couldn't have known what was coming.' Clara was quiet on the other end of the line. As Shane entered the room again with two glasses of water, Bonnie said, 'Is it true what you said on your form? The secret you'd kept?'

'Yeah. I'm sorry.'

83

Bonnie immediately began searching the internet when Clara hung up. Within a few clicks she had opened YouTube and was watching the opening credits to *The Fortress*.

'He's released the first episode.'

'Yes. We know. The team have been watching it.'

'Why would he do that?'

'I expect it's what he was planning all along. You were told it was a five-week recording process, which meant plenty of time to clear up and clear out before anyone became suspicious. Then, when the coast was clear, broadcast it.'

'To show off his crime?'

'Or his achievement.'

'Achievement?'

Shane placed his headphones on and adjusted his microphone.

Bonnie wanted to leave. She needed to see the footage. But she also wanted to know what Shane knew.

'Before we start, can we discuss who else survived?'

'Well, things have changed.'

'How do you mean?'

'Something has been bugging me this whole time. Why eight contestants? You have been very clear that this whole game was based on the deadly sins, the *seven* deadly sins. So why eight contestants?'

'Because one will survive.'

'But surely all contestants need to be tested? Shouldn't it be one in seven that survives? And this got me thinking that maybe one of your group wasn't a genuine contestant. And now we have the first episode released and you know what's odd?'

'What's that?'

'There are only seven contestants.'

'That can't be right. There were eight of us: me, Dennis, Maria, Charlie, Russ, Grant, Jaide and Jacko.'

'Bonnie, why did you agree to this interview?'

'What do you mean?'

'I mean, was there something you wanted to tell me? To tell the audience? Something you've been hiding?'

Bonnie sat in stunned silence as Shane began recording again.

84

Expect the Unexpected Podcast
Season 2, Episode 1: 'The Fortress'

'Well, we have something of a first here on Expect the Unexpected, listeners. A break in the case has occurred during my interview with Bonnie Drake, the sole survivor of The Fortress. At ten a.m. this morning, episode one of The Fortress was released online. People across the country, and probably around the world, have been watching the doomed contestants arrive and undertake their first few challenges with no idea what was to come.

'No doubt you'll have all watched it by the time you listen to this, so I know you'll be wanting me to ask one critical question.

'Bonnie Drake, why are you not in the episode?'

'I beg your pardon?'

'It shows everything from the group working out how to get into the building and completing the Morse code challenge, to making the initial nominations and doing the escape room duel. These are all things you have told us about today, but you are nowhere to be seen. Why is that?'

'I was there. I helped Jacko unlock the door, I arrived late for the nominations looking rough and hungover. I was there for all of it. It's not possible that I'm not seen.'

'*Wow. That's not the answer I was expecting.*'

'Why? What were you expecting?'

'*That you'd have an explanation.*'

'Such as?'

'*I think we've already established there were most likely two of you doing this.*'

'That's crazy. I had nothing to do with this. You clearly have some insights into the set-up on the fort: the cameras, the automated doors, the heating system. Surely you can't think I'm capable of all that?'

'*You wouldn't be the first person to brag about their crimes or want to control the narrative. What other conclusion is there for people to reach?*'

'That the bastard cut me out to . . . I don't know . . . discredit my account of things or destroy me as a witness.'

'*Did your partner think you were breaking some code of silence by speaking to me? Is that why he betrayed you and released the evidence that you were never there?*'

'I think we should stop the interview here.'

'*Are you sure? Imagine how that will look when this podcast is released.*'

'I don't care.'

'*If you really had nothing to do with it, don't you need to stay and clear your name? You are asserting that you were there as a contestant despite the fact that you can't be seen in episode one. That the real perpetrator has simply cut you out. But there are many other things you have said in our conversation that worry me.*'

'Like what?'

'*At the start you said that everything in that place was a*' clue and you should have paid more attention. Did you mean everything in this interview is a clue?'

'No. I told you: I meant everything about where *The Fortress* was set, how it was designed and the initial challenges we were made to do was telling a story. It's like you said, Charlie was wrong to think that finding a star to open the door was a reference to us all becoming famous, because it was linked to the devil. We were being told we were entering hell.'

'OK, but now we have the footage from the episode, which disputes your recollections.'

'How? How exactly does it dispute what I've said? I wouldn't have come on this podcast if I had anything to do with any of it. That would be stupid.'

'You said in this very interview that it was you who revealed the Morse code sentence: "Calling for help is useless, no one is coming." Is that correct?'

'Yes.'

'And yet we have all just watched Maria do it. How do you explain that?'

Bonnie was thrown, her mind blank for a moment as her anger at being challenged this way clouded her thoughts. It had been her. Charlie had said something far too optimistic about help was coming, no one being useless for calling and then . . .

'I only moved the papers. I didn't say it out loud. I put the words in order and then Maria probably read it aloud.'

'Probably read it aloud?'

'I don't recall. But if you saw her saying it on screen, she must have.'

'Because the footage on screen is fact.'

'I wouldn't go that far. It's a skewed version of the facts.'

'Couldn't we say the same about your account? For

instance, you said that the door to the cellar was open when you returned to your room after the first duel, then on your way back up it was closed. But we only have your word for that? You could be saying that to give the impression someone else was there.'

'Why would I do that?'

'You tell me.'

'That door was open and I knew there was something off about it.'

'You also said you woke a couple of nights later to find Dennis alone in the kitchen just after he'd seen the tweet about Russ suffering.'

'Yes, that's right.'

'How did you know to join him at that specific point?'

'Pardon?'

'You said the tweets were scrolling, so how come you, and only you, just happened to join Dennis a moment or two after he'd seen that tweet?'

'No, the tweets weren't scrolling in the middle of the night. I don't know when Dennis saw them, but they could have been there for hours. A noise woke me up.'

'And yet you were the only person who reacted to that noise and joined Dennis. Isn't that convenient? It seems to me that you were in the midst of key events in a very helpful way.'

'There were only eight of us. I bet everyone's account would put them in the midst of the key events.'

'But no one else is here, are they? So we only have your word for that. Speaking of Dennis, is it not also significant that when he convinced the group to refuse to play, after you were locked in the basement, it was you who talked people around?'

'That's twisting things. I simply couldn't cope with the music and the darkness any more.'

'But even earlier than that, there's the fact that you were

338

singled out by name, or at least Clara's name, to be told the group had unlocked the first secret: that no one leaves. Why were you chosen when by your own admission you'd been keeping a low profile?'

'I don't know. I was standing alone by the screen.'

'So you were picked at random?'

'I expect so.'

'Where was everyone else?'

'Just a few metres away, by Russ's door.'

'But you didn't join them?'

'I did later.'

'Why not then? Why not go and check on his well-being like everyone else? Wasn't that the most important thing happening?'

'Of course, but the corridor wasn't that big. We couldn't all be in one place at the same time.'

'So you've gone from saying, "There were only eight of us," to saying, "There were too many to fit in the space."'

'The space outside Russ's door, yes!'

'You kept your distance from the group a fair bit by the sounds of it. Why was that?'

'I don't think I did. No more than others.'

'You didn't like them much, though, did you? You thought Grant was arrogant, that Charlie was a bimbo, that Russ was a fake, that Jacko betrayed his mother to get on the show, that Dennis and Maria let you down, and then we have Jaide. You really didn't like her, did you? All those scowls she gave you coupled with her aggressive manner and intimidating appearance. You even said you were suspicious she might have been in on it at one stage, and yet you're offended that someone would suggest the same of you.'

'That's not fair. I've not said anything about Jaide that wasn't the truth as I saw it.'

'As you saw it. Well, we did some research about all of you

and do you know what we discovered about Jaide, this rude, aggressive competitor who took against you? She worked for a children's charity, had done for over five years, and she volunteered every weekend at the homeless centre. Her colleagues said she had a massive heart and bags of empathy for those less fortunate than herself. So I'm wondering, why did she take against you?'

'I . . . I don't know. Only she would have known that. I tried to be nice, but she just didn't like me.'

'Hmmm.'

'What does that mean?'

'When you were telling me at the start about how you didn't want to stand in for Clara, you said you'd told her it would ruin your reputation. Do you have a problem with people who go on reality TV shows?'

'No. Look, this isn't fair. None of this is any evidence that I was involved in it.'

'You said you went there in place of your sister because she had broken her leg?'

'Yes.'

'And she had applied to go on the show because following the death of your mother you had defaulted on the mortgage and faced eviction?'

'Correct.'

'So how do you explain why your mortgage company told us there have been no issues related to your account?'

'That . . . that's not true.'

'And when my colleague spoke to the radiographer at the hospital where Clara apparently had her leg placed in a cast, he said he couldn't remember her, even though her face has been everywhere since you escaped The Fortress? *Don't you think that's odd?'*

'Not really. There's probably more than one radiographer.'

'Is it not really the case that you used the story that you were stepping in for Clara to give you an excuse if anyone questioned anything odd in your behaviour or motives?'

'No! She begged me to go on the show for her.'

'And you just did it? Because she begged you? You can see that this sounds a little tenuous, right?'

'It's the truth. I have Clara's application form to prove it and she will back me up on everything.'

'It's hardly watertight, though, is it, the word of your sister?'

'Why are you doing this? I thought you were trying to help me.'

'Would you mind telling our listeners what you do for a living?'

'I expect most people know, it's been in the papers. I'm studying for a PhD.'

'In?'

'Psychology.'

'Is it not true that over the years psychologists have been famous for placing unwitting people in extreme situations just to see how they will react?'

'That's all historical. It's not allowed any more. There are strict codes of ethics to adhere to now.'

'So you can't run these experiments in a university any more?'

'You can't run them anywhere.'

'So if someone were studying, let's say, the impact of psychological distress on performance, a reality TV show would be a good front for that?'

'What are you getting at?'

'I'm getting at the fact that your PhD thesis is titled "The Impact of Psychological Distress on Performance", and The Fortress did exactly that. It set a range of performance tasks both physical and mental and then exposed contestants to all *forms of psychological distress. What's really fascinating, though, is how you selected your contestants, or more importantly* why *you selected them. Because I think that despite your assertion that you don't have a problem with people who go on reality TV, you in fact judge these people to be lesser in some way because they want to be famous or think they are smarter than everyone else. Was it you or your partner in crime who chose to focus on the seven sins? Because I think this came from people who genuinely believed they were serving some greater good. Your PhD might well be the overt reason for this, but covertly I think you wanted to punish the sinful for their sins. You wanted the world to know that people who obsess about fame and fortune are damned. You were making the world listen to the truth of things by sending a clear, unequivocal warning to every person: don't sin. And I think you came on the podcast out of arrogance and some twisted belief that you could spin a tale that confirmed your innocence. But you underestimated me. And I'm going to make sure you pay for what you did.*

'*Thank you for joining us today, listeners. If you enjoyed this episode, please pass it on to others; word of mouth is how we survive and prosper. And remember, we appreciate it when you help those who help us. This month our sponsor is SecureIT. The digital home security system that keeps you safe all day, every day.*

'*I've been Shane Fletcher and this is* Expect the Unexpected, *the podcast that blows your mind with crimes that beggar belief.*'

85

Bonnie's voicemail kicked in again. The interview must have resumed. Clara returned to the episode, moving the little red dot back to the beginning and restarting. It made no sense. Why was Bonnie nowhere to be seen? Not even at the beginning, when they showed the application videos for all the contestants. Clara focused hard on the screen, this time watching for shadows in the background or a flash of Bonnie's hand or clothing. She had to have been there. Why else would she have been found soaking wet and injured on a beach on the Isle of Wight?

The weeks while Bonnie was away had dragged for Clara. She had felt sorry for herself, sitting on the sofa watching dross every evening, feeling jealous at the fun her sister was having. Fun that should have been hers. This had been her chance to prove she was just as smart as Bonnie, publicly to the world, and now everyone was going to be saying how clever Bonnie was – again. It was so unfair.

She had always felt this inner bitterness towards her big sister. Clara would often find Bonnie and their mum whispering something they didn't want her to know, especially when Mum was ill. Even at school, Clara was constantly told by the teachers how clever and polite her sister was. It was a tough act to follow, especially when you weren't so academic and had an actual personality rather than simply doing what everyone wanted you to. Perhaps this bitterness was why she'd sent the application form across to Bonnie earlier without any warning about what she'd written.

Of course, ever since the hospital had called to say Bonnie had been in some kind of accident and then a coma, she'd been feeling really crappy. All those nights she'd felt sorry for herself, Bonnie had been suffering and scared. Clara needed to watch the episode because her imagination about what she had put her sister through was vivid and awful and part of her hoped that reality wouldn't be half so bad.

But this was getting weird now. There were not even any shots of other contestants looking at, or speaking to, someone off camera that could be Bonnie. Clara began to read the comments below the episode.

NicEast 1 hour ago
No sign of the sole survivor Bonnie Drake in this episode. Anyone else think that's odd?

Davecakes765 2 hours ago
How sad to watch these folks playing games without a care. Maria was amazing. Her family should be so proud.

Jojo 32 minutes ago
Who pretends to be part of something so tragic? I think Bonnie needs help. This is another level of attention grabbing.

Cathcart 1 hour ago
People lost their lives. It's sick to say you were there when you weren't. Bonnie Drake will be famous for a whole different reason now.

Clara turned her attention to Twitter, hoping such comments were limited to YouTube. But as she began to read the trending hashtag relating to Bonnie Drake, her heart sank.

Clara slammed the laptop shut. She remembered Bonnie saying that going on the show could ruin her reputation and Clara had thought she was being so dramatic. It was only a stupid show. No one's life gets ruined. But she had been wrong. Oh, so wrong.

She WhatsApped Bonnie, hoping her sister would see the message before reading any of this trash.

Sis, call me ASAP. BEFORE you do anything else.
Promise me xx
14.45

86

Bonnie watched Shane packing up his equipment. A voice in her head screamed for her to say something, *do* something, but she couldn't move. It was like she was back in the basement again, helpless and afraid. She felt hot and clammy, her mouth was dry and her head pounded. This man was going to convict her in public opinion. Even if the police dismissed his theories, this would follow her around for the rest of her life. There's no smoke without fire. People would always wonder.

She should have left as soon as he'd turned on her, but he'd cracked cases before. She wanted to trust that he had a good investigative mind. The Director was obviously trying to diminish her account and that made her so angry. How dare he make out she was never there. How dare he deny her that. He'd killed her friends and ruined her life. She would not let him get away with it. No way.

Shane reached across the desk and took her phone.

'The police asked me to keep hold of this and to make sure you stay here until they arrive.' He sounded angry. He really believed she'd done this and tried to use him and his podcast. It was a whole level of ridiculous that she couldn't begin to comprehend.

He sealed the plastic box in which he'd packed the two

microphones, the recording device and his notes, along with her phone. Then he lifted it off the table.

'For what it's worth, you deserve everything you have coming to you.' There was real venom to his words. Gone was the smile-filled podcast voice.

Bonnie thought about walking out. The door wasn't locked, but the one into the reception had been. Shane had buzzed her in. He'd only stop her there. She may as well wait for the police and try her best to explain. Plus she needed her phone.

She'd heard about investigators who become tunnel visioned and look only for evidence that backs up their suspicions. The fact she'd been edited out of the first episode had set Shane off on a theory that had him forensically unpicking her interview comments to zero in on anything that might back up this idea. And even though his theory was flawed, it was frightening how plausible he'd made it all sound. Bonnie forced herself to dampen the panic. She could get angry about Shane later. For now she needed to focus on some of his observations.

The police haven't revealed how many bodies they found.

This was the one that had freaked her out the most. Had someone else survived? If so, who? Jacko and Charlie were locked in rooms when she left, so it had to be Grant, Maria, Dennis or Jaide. She knew for a fact that Maria and Grant had died because she'd spoken to their devastated families, and she couldn't bring herself to think Dennis was anything other than an upstanding member of society, but then Shane had said Jaide was this charitable person who apparently liked everyone except for Bonnie. Truth be told, she couldn't bring herself to think any of them were involved.

Plus, like Shane had said, whoever did this was not only obsessed with sins; they were also smart and well funded.

He didn't torch the whole place. Is it a clue? Is this guy still playing?

Clearly he *was* still playing. Releasing the footage without her in it was at best discrediting her word, at worst portraying her as a fraud. She wasn't at all surprised he'd left the majority of the building intact.

You were very lucky.

How was that lucky? Why had she survived? If the group hadn't forced her into that room, she wouldn't be here. She'd have died in the fire like everyone else.

She drank the last of the water and put her head in her hands. Why was this happening to her? It wasn't fair. She felt dizzy with it all and she wanted the whole thing to be over, to go back to her life. To have time to mourn her mum and work out how the hell to pay the mortgage. Would anyone employ her after this? She had come here for Shane's help and all she'd managed to do was make it worse. If she'd met with him yesterday, before the episode had been released, how different it would have been. Even if she'd come in tomorrow, it would have been better. She'd have been able to prepare.

She rested her head on the table, no longer having the energy to sit up straight. Thinking of it all made her queasy. If she had her time again, she wasn't sure she'd fight so hard to swim to the surface. She could have stayed there in the peace and quiet and not had to face all this. They could have said what they wanted and she wouldn't have cared. She'd be with her mum. Damn that instinct to swim. If only she'd been more like Clara and refused to go anywhere near the water.

Bonnie tried to raise her head.

Clara can't swim.

The room spun and she began to retch. It took all her effort to push her head up from the table top.

Clara can't swim. Oh God.

'Hello?' she tried to shout but her voice caught in her throat, and she retched again. She needed to get Shane back in here and tell him. He would know what to do.

As she attempted to stand, her legs gave way and she fell into a heap on the floor.

87

Clara paced and checked her watch. Bonnie had promised to be back by five. They were meeting one of her old school-friends for dinner in town. Harriet had travelled to Leeds from Bristol especially to see Bonnie and was only home for one night. Clara knew Bonnie wouldn't want to miss it. The plan was to catch the six o'clock train and Bonnie needed to change.

She tried Bonnie's phone one more time and once again the call went to voicemail, so she checked WhatsApp. It said she was last online over two hours ago. She hadn't even read Clara's messages. How long do these interviews take? She knew things had changed with the airing of the episode, but this was getting ridiculous.

Clara opened Google on her phone and searched for the *Expect the Unexpected* podcast. If she could at least find out when they were expected to finish, she could text Harriet to let her know how long they might be delayed.

There was no number on the website, only a Contact Us form. She typed out a quick message saying she was Bonnie Drake's sister and urgently needed to know when Bonnie's interview with Shane might be finishing. Then she pressed send. She didn't hold out much hope of someone responding so went back to drying her hair, hoping Bonnie would walk through the door any minute.

Since watching the episode, it had been bugging Clara that Bonnie had been hiding things from her. She had said so little about what had happened in that place and yet she was happy to spend hours and hours offloading to a stranger who was then going to broadcast it to the world. Did Clara not deserve a heads up? It wasn't fair to keep her in the dark. Bonnie knew Clara was upset about having convinced Bonnie to go on the show. Was this some kind of punishment? Would she be blaming Clara for everything in her frank and honest chat with Shane? Perhaps Clara should have explained her application form comments and apologized.

She turned her head to dry the other side of her hair and noticed her phone screen was lit up with an incoming call.

'Is that Clara Drake?'

'Yep.'

'This is Amra from the *Expect the Unexpected* podcast. You just sent us a message.'

'Oh, thanks for calling back so quick. Sorry to be a drama queen but Bonnie and I have plans tonight and she said Shane thought it would only take a few hours. I know everything's changed with the episode going out online, but do you know when they might be done?'

'Is this Bonnie Drake from the *Fortress* thing?'

'Yes. Why? How many Bonnie Drakes are you interviewing?' Clara gave a small laugh.

'That's the thing. We're not interviewing her at all. I checked with Shane and he's had no contact. In fact he's in Denmark right now . . . Are you still there?'

'That can't be right.'

'Sorry. I recognized her name, so I thought I'd better come back to you asap because what happened to her was awful.'

88

When Shane came back into the room, Bonnie experienced a brief moment of hope. He was still here. He would help her. If she could just tell him what was going on. But then he stepped over her and began to wipe down the table they'd been using with a cloth that smelled of bleach, and Bonnie noticed he was wearing gloves.

It should have been obvious. If she'd been paying more attention, she'd have questioned how quickly Shane had managed to watch the newly released episode and modify his interview questions to pull holes in her story. All in the time it had taken her to call Clara.

Then perhaps she wouldn't have handed him her phone.

Or drunk the water he'd given her.

Too late. She expected the sandwich she'd eaten at lunchtime was the real problem.

But still it made no sense. Her mind couldn't compute how this whole nightmare had been created by an ex-police officer-cum-social media star. His podcast was one of the most popular in the UK. It had won awards. Solved crimes.

Bonnie recalled something Maria had said when they were discussing Jaide and Grant: *You see what you expect to see and not what's really there.*

'If you're wondering why I'm doing this to you, you brought it on yourself, just like the others did. You may not have applied to be on the show, but you fraudulently came on it.' His voice was deeper than when he'd been conducting the interview and that venom she'd heard when he'd said she deserved everything that happened to her dripped from every word. 'And so your punishment will fit the crime. You will be remembered as a fraud.'

Remembered?

'I had no choice. You ruined everything. It was all planned so meticulously. I should have had all the time I needed and then you turn up – a cuckoo in the nest pretending to belong.' He wiped down the legs of the chairs as he talked. 'I didn't understand why at first. I asked *Him* why did this happen, how could she have survived, is it a test? I had done everything *He* had asked of me.' Shane finally looked at Bonnie as she desperately fought to keep her eyes open. 'And then I realized you were a gift.'

He crouched down and to Bonnie's horror pushed her hair away from her face.

Get off me, you sick fuck, she screamed in her head but no words would come out.

'When I pitched my ideas to various production companies they told me that I didn't have a commercial mind. But wait until they see the viewing figures for *The Fortress*. This thing is going viral. Everyone will hear the message that this world has turned once more to ruin. People's obsession with sharing everything about themselves through social media and TV shows, it is the antithesis of the Lord's command. It was the same with her. She was too busy looking in a mirror or down the lens of a camera to pay attention to what was important. To sin is to turn away from *Him*. It is despicable and disgusting and through me *His* retribution will be swift.'

'What are you trying to say?'

Shane laughed as he stood up and, if there had been any doubt left in Bonnie's mind that he was the Director, it was gone. Because for all the masking he had done of his voice during the podcast and in his *Fortress* announcements, there was no mistaking his laugh.

'As it turned out, your escape was the best form of publicity. It ensured everyone knew about *The Fortress* before it went live. And then I realized that only one thing was more powerful than watching people pay for their sins, and that was the one thing that you and you alone could provide – describing what it feels like to be a sinner standing at the gates of hell. All I needed was the right vehicle through which you could share your story. Being able to label you as the fraudulent sinner you are at the same time was the cherry on top. I know what you're thinking. I can see it in your eyes. You think I'm the sinner. That taking the lives of others is never justified. But you are wrong. *He* sacrificed his only son to save our souls, so think what *He* expects of us.'

You are batshit crazy.

'I can see you're not buying it, so I'll leave you with this.' He stooped down low, his breath warm on her face as he whispered the words into her ear. 'Puzzle me this. Would you kill a sinful soul to honour thy father? Would you kill thy mother to save an innocent soul?'

He laughed again and it turned Bonnie's stomach.

'Now then. Enough chit-chat. Shall we set up your final scene?'

89

Bonnie forced her eyes open. The lights were bright and everything was white.

Am I dead?

She couldn't be because the floor below her felt cold and she could still smell bleach.

She dragged herself to the toilet bowl and put her fingers down her throat. It might be too late to rid herself of any poison but she had to try. She couldn't let this bastard get away with it.

Bonnie sat back and looked at the door. Her head spun and the effort to drag herself up had worn her out. Sweat bubbled on her forehead and dripped into her eyes. She needed a minute.

Russ and Jacko's rooms were like this.

Locked and lonely.

The world lost focus and Bonnie felt like she might pass out again. She dug her fingernails into her palms until it hurt.

He locked everyone in. So he could take his time. See them panic.

Do something.

Who lasted longest?

A tear fell from her chin and landed on her hand. *I'm sorry, Clara. I let you down again.*

Maria? Dennis? Super Grant?

Do something.

He watched them burn.

Do something. Now.

Bonnie closed her eyes and tried to concentrate. *What would Grant do?* He had been the most competitive. He would have fought to the last. What would he do, here and now?

She had not seen anyone else in the building. Shane had met her in reception after she called the number he'd given her. But it was one of those rent-by-the-day office spaces so there must be other people here somewhere.

'He-fp.' Her lips wouldn't form the words properly and she had no volume.

Her handbag lay near by; its contents partially spilled on the floor. She reached out as far as she could with her left arm.

Her fingers couldn't quite reach the strap. She stretched further, afraid that if she lost her balance she might not have the strength to sit again. Her index finger made contact with the leather and she wriggled it along the floor to get a better grip, eventually managing to pull the strap slowly towards her. Her purse, a hairbrush and a box of painkillers remained on the floor but she ignored them. When the bag was at her side, she took a moment to gather her energy before rummaging through the contents. She found a receipt for the morning coffee she had bought on the way here – that would do – and she also found an old lip liner that she couldn't remember putting in there.

She flattened the receipt on her leg face down so she could write on the blank side.

What had he said?

Puzzle me this.

It made her think of Jacko. He always spotted the phrases that were out of place. She swallowed back the tears and concentrated on writing down the words. It took all the energy she had to make the letters look like they should.

She tried her best to recall what he'd said next about killing sinful souls but her brain wouldn't work. This was important. She had to remember because he'd been gloating and he knew he'd won so maybe he said something he shouldn't have.

Try to remember.

The dizziness engulfed her and just for a moment she allowed herself to sink back against the wall and close her eyes.

90

Clara chewed the nail on her right index finger as she walked along the street. It had been nearly three hours since she had last spoken to Bonnie. She had called the number for Bonnie's police contact, DS Piper, whose card Bonnie had pinned to the fridge, and asked for her help. The DS had not been impressed by Bonnie's decision to speak to *Expect the Unexpected*, but when Clara explained that someone had used the podcast to con Bonnie into meeting them and that Clara couldn't now reach her, her tone had changed. DS Piper had called back within twenty minutes to say they'd traced Bonnie's phone to an office for hire in Leeds city centre and that the local police were making a check. She had told Clara not to go there. She would call back as soon as she had news, but Clara had already requested an Uber through her phone app. Her leg was no longer in a cast but she hadn't been cleared to drive yet. She figured there couldn't be that many office-for-hire businesses in the city, and she was right. A quick Google revealed three possibilities and so she'd directed the driver to each of the addresses in turn, until she spotted the police car parked outside the last one.

Clara could not believe this was happening. She felt sick with fear and guilt. She had done this to Bonnie. It should have been her on that show. And now someone had edited Bonnie out of the *Fortress* episode with a forensic attention to detail and Clara felt sure this was intended to make Bonnie look like a liar. Was that because she knew something or had seen something important? If so, it made sense that the person behind this would want to shut Bonnie up.

Clara crossed the road. The glass-fronted reception had WIZU WORKSPACE emblazoned across it in large letters. It was nestled between a cafe and a Boots. Inside she could see two police officers talking to a tall dark-haired man. She didn't want to interrupt anything but she also needed to know if Bonnie was here.

'I'll be with you in a moment,' said the dark-haired man as she walked in. 'Like I said, I only started an hour ago as my colleague had a dental appointment. According to the log, only one room was hired today but they signed out before I arrived.'

'Who was that?'

All three men looked at Clara when she spoke.

'Sorry, I'm Bonnie Drake's sister.'

The taller of the officers frowned and looked to be about to chastise her but his colleague spoke first.

'If you could wait there and let us handle this, please.'

Clara nodded and looked at the receptionist, who looked quickly away. He had obviously been staring at her. No doubt he recognized her face or Bonnie's name from all the media reports on *The Fortress*.

'It was a Mr H. Styles,' he said, showing the officers on an iPad.

'Was he alone, do you know?'

'Err, it should say on here. One second. People book online and then simply sign in. We only need the main signature. Sorry, it doesn't say for how many people.'

'H. Styles as in Harry Styles,' said Clara. 'You don't take ID? People can just give you any fictitious name?'

'It's just office space,' said the receptionist.

'Thank you,' said the officer who had asked Clara to stay out of it.

'He was pretending to be Shane Fletcher from the *Expect the Unexpected* podcast.'

'Well, it appears they all left,' said the taller officer.

'I want to see inside,' Clara said.

'Miss, please can you leave this to us?'

'Can I book a room, please, for now?'

'Err, we're closing.' The receptionist looked from Clara to the officers. 'I'm about to lock up.'

'We will take a quick look around if that puts your mind at ease,' said the shorter officer to Clara.

The receptionist buzzed them through and Clara followed the officers to the room H. Styles had used. It was painted green and white with a few abstract pictures on the wall. In one corner was a large fake pot plant and in the middle of the room there was an oblong wooden table surrounded by green chairs.

Clara looked around the space for any sign of her sister. She was too late. She should have realized sooner that something was wrong. She should have made Bonnie check this guy out before coming here. They had looked at the *Expect the Unexpected* website but the only photograph of Shane was a side profile where he wore a Sherlock Holmes-style monocle and deer-stalker hat. They should have googled him so Bonnie knew exactly what he looked like before she came here. And Clara should have insisted on coming with her. Mum would never have let Bonnie come alone after what she'd been through. Bonnie would never have let Clara come alone.

'Smells very clean in here. Do you usually use bleach?' The tall officer looked at the receptionist.

'I don't know. I don't do the cleaning.'

The officer nodded and walked around the small room. 'And this is the only room they'd have had access to?'

'Yes. Apart from the kitchen and the toilets. The offices are all opened with a unique QR code.'

The officer looked at Clara as he said, 'Can we quickly check the communal areas, then?'

There was a faint smell of bleach in the kitchen area too but again no sign of Bonnie. It was the same story in the washrooms.

What now? Clara felt the panic rising. The police would leave here and then what? If this was the last place her phone had been traced to, that meant it had since been switched off or run out of charge. How would they find where he had taken her now?

'Can you get hold of your colleague who was working here today?' said the friendly officer.

'Sure, I have her number at the desk.'

Halfway along the corridor back to reception, the friendly officer stopped. 'You said no one else was in here today.'

'That's right. The next booking is tomorrow at nine a.m. Like I said, I'm about to lock up.'

'So why is the disabled toilet door locked?' He pointed at the little red marker on the door handle.

'I . . . I don't know.' The receptionist looked at the officers. 'I was told we were empty.'

The officer knocked on the door. 'Hello? Is someone in there?'

There was no answer.

'Maybe the lock fell into place on its own?' said the receptionist.

The officer knocked again with one hand as he removed something from his pocket. It was a ten pence piece. After waiting a few seconds for a reply, he inserted the coin into the rear of the lock. 'I'm opening the door now,' he said loudly.

He twisted the lock and stood to block Clara's view as he opened the door. But Clara could still see enough.

Bonnie lay slumped on the floor by the wall. Her hair was wrapped around her head and her T-shirt was half untucked from her jeans.

'Bonnie!'

The nice officer blocked her with his arm and spoke softly. 'Let us.'

She heard the taller policeman requesting an ambulance as she and the receptionist watched his colleague check Bonnie's vitals and start to give her CPR.

Clara willed Bonnie to get up. *Come on, sis, please.*

'Should I take her back to reception?' the receptionist asked the taller officer. 'This doesn't look good.'

'I'm not going anywhere,' said Clara before the officer had a chance to reply.

As the minutes ticked by, the nice officer continued giving Bonnie CPR but she still had no heartbeat when the paramedics finally turned up. A female paramedic took over CPR as her male colleague switched on the defibrillator. He then took a pair of scissors from his bag and cut Bonnie's T-shirt from the bottom to the top.

Inside the left cup of Bonnie's bra Clara could see something white poking out. The female paramedic removed it, looked at it and then handed it to the friendly officer.

'Looks like this is for you.'

Clara saw it was a folded receipt with large shaky letters written on it.

'I'd better call the boss,' said the receptionist.

'Is she going to be OK?' Clara asked.

'She's in the best hands,' said the female paramedic.

The friendly officer joined Clara in the hallway after reading Bonnie's piece of paper.

'Can you make any sense of this?' The officer held up the receipt. The words were untidy and sloped across the paper. It looked nothing like Bonnie's handwriting and Clara wondered what situation Bonnie had been in when she had written it and why she had stuck it in her bra. How much of a risk had she been taking? Clara's stomach dropped as she realized Bonnie might have hidden it there, knowing it would be found post-mortem.

Clara read the note out loud. 'I think it says, *Puzzle me this. Ill sinners honour father. Kill other to save . . .* Sorry, I can't read that last word.'

'Could that be *kill* sinners to honour father? It looks like there's a K there – and is that the number two like below?'

Clara studied the letters again. 'Yeah, maybe. What does it mean?'

'I was hoping you could tell me. I'll pass it on to the DS. It might be important.' The officer folded the paper and placed it in an evidence bag.

'We have a heartbeat,' said the female paramedic. 'We're taking her to Jimmy's. You can come if you're family,' she said to Clara.

91

The Director

What a triumph.

Even with the Bonnie Drake factor, he had still managed to deliver perfection. When he'd discovered she had survived, he had to admit he'd panicked. He had thought the game was up, and that the police would be knocking on his door sometime soon. But he had underestimated himself. He had covered his tracks better than he thought.

And that left room for vengeance.

He was incensed to learn she was an imposter. The selection of the candidates had been meticulous and everything relied on them being exactly the right person. She had ripped that apart, lied, cheated and caused him one hell of a headache.

He had to make her pay.

The podcast invite had been sublime. It had taken a good few weeks to convince Bonnie but he'd researched her well and knew which strings to pull. She would want to do something worthwhile. She would want to help the families achieve justice. She would want the world to know the truth.

And then it was simply a matter of carefully editing her out of the episodes and acquiring a good amount of her hospital-prescribed painkillers off the internet. By making her look like a co-conspirator, who after being caught in her lie had taken her own life, he had killed two birds with one stone. He had presented a viable suspect to distract the police and delivered his seventh soul as promised.

He knew what he had done surpassed the norm. He had a power within him that allowed him to ensure vengeance was served to those who deserved it. That included his mother – who had mentally and physically abused him as she became more addicted to drugs and obsessed with her fame. She resented him for holding back her career and berated him for being stupid like his father. But she was the stupid one. Despite her looks and high IQ. Despite the column inches dedicated to her every movement. Despite her fame and fortune. She had been weak and rotten on the inside.

Making her pay had been the start of it all. After that he knew he was destined for greatness and it was only a matter of time before the Lord showed him the way.

He had first seen the Solent sea fort from a small motor boat he and two colleagues had been sent to it on. He was in awe of its magnitude; this tool of war rising from the depths of the ocean as if emerging from hell itself. He was part of an engineering team who had been contracted by ITV to create a set for a new reality TV show on site. It was to be an escape room-based game show but, within three months of the build, Covid had hit. It was first paused, then postponed and eventually abandoned. When he received the email informing him he was no longer needed, it was the single most significant day of his life. The coincidence of working on a TV game show had not passed him by. His mother had been the first ever winner of *Puzzle Me This*, the Channel 5 rival to *The Krypton Factor* back in 1999, and now he had access to a remote, abandoned TV set. It was a sign.

After that – apart from Bonnie Drake – everything had gone to plan. And now he could sit back and soak up the glory. The *Fortress* episodes would continue to stream and the world would watch right to the bitter end because they would not be able to stop themselves.

92

'DS Piper, it's Clara again. Clara Drake.' She stood in the car park of the hospital as calls weren't allowed in intensive care.

'Hi Clara. How is she doing?'

'The same. It's going to be a long road. It might take days, weeks even, until they know what the extent of the damage is. We have no idea how long before we got there she had stopped breathing.'

'I see. That's not the best news for any of us. I'm sorry.'

'Did you know he released the podcast recording and it claims Bonnie was tied up in all of this? That's a total lie, you know that, don't you? He's trying to ruin her. Can't you take it down? And the episode, for that matter?'

'We will fully investigate all the claims. I assure you we're working hard here but, until Bonnie wakes up and tells us what happened, we have very little to go on.'

Investigating all the claims? What did that mean? Did that mean the claims he'd made about Bonnie?

'That's why I was ringing. You see, I was thinking about that note she left – I've got a lot of time to think, sitting in here – and so I googled some of the phrases to see if there were any religious links and stuff. Did you know *Puzzle Me This* was a TV show?'

'Yes. It was a quiz show, I believe. We looked into that.'

'Did you know that the first person to win it – Izzy Baxter – was murdered? Someone stabbed her in her own home.'

'It was a very different crime to this one, though. There's nothing to suggest a link.'

'Oh, I see. Right. It's just . . . sorry, can I ask, if you don't mind, whether her son was ever a suspect?'

'From memory, I believe her child was very young when it happened.'

'No, I mean the older one. There was a teenage son. I listened to a podcast on the case last night. Sorry,' Clara said when she heard the detective sigh.

'It's OK, go on.' The detective was humouring her, probably because she felt sorry for her and Bonnie.

'Well, they said on the show that she'd had a son in her teens so he would have been fourteen or something when she died. And that they'd tried to track him down, but he'd just disappeared, you know, dropped out of school, left town. Don't you think that's weird?'

'Maybe he didn't want to hang around the place his mum got killed.'

'Or . . . maybe he scarpered because he didn't want to speak to your lot. They also said on this show that his mum was rich, like, really rich. She'd made a ton of money doing commercials and modelling after winning *Puzzle Me This* – and guess who that would have gone to?'

'The next of kin.'

'Exactly!'

'I'll bear it in mind.'

'No, wait, that's not all. In the note Bonnie wrote, the last line said something about "kill other to save something".'

'I remember, yes.'

'Might it say kill *mother*, not other? I mean the first line is "kill sinners to honour father", so it makes sense that the next line was "kill mother". As in mother and father.'

'Maybe.'

'And if it says "kill sinners to honour father", could the next bit be "kill mother to save self"? Maybe Izzy Baxter was a crappy mum.'

The line was quiet.

'Hello?'

'I'm still here. I'm just looking at the image of what she wrote. It's impossible to say what that last word is – it's no more than a wavy line, but . . . there is a mark before the word you thought was "other" that could be an M. But that still doesn't prove anything, Clara.'

'OK, so what about this? I worked this out myself last night; it wasn't on the podcast. Bonnie and the others went into *The Fortress* on fifth September, yeah? Well, guess what show first aired on fifth September exactly twenty-five years ago.'

'You're kidding.'

'I'm not. It's on Wikipedia.'

'Clara, can you leave this with me? I think we need to do a bit of digging. But, well done, this could be helpful.'

'It's Bonnie we have to thank. She spent all her time in that place scared she'd never escape this man and now he has her locked inside her own body. How unfair is that? If you find him, if Izzy Baxter's son is him, I want you to remember that.'

Clara hung up, unable to carry on speaking through the tears.

93

'All right, Gabe? We haven't seen you for a while.'

Gabe exited through the gym's turnstile.

'Yeah, I had some family business to take care of.'

'I hope everything's all right, mate.'

'Yeah, all sorted now. Thanks.' He waved goodbye to Mikey on reception. He was a nice lad, if a little over friendly.

The cold weather outside was a stark comparison to the warmth of the gym and he walked swiftly to his car. It was only a ten-minute drive home. He used to have a much nicer motor but he'd traded it in for a modest Seat Leon. He not only needed to divert all his funds to his special project; it also made sense to be less conspicuous for a while.

He drove past the end of the road where his mother had lived and died. He had chosen to live near by on purpose to remind him of two key things: that he had been chosen to fulfil an important purpose and that he could get away with it. He suspected the Lord might have a hand in this. He had lived for years in homeless shelters, expecting that if he emerged back into society he would be instantly arrested, but then he met Tobias and everything changed.

Tobias had him reading the Old Testament with its tales of God testing man and vengeance being served. Then he directed him to Revelation and his mind was blown. This was a God he could get behind. He had always thought Christianity preached nothing more than love and forgiveness and it was a delicious surprise to realize there was so much more to it. That was when he knew in his heart he had been chosen, that he was special and that he had an important message to spread.

He parked up outside his house.

'Fergus Baxter?'

Gabe was reaching for his gym bag from the car when someone said that name, the name his mother had given him. He froze for a second, just long enough to gather his thoughts before he turned to face her.

'Sorry, who?'

The woman was not alone. She stood with two uniformed officers.

'DS Piper. We have reason to believe you are Fergus Baxter, Izzy Baxter's son, and I'm arresting you on suspicion of murder.'

'What? That's ridiculous. I'm Gabe Abrahams. Always have been, always will be.'

'Well, you won't mind coming to the station to do a DNA test, then, will you?'

'Why, who am I supposed to have murdered?'

The police officer opened the back door of the patrol car as she reeled off his rights.

'Seriously, who am I supposed to have murdered?'

'If you have a solicitor, you can call them, although if you've done what we think you've done, I expect calling for help will be useless.'

Gabe Abrahams looked at the wry smile on the detective's face. The sin of pride. She would pay for that.

94

'Hey, sis, I brought you some more flowers.'

Clara looked around the room at all the half-dead bouquets and imagined Bonnie saying, *Great, just what I need.*

'I met with Dennis's ex-wife yesterday. She's lovely and has friends who worked with Dennis in the Crown Prosecution Service, so she was able to explain lots of things about the case. I told you they hadn't found any physical evidence of Fergus Baxter on the sea fort, but they did find a command centre on the main level where he must have based himself. It had a sofa bed and a fridge and a loo. He was there the whole time, locked away in his den. I reckon that's why in the podcast he kept going on about whether you thought someone was there with you. The dipshit was showing off. DS Piper said he'd stripped it all down and cleaned it, but one of the doctors told me it's almost impossible to remove every trace of yourself, so hopefully something will turn up. They do have digital evidence of him buying some of the equipment that was used. Sheila – that's Dennis's ex-wife – said his defence would no doubt try to say these were all items bought legitimately when he was contracted by ITV, but the specific models bought and the dates will hopefully prove that's not the case.'

Clara smoothed down the sheets covering Bonnie.

'They had managed to find some of the actors he'd hired to work the selection events and take you over on the boat, but Baxter was smart. He'd booked them and briefed them over the phone with a prepaid mobile, so there was no digital trail back to him. It was your note that caught him. There's no way they'd have tracked him down without it. They looked into Izzy Baxter's son and found he'd disappeared so he was either dead or he'd changed his identity. But then they managed to track down a schoolfriend who said Fergus had lived on the streets after his mum died and then got all weird and religious. This friend said the last time he'd seen him, Fergus had been off his head and demanded to be called Gabriel, like the angel. What a knob. The police then went to a company ITV had hired to modify the sea fort into an escape room pre-Covid and it turns out they had employed a guy called Gabriel Abrahams.' Clara loved this story. She had told Bonnie many times over the weeks, but she wanted her sister to know how important her note had been in catching the bastard. She was also very proud to have worked out who he was from her own research. DS Piper had said Clara should consider becoming a police officer because she'd make a good detective. Not so scatty-cat after all.

'And DS Piper told me they were planning to quiz Fergus about his mother's murder, too, at some stage. She also thinks he may have done it. Killed his own mother when he was a kid. It's just shocking, the whole thing.'

Clara moved around the room sorting through the dead flowers and throwing them away. As she did she updated Bonnie on other things, like the fact that their neighbour Shelley had a new man who was ten years her junior, and the fact that Clara had applied for a new job so was finally putting her degree to some use.

Once she was done, she sat down again next to Bonnie and kissed her hand.

She came every day without fail and sometimes with friends, neighbours and even Bonnie's PhD supervisor. None of them knew if it helped but at least they were doing something.

'I know you're trapped in there, sis, and I expect it's scary sometimes, or maybe it's just peaceful, I don't know, but I wanted to say take your time. You have food and water and you're safe, no one is trying to harm you or test you. You can take as long as you like, just promise me one thing.' Clara stroked her sister's forehead and moved her hair from her eyes. 'Come back to me, someday. I miss you and I want you home.'

95

Two Months Later

The REAL *Expect the Unexpected* Podcast
Season 2, Episode 5: 'The *Fortress* Fraud'

'Hi, everybody. This is the actual Shane Fletcher on the real
Expect the Unexpected *podcast. Today's guest is Clara Drake.*
You may well know her sister Bonnie, who was interviewed on
a fake version of our podcast that was released a short while
ago with the sole purpose of smearing Bonnie's name.

'We have decided as a team to try and put the record
straight because, although we had nothing to do with this
fraudulent broadcast, the fact that it used my name and the
reputation of Expect the Unexpected *to traumatize Bonnie*
and her family is something we all feel some responsibility for.

'We have invited Clara here today to help us set the record
straight. And we are also joined by Professor Harriet Fallon,
an expert in the psychology of religious fanaticism.

'Thank you both for joining us. Can I start with you,
Clara? First off, can we ask how your sister is?'

'She's OK, thank you. We have been told she is
responding well to all the tests so we're hopeful that there's

no lasting damage. But she hasn't woken up yet. I personally don't think she's ready. I think she probably feels safer where she is.'

'*That sounds totally understandable. Please do pass on the best wishes of all of us here at* Expect the Unexpected, *along with our sincere apologies for any part we have played in what happened to Bonnie.*'

'Thank you. I will.'

'*Have the police given their permission for you to speak to me?*'

'Well, they would rather I didn't, but they accept my reasons. There are some things I can't discuss but I will do my best to work around those.'

'*So I listened to the fake podcast and it was a very realistic copy of our output. He had the music, the sponsor pitches and by all accounts pulled off a decent imitation of my accent. This was a man who went to great lengths to get the details right. I guess a good few would have believed it was us. Bonnie certainly seemed to believe he was me throughout. Do you think she worked out he was a fraud at any point?*'

'Maybe when she began to feel ill. The doctors said she'd ingested large amounts of the painkiller she had been taking since the head injury she sustained escaping from the sea fort. I spoke to her during the recording and she said he'd given her a sandwich, so we think he put it in that. She would have felt dizzy and queasy before she passed out.'

'*And she has you to thank for alerting the emergency services after you'd contacted Amra on my team and she'd told you I was not interviewing Bonnie. Presumably at that point you didn't know what his fake podcast contained?*'

'Not at all. I kind of assumed there was no recording and that she'd been invited there simply so he could finish the job. It was only when friends contacted me the next day to say it was out that I understood the lengths he was prepared to go to. He didn't only want to take her life, he also wanted to destroy her reputation. Sadly for him, she had the wherewithal to write down a few things he'd said and hide the note. Without that I think he might have got away with it.'

'OK, can we clear up a few things that I'm sure listeners are curious about, then? Is it true that Bonnie subbed for you on the show because you broke your leg after being selected?'

'Yes, and the team at Leeds General Infirmary can confirm that I did break my leg.'

'And you did apply in the hope of winning the prize money?'

'Yes.'

'And your bank never spoke to this man to confirm no monies were outstanding?'

'They told me they would never share such information, but it is true that our debt has been settled. Friends of ours set up a GoFundMe appeal when Bonnie first came home and people were so generous we were able to settle the debt and I've started a new job as a community support officer with the police, so for now we are able to stay in the house.'

'It's a good thing we're letting people know this man's claims about your sister are lies, then. People can get very tetchy about being conned out of their money. And congratulations on the new job. Is that inspired by everything that's happened?'

'You could say that, yes. I'm not sure I'm detective material but at least this way I can help to protect people.'

'It's a great organization to be part of. I loved my police career. And speaking of careers, I have to ask about Bonnie's PhD. Can you tell us about that because I have to admit when I heard that detail I thought uh-oh, busted.'

'It was a total lie. Bonnie's PhD is about the impact of Alzheimer's on social skills. Our grandpa suffered from it and became really isolated because he couldn't talk to people right. It has absolutely nothing to do with how people cope when under pressure and in distress.'

'*He just made that up?*'

'He just made it up. Lied about everything, including pretending Bonnie had never been a contestant.'

'*So what can you tell us about him?*'

'His real name is Fergus Baxter, although he goes by Gabriel Abrahams these days. But the police would not have found any of this without Bonnie's note and the details she included. They led the police to identifying his real mother, Izzy Baxter.'

'*I remember her. She was like Carol Vorderman only a bit more page three in style. For a time you couldn't open a paper without her being in it, especially when she dated an American film star. I think his name was Corey something. There were a lot of Coreys around at the time.*'

'*For those of you who don't know the story of Izzy Baxter, she was murdered five years after winning* Puzzle Me This, *which was a game show based around IQ challenges in the late nineties. It was very sad what happened to her and, as far as I know, it still hasn't been solved.*'

'I think this whole thing was linked to his mother's death.'

'*Well, it can't be a coincidence that* The Fortress *was a modern version of* Puzzle Me This. *One of the things that intrigued me personally was how the victims were chosen. Can you tell us what you confessed to in your application?*'

'Envy. I've been envious of Bonnie my whole life – recent experiences excepted, of course. I think lots of younger siblings want to be like their big sisters but I had that feeling on speed. It made me angry how easy life came to her. She was so clever, and everything she tried, from swimming to playing netball, came easy to her, while I struggled to be anything other than mediocre. And I not only confessed it to be the thing I was most ashamed of in my application, I also said the thing I most desired was to prove to the world that I was just as good as her.

'And in terms of how he selected us, I managed to track down most of the applicants from my selection event and they had all confessed to being envious in one way or another, so it didn't matter which one of us passed the final test. He ran separate selection events with applicants who had all confessed to the same sin.'

'But he wasn't at your selection event?'

'He hired actors. He stayed out of sight the whole time.'

'He was meticulous in his planning.'

'And yet he still underestimated Bonnie.'

'And her sister. Professor Fallon, can I bring you in at this point? What is your take on this man, from what you've heard?'

'To start with, I'd like to express how sorry I am for the families of all those who died at this man's hand, and for what your sister has endured, Clara. Now, we don't know what his exact ideology is but we can guess from the name he adopted, Gabriel Abrahams, and his reference to Revelation, the beast and six-six-six in the *Fortress* design that it is founded in Christianity.'

'Because the seven sins are depicted in other religions, too?'

'Some version of deadly sins are found in most religions, yes, as they sit at the core of controlling our destiny: avoid these sins and you will go to heaven or live a good life. It sounds like this man had been mentally hijacked by his beliefs, which eroded his capacity for rational thought.'

'How does that work, then? Because he was clearly rational enough to plan and execute this TV show and the podcast with great attention to detail.'

'Indeed. What we see with religious fundamentalism is that, unlike most religious people, who take great well-being benefits from their faith, when a person's belief is based on the absolute authority of a religious text, it discourages logical reasoning or scientific proof.'

'So they are incapable of having their world view challenged?'

'More than that, they are unable to challenge it for themselves. It is akin to being infected with a mental parasite that looks to sustain its own survival, and it does this by causing the host's mind to process information in a biased, irrational way.

'Now, this does not mean the person is incapable of planning and executing something with great attention to detail. In fact, they may become more obsessed with getting everything right because it is a representation of their beliefs; it is their gift to God.'

'So he may have thought he was making some kind of offering or sacrifice?'

'I would expect so, yes. From what Clara has just told us about his family history, he may view those who participate in such TV shows as deserving of punishment.'

'So this does all go back to his mother. He was fourteen when she was murdered. I wonder if he thought her fame had caused her death and taken her away; that she was at fault. I expect that kind of thing is enough to set a young lad off on the wrong track.'

'I have studied people who have done worse with less of a reason. There was a great deal of symbology in how he designed things. To directly punish sinners for their own sins is a clear message to all of us that we shouldn't sin.'

'You make a great point, because he went on to try and punish Bonnie too for her sin of fraud.'

'And do you know why he chose to replicate your podcast?'

'No, although we think maybe because it has a strong listener base so he could reach a lot of people, plus it had been in the press recently for assisting with another case.'

'And it beggars belief.'

'What do you mean by that?'

'The phrase "beggars belief" was coined by John Whitley in 1830 when he wrote about heathens who deny the Bible in his religious text, *The Scheme and Completion of Prophecy*. I think if he heard that phrase in your podcast slogan he would have seen it as a sign.'

'He might have thought God told him to use Expect the Unexpected?'

'I suspect there is no might about it. Many religious fanatics totally reject the idea of a coincidence. Everything is there for a reason and is interpreted as a message from God.'

'Like you say, how do you reason with that? Tell me this, though. When I think of religious fanatics I imagine they are part of a group that has encouraged them to have extreme views. Is that how it usually works or am I totally wrong here?'

'There are no hard and fast rules. Most fanatics become more extreme in the face of opposition, whether they are in a group or standing as an individual. They have a strong perception of "them versus us", with *them* being good and *us* being bad, so anyone who challenges them merely acts to entrench them more.'

'But in your experience, are there people out there who would tell him what he did was right and justified?'

'If the world can create one extreme thinker, it can create more.'

'That is a sobering thought. I kind of hoped Fergus Baxter was a one-off.'

'If he were, I'd be out of a job.'

'*Look, thank you both so much for coming to talk to me today. I hope this has not only set the record straight for Bonnie but started to give our listeners some understanding of what may have motivated Baxter. I'm sure there's much more our listeners would like to know so perhaps you could both come back, hopefully with Bonnie too, once the trial is done. And, Clara, we wish you all the luck in the world getting a strong conviction.*'

'Thank you and thank you for having me on. It's been helpful to hear your insights and to have the chance to clear Bonnie's name. She told me before she took my place on *The Fortress* that she was scared it would ruin her reputation, so I'm making it my mission to ensure that doesn't happen.'

'*Happy to help.*

'*Well, thanks for listening, folks. We have no sponsor today. This one we are funding ourselves as it felt like the right thing to do. Next week I'll be talking to Philippe Hassan and taking a deep dive into the unexpected ways people con us with fake news on social media.*

'*This is Shane Fletcher and you have been listening to the real* Expect the Unexpected, *a podcast that blows your mind with crimes that beggar belief.*'

96

Bonnie slowly reached for the cup of tea Clara had brought her. Her movements were still stiff and a little painful after many months in a hospital bed. It felt so good to be home, for it to finally be over. The doctors had no real explanation for why she had stayed in a coma for so long – perhaps it was due to her having been in an induced coma so recently, or maybe her body simply needed time to rest and escape from all that had happened.

'The mind is a curious thing,' her psychology professor had said during his last visit. 'Sometimes it knows best what it needs, so don't worry about it.'

The neighbours had decorated the front of the house with bunting and put a large welcome home banner between the upstairs windows. When Bonnie had opened the front door and stepped into the hallway, Mum's hallway, she had finally felt free.

Her memories of the whole ordeal were fragmented and vague, but the most important thing was that Fergus Baxter was exactly where he deserved to be – locked away awaiting trial – and she and Clara were closer than ever. The trauma had brought them together: the Drake sisters against the world. Mum would have been so proud.

She heard the doorbell ring and hoped it wasn't a visitor. She was still in her pyjamas and hadn't even brushed her hair yet.

'How's the patient today?' It was Shelley, their next-door neighbour, her voice loud in the corridor downstairs.

'More flowers?' Clara said.

'These aren't from me. That woman asked me to bring them in.'

'Doesn't she want to come and say hello? Bonnie's awake.'

'She said she didn't want to disturb you but asked me to say you guys are an inspiration.'

'Bring them up.'

Bonnie sighed inside. They were coming to see her. She swung her legs off the bed. There was no time to get dressed but she could look less like a helpless patient.

Shelley walked in carrying a large bouquet of lilies.

'Morning, superstar. These were just delivered, and they smell wonderful.'

Bonnie couldn't deny that the smell coming from the huge flowers was beautifully sweet but that wasn't what bothered her. Her mum's wreath had been made of white lilies and the florist had told her and Clara they were a traditional funeral flower. And now someone had sent her a bouquet of the same flowers, only these lilies were such a deep purple colour they looked almost black, apart from the single white one in the middle.

'You all right, sis?' said Clara, seeing the look on Bonnie's face.

Bonnie stood as quickly as she could and walked to the window. The woman was still in the street. She had her back to the house and was about to climb into a taxi. She had short cropped auburn hair and was wearing a tailored trouser suit with heels. This was not the attire of your typical university

384

worker, so it wasn't someone from work and it certainly wasn't a friend as far as she could tell.

'Did she say anything else?' Bonnie said, without taking her eyes off the woman.

'Just that you're living proof that the sibling bond is stronger than sibling rivalry, or something along those lines.'

Even before the woman in the street glanced back and met Bonnie's gaze, something she had forgotten revealed itself. Something she had realized at the end of the podcast interview, just before she passed out.

'Clara can't swim.'

'What? What did you say?' Clara said.

Bonnie had been so upset that day when Clara sent over the copy of her application form that she'd initially missed the clue. Clara had written how hard it had been to live in the shadow of someone that even their mum thought was more intelligent and destined for success. She wrote how much she had hated Bonnie for this and Bonnie had been distracted by that word. Hate was a strong emotion but of course she'd missed the point. Hate wasn't Clara's sin, envy was.

Her sister was always meant to be in that room, to climb through that window and to end up in the sea. The ladder must have been rigged to fall, somehow. Because another fact Clara had written on the form was that she couldn't swim.

Bonnie couldn't remember the exact words because she had been concentrating on squeezing her body through that small window, but they were something along the lines of, 'Come back in . . . If you fall, you'll drown.' Why would someone say that unless they knew Clara couldn't swim? And they could only have known that if they'd read the application forms.

Charlie looked different. The bimbo was gone. The smart-suited redhead in her place wouldn't have gone amiss in a high-fashion magazine. She met Bonnie's gaze with a smile. But even though she wore large sunglasses, Bonnie could tell it was not a smile that met her eyes.

Charlie had needed to look to the group like she was facing a sin, hence being selected for envy, but by getting Bonnie to go into that room with her it ensured 'Clara' was the one who was really punished. Charlie never intended to climb out of that window and telling Bonnie to come back in was for effect. To make it look to the cameras like she was scared for Bonnie, when in fact she was manipulating her to do exactly what they needed her to do. No doubt when all the other contestants were all safely locked away, the Director simply opened the door so she could walk out. The whole thing was done to make sure Charlie looked innocent of any involvement.

Fergus had even hinted at it throughout his interview. *Why were there eight? One of you mustn't have been a real contestant. How many bodies did they find?* He had wanted her to know he had an accomplice and that she had been smart, oh so smart.

Bonnie could now see how this woman had spread her poison around the group to ensure they all wanted Bonnie in that room. At the time she had thought it was Grant, but wherever he was, Charlie was his shadow. She had even done a number on Bonnie, winding her up about Grant and Jaide, feigning concern as she fed the drama. And then the other things fell into place: the drinking of their last bottle of water, the missing crate of supplies. It had been Charlie who had called everyone away from the central room and the crate of food Grant had been protecting because smoke was once more filling Jacko's room. And Bonnie now felt sure that when the lights went out and the music came on, it was Charlie who went and moved it. Had she also removed Bonnie's shoe from wedging open the flap in Jacko's door and thrown it over to Grant? Probably.

But why? Who was she really and what did she have to gain?

You're living proof the sibling bond is stronger than sibling rivalry.

'Clara, did you say Izzy Baxter had two children?'

'Err, yeah. Her youngest was found walking her blood through the snow outside the house after she died.'

'That's awful,' said Shelley.

'And it was a sister, yeah?'

'Yeah. She was adopted apparently, so hopefully she knows nothing about her sick brother.'

'Oh, I think she's fully aware. And in receipt of her mother's inheritance, by the looks of her designer clothes.'

'What are you talking about?' Clara came to the window but Charlie and her taxi were long gone.

Would you kill thy mother to save an innocent soul? Those had been the words Fergus Baxter had whispered in her ear before she passed out. He had killed his mother to save Charlie. Charlie had told them all a sob story at one point about telling someone her mum used to hurt her, after which her mum never did it again. Presumably because she was dead. So did Charlie feel obliged to pay her big brother back? Indebted to him? Eternally grateful? Bonnie had no idea. But what she did know was that Charlie was a woman of means who was good at playing a role and faking it, and who knew where Bonnie and Clara lived.

She took the card from the bouquet, counting seven black lilies to go with the one white, and knowing full well what it would say even before she read it.

ONLY ONE SURVIVES

Acknowledgements

The journey to writing my first stand-alone thriller started in a conversation with Frankie Gray at Transworld. Since I had published four books in the Dr Bloom series, Frankie thought it might be good to stretch myself with a fresh challenge. It was an idea that filled me with both fear and excitement. The Dr Bloom characters felt safe and familiar. What on earth would I do with a blank sheet of paper?

Enter my new editor, Finn Cotton, who has been the most significant influence on the evolution of this story. I sent him three stand-alone ideas, he liked one, and we began bouncing ideas back and forth. The time he took to help me to form the idea was incredibly generous and something I am hugely grateful for. I did, however, make the mistake of telling him to push me as I wanted to produce my best book yet. He took me at my word and worked me hard: 'Make it more believable, make the characters more vivid, provide more emotion, make us care,' were just some of the notes he sent back. It was tough at times, but I am so proud of the result, and I absolutely could not have done this without you, Finn, so thank you, you totally awesome human.

Thanks also to the amazing Irene Martinez for designing the cover and to copy-editor Charley Chapman and the proofreading team, Holly McElroy, Barbara Thompson, Lorraine McCann and Rachel Cross, for refining everything so well. A big thanks to Melissa Kelly and Chloe Rose for all your wonderful PR and marketing work, and Tom Chicken and Emily Harvey for all your efforts on UK sales. It continues to be a pleasure working with you all.

I also need to say a general thanks to the Transworld team for their warmth, support and flexibility when my niece became ill during the writing of this book. You allowed me the time to focus on my family and for that I am ever grateful. You are wonderful people.

So, why a reality TV-based, escape room thriller? Well, in the basement of the psychology department at my university, there was a nursery school in which one whole wall was a two-sided mirror. Students such as myself would file in to a thin, dark room on the other side of that wall and watch. It was a sneak peek into how kids behave when they think no-one can see them. And we saw some fascinating things – like the boy behind the bookcase who hit three or four children as they were sent to fetch a book, only to then join them crying at the teacher's table. A sign of intellect or criminal prowess? Only time would tell.

This was way before I had ideas of being a crime thriller writer, I just wanted to study people and find out what makes them tick. And TV was about to help out with that, big style, because, a few years later, in July 2000, *Big Brother* launched, and a new era of reality TV was born. Here was the chance for all of us to stand on the other side of that two-way mirror and see *how real people behave in the real world*.

Twenty years later, it turns out the two-sided mirror is not enough. What we really want is to watch real people in *extreme* situations, and we don't mind if this has to be stage-managed. Many reality TV shows today employ psychologists to help them to pick the right 'characters', and much time is spent on designing the best scenarios to elicit an emotional reaction. So, if the scenes are staged and the characters hand-picked, what is real? It turns out this question is what many people have come to most enjoy about such shows. We have to figure out what part of the show is *Reality* and what part is *Television*, so we become ever more engaged in the experience. We become part of the game.

All this got me thinking: if reality TV shows have to keep evolving to apply ever increasing pressure on participants so that they react in ways that keep us interested and entertained, how far would they go?

And if someone making such a show really hated the genre and the kinds of people who chose to participate – people they see as fame-hungry, shallow, attention seekers – what then? What dire situation would they be willing to put people in to grab attention and make the public watch. This is the premise of *The Escape Room*. A reality TV show to end all reality TV shows.

Thank you to Clare at X-It Games for talking me through all things escape room. Your insights into how such things are designed and run helped me to create something so much more realistic. And when it came to checking whether my recreation of an escape room and a reality TV show were any good, no-one was better placed to judge than my sisters, Elizabeth and Joanne, who are big fans of both. Thanks for taking the time to read the early draft and giving me all your enthusiastic feedback. You encouraged me to keep going, and I hope you like the final version. Also, thanks to my mum and dad for your love of a good story and all your support.

A stand-alone book meant a pseudonym was needed, and, as luck would have it, I had just married the love of my life, Jamie Smithson. I was not taking his surname in real life, so becoming a Smithson in the book world felt like the right thing to do. Thank you, hubby, for the constant love, encouragement and laughter. You are my partner in crime. Thanks also to Erica, Ella and Henry who keep us busy and make us happy. This book you definitively *cannot* read until you're older!

Finally, my biggest thank-you has to go to Amelie. You are an inspiration.

About the Author

L. D. Smithson was born in Staffordshire and now lives in Ilkley with her husband and their three children. She is an occupational psychologist and a crime writer who has published under another name.